PENELOPE
IN
RETROGRADE

PRAISE FOR
PENELOPE IN RETROGRADE

"An ex-husband, a fake boyfriend, and a snarky, weed-growing grandma are just a few of the guests at the Banks's family Thanksgiving that make Brooke Abrams's debut unputdownable. *Penelope in Retrograde* will make you laugh a lot, cry a little, and want to call your dysfunctional family to tell them you'll be home for the next holiday. Spice Girl's Honor."

—Ali Brady, author of *The Beach Trap*

"*Penelope in Retrograde* sucked me in from the very first page! Abrams's voice is a standout—she had me laughing on one page and tearing up on the next. With sparkling wit and characters I want to be best friends with, Abrams has crafted a story that cuts right to the heart of what it means to be a family, and she does it beautifully. This book is perfect for anyone who has ever struggled to find their place. Abrams has penned a brilliant debut, and I can't wait to see what she does next!"

—Falon Ballard, author of *Just My Type*

"Brooke Abrams's *Penelope in Retrograde* is the ultimate feel-good novel. It's utterly charming, laugh-out-loud funny, and interspersed with genuine, heartfelt moments. Abrams's dialogue sparkles, and her characters come to life in all the best, most relatable ways. I loved it."

—Kathleen West, author of *Home or Away*

PENELOPE IN RETROGRADE

A Novel

BROOKE ABRAMS

LAKE UNION
PUBLISHING

Text copyright © 2023 by Brooke Abrams
All rights reserved.

No part of this book may be reproduced, or stored in a retrieval system, or transmitted in any form or by any means, electronic, mechanical, photocopying, recording, or otherwise, without express written permission of the publisher.

Published by Lake Union Publishing, Seattle

www.apub.com

Amazon, the Amazon logo, and Lake Union Publishing are trademarks of Amazon.com, Inc., or its affiliates.

ISBN-13: 9781662513251 (hardcover)
ISBN-13: 9781662513268 (paperback)
ISBN-13: 9781662513244 (digital)

Cover design by Philip Pascuzzo
Cover image: ©Mike Harrington/ Getty; ©Dimitris66 / Getty; ©4x6 / Getty

Printed in the United States of America

First edition

For Matt, who always accepts me exactly as I am

Do not swear by the moon, for
she changes constantly.

—Adapted from William Shakespeare's *Romeo and Juliet*

Chapter 1

If it wasn't for the Smut Coven, I wouldn't be here right now.

For reference, *here* is the San Diego airport on one of the busiest travel days of the year: the day before Thanksgiving. It's hell. Actually, it's more like the place you stop on your way to hell. Purgatory? Limbo? The DMV? I'm more spiritual than religious, so the exact term escapes me. I do, however, know that as loud and crowded as this airport is, it is not hell. Hell is where I'm going next.

Hell is my parents' home on Thanksgiving.

For the past ten years, I've successfully avoided the place, like a master criminal always managing to stay one step ahead of the law. I set reminders one month, two weeks, and three days before all major holidays to ensure that I'm never without a conflict. I always have a deadline I can't get out of, a cold I can't get over, or a household emergency that can't be ignored. If necessary, I have all three. I keep meticulous notes on my excuses so they never repeat, thus ensuring that a separate conflict connected to my pretend conflict doesn't arise. Being the misfit of the family takes a lot of planning.

"Penelope, are you sure you don't want me to send your father to pick you up?" My mother, Silvia Banks, lowers her voice through the phone. "I don't like the idea of you trying to hail a taxi after dark. It's not safe. All the cabbies know you're unarmed thanks to the TSA. You might as well hold up a giant sign that says *Kidnap me*."

Ladies and gentlemen, my mother.

"First, I live in San Francisco, not South Dakota. I can take care of myself." I strain under the weight of my luggage as I hoist it over my shoulder, trying my best to avoid jostling Ozzie, my elderly Pomeranian, in his rolling carrier. "Second, I don't think anyone's hailed a cab from the airport in the last ten years. And third, I'm never armed. Not unless you count hand sanitizer as a lethal weapon, which it kind of is, I guess, if you forced someone to drink it. At the very least, you could probably blind someone with it."

"Penelope, I know you think your father and I are old fashioned, but crime isn't the sort of thing that goes out of style."

I do think my parents are old fashioned. In fact, I'm willing to bet that the greater part of people born after 1970 would find my parents old fashioned. In their defense, they are old. They're both in their late seventies and so ridiculously prim and proper, they make Martha Stewart seem edgy. To be clear, I'm talking pre–Snoop Dogg Martha. They like their bedsheets to have hospital corners, their drinks to have coasters, and their daughters to have nice reliable jobs with health benefits. They'd also prefer their thirtysomething-year-old daughters to be married and stay married, though they're completely fine with the chosen spouse being male, female, or any gender in between. They're old fashioned, not assholes.

I encompass virtually none of those qualities, which makes me somewhat of a curiosity to my parents. I'm a midlist romance author, which means my paychecks aren't bad, but they're also not exactly reliable. The same can be said for any relationship I've been in that hasn't involved a fictional character I've written. I was married—emphasis on *was*—and I've never owned a coaster in my life. To my parents, I'm basically a human version of an air plant. I'm alive and thriving, but they don't really understand the science behind it.

"I'm going to book a rideshare just as soon as we hang up, Mom. I do it all the time. I even put in my preferences that I will only accept rides from people who aren't kidnappers or murderers. So far, it's worked out well."

"I don't like those rideshare things." My mother's voice is muffled, most likely by one of the cream puffs she's hidden in the butler's pantry.

"My water-aerobics instructor caught pubic lice from one. Do you have something you can sit on?"

The energy it would take to unpack my mother's concern for my genitals is too much for me to exert, especially now that Ozzie has taken to scratching his in the corner of his crate. I nudge it with my hip, hoping the five-pound ball of fluff gets the message.

"I promise I won't get crabs, Mom," I say a little too loudly, considering how jampacked the terminal exit is. I don't mind the raised eyebrows or stink eyes, though. I write sex scenes for a living. These people don't scare me. "Now, I've got to go if you want me to make it in time for drinks."

"All right, dear. Oh, one more thing. Are you wearing something nice or just your regular sort of clothes?"

"I'm actually fully nude. I studied up on how livestock auctions work and decided that it was better to let the lucky gentleman you've suckered into coming over tonight know exactly what he was purchasing ahead of time. I've even considered labeling the best parts like they do with cuts of beef."

"That's not funny, and I hope you don't plan on being vulgar like that at the table in front of your father's new associate. It's not a setup. I just hate to have an uneven table, and Martin had no place to go. He's new to town, you know. Originally from Kentucky. Your father's very impressed with him. He graduated first in his class from Yale, you know."

I do know. As of eight o'clock this morning, when my mother decided to spring the news on me of a gentleman caller joining us for the holiday, I officially know everything there is to know about Martin Butler without ever having to look him up on the internet. That is exactly how desperate my mother is to make sure that I fall in love and have one hundred of Martin Butler's babies. Because falling in love and having babies is the answer to all your problems, according to my mother and the majority of Hallmark movies.

"Are you still on the line, Penelope?" My mother's voice snaps me back into the present. "You're not even here yet and you're already ignoring me."

"It's impossible to ignore you, Mom. You're like one of those blow-up things with wild arms they stick out in front of car dealerships."

"I'm going to choose to ignore that, Penelope."

Typical.

"Did I mention your sister thinks Martin looks like that famous Christopher? Oh, which one did she say?"

"I hope it's Walken."

"Hemsworth!" She shouts it like she's just gotten bingo. "Anyway, he's very handsome and smart. I told him you write books, and he seemed very impressed by that."

"Did you tell him I can also read? Or that I can walk, chew gum, and sing 'The Star-Spangled Banner' backward at the same time? What about my boobs? In my experience, men seem to really like them."

"I don't know why I worry about someone kidnapping you." My mother groans. "They'd bring you back within an hour. Hurry home, and for the love of god, do not drink any caffeine."

"No promises."

I hang up the phone and plop down into an empty seat in the food court. The smell of salty fries mixing with hot pepperoni pizza makes my stomach growl. My parents are the type that believe dinner is best served over a three-hour period, starting with half an hour of cocktails and conversation, which means if I don't eat now, I will die of hunger with a martini in my hand.

Ozzie whimpers in his crate. It would be cruel not to get him his customary slice of meat lover's, and even crueler for me to make him an orphan because I passed up a slice of greasy airport pizza. The line isn't too long, so I drag Ozzie and my luggage over while pulling up the Dryver app on my phone.

"A slice of meat lover's pizza and a slice of pepperoni with extra garlic," I say once we reach the front of the line. Extra garlic might not be the wisest choice, but Martin should know up front that I'm the sort of woman who will always sacrifice fresh breath for a satisfied belly. "Add red onions too."

"Alone for Thanksgiving?" the cashier asks. He leans over the counter and smiles at Ozzie. "Oh, never mind, there's your little date. Such a cutie."

"What did you just ask me?"

"Uh . . . if you were alone?"

His name tag says Karl. Karl with a *K*. He looks like a Karl with a *K*. All entitled and judgy. The teenage acne and oversize plastic frames almost had me fooled into thinking he was some *Pretty in Pink*, Jon Cryer nice guy. But he's not. Karl is no Duckie Dale. I narrow my eyes and push the 10 percent tip option on the card reader instead of 20 percent.

"My husband is dead, Karl."

"Oh my god." My receipt shakes like a leaf in his hand. "Are you serious?"

"No, but what kind of person asks someone if they're alone in an airport?" I snatch the receipt from him. "I'll tell you what kind. Serial killers. Are you a serial killer, Karl?"

"No!" Karl frantically waves his hands in front of me. "I thought I was flirting. I promise I wasn't thinking of killing you."

"Oh." I wish I could say this was the first time that something like this has happened to me. You'd think that a woman who writes romance books for a living would be a tiny bit more perceptive when it comes to flirting. "Sorry I called you a serial killer."

We stare at each other in awkward silence. There's a small line of people behind me that had no idea they'd be getting dinner and a show when they stepped in line for pizza.

"Do you want Parmesan packets?"

"Obviously."

Ozzie and I take our slices to a table at the back of the food court. It's the farthest I can get away from Karl and people without breaking any laws of science.

I pull out my phone and open the Smut Coven group chat.

Penny: I scared a cashier who was trying to flirt with me.
Jackie: Again?
Chelsey: Did you make this one cry?
Penny: No. I called him a serial killer though.

The Smut Coven consists of me and my two closest friends, Chelsey Hicks and Jackie Von. Like me, Jackie and Chelsey are romance writers. We met at a local writers' group, not long after I moved to San Francisco, and started critiquing each other's work. When Jackie and Chelsey's lease was up, they moved in with me, and the Smut Coven was born. We've been roomies for the past nine years, and as of a month ago, we're now business partners. Or at least we will be if we can come up with the cash to officially open our romance bookstore.

Chelsey: That wasn't very Pisces of you.
Jackie: Cut yourself some slack. It's your first time home in forever.
Jackie: And you're there on business. Not pleasure.

That's the truth. I've always been envious of people who go home for the holidays or even just on a whim without having to book extra sessions with their therapists to prep first. It's not that my parents are bad people. They recycle, send handwritten thank-you notes, and I'm willing to bet they're lifelong donors to the ASPCA because of that Sarah McLachlan commercial. They're good people. They're just so radically different from me that whenever we spend time together, we always end up turning into the worst versions of ourselves.

And I know it's me. I'm the problem.

My twin sister, Phoebe, posts pictures on social media all the time of her with our parents at brunch at the Del Coronado or at home having a barbecue, and they all look so happy. I know social media is the highlight reel of our lives, but the reason Phoebe posts so many pictures with our parents is because she's with them all the time. By choice. Even now I'm not coming home by choice. It's a necessity.

Penny: Business. Not pleasure. I can do this.
Chelsey: Mercury is in retrograde.
Jackie: Ugh. Of course it is.
Penny: Mercury is so rude.
Chelsey: You've got this.
Jackie: There's a new moon in two nights.
Chelsey: That's a good sign!
Penny: Maybe. I'll keep you guys posted.

I scarf down a few bites of pizza as I look at the rideshare app on my phone. As expected, the holiday means fewer drivers—the number of which allow pets is already minimal—and more passengers. I plug in my parents' address on Coronado Island and watch as a little car widget dances across my phone screen promising that it's looking for a match that will *offer a speedy and friendly drive.* I pour a little of my bottled water into Ozzie's travel bowl and polish off the crust of my pizza. *No Rides Found* flashes across my phone screen.

"Please consider editing your preferences to increase your chances of finding a friendly Dryver near you," I mumble to myself as I scroll through the list of preferences. "Smoking is out of the question. Right, Ozzie?"

Ozzie actually likes the way gross stuff smells, as is evidenced by the way he greets new friends at the dog park. My mother, on the other hand, has a nose that could rival a dog trained to sniff out drugs and illegally transported fruit at border checkpoints. If I show up smelling like cigarettes, she won't let me in the house without first squirting me down with a hose. I decide that smoking is nonnegotiable, which leaves only one other possible option to yield different search results. *The more the merrier!*

Shit.

People. Strangers to be exact. Strangers like to make small talk, and if Karl has taught me anything, it's that casual conversation isn't my strong suit. Suddenly, secondhand smoke doesn't sound so bad. Unfortunately, my mom would probably burn my clothes, leaving me with only my old prom dresses hanging in my closet to wear. I can't spend the next three days dressed in floor-length ball gowns in hideous shades of aqua and pink.

"Fine," I say to no one as I push the silly button that looks like a tiny stick figure orgy. "The more the freaking merrier."

I wait as the little car widget spins and spins. So help me, if this doesn't yield any results, I'll be forced to take the bus, which on the unpleasantness meter is somewhere between pubic lice and talking to my father for an entire car ride without a drink.

"Your friendly Dryver will be at your location in three minutes," my phone announces robotically.

Three minutes? Geez! It's going to take me twice as many minutes just to get all my stuff together.

I force Ozzie back into his crate and am met with one of his old-man growls. I apologize as I plop my luggage on top of his crate and start booking it toward the ground transportation pickup terminal. Running is the sort of thing I don't enjoy, for two reasons. One, it's running, and two, it's not walking.

"Your friendly Dryver is approaching," says my phone. "Please be ready at the designated Dryver pickup location."

"That's the fastest three minutes I've ever seen," I mutter under my breath.

The sliding terminal doors are in sight when I realize I'm not sure what the car that is picking me up looks like. I struggle to keep one eye on my phone and one on the sea of people in front of me. A beige minivan. Oh, lovely. Room for an entire polka band from Sheboygan. I spot the van as soon as I'm outside.

"Penelope Banks?" the driver asks. He looks younger than the majority of my lingerie collection, which is concerning for multiple reasons. "Traveling to Coronado Island?"

"That's me," I say. "Should I put my bag in the back or is that where you're keeping the band?"

"Band?"

"Never mind."

"If you say so. My name is Aidan, and I'll be your friendly Dryver." Aidan takes my bag. "The other passenger should be arriving shortly. Please, take a seat."

A clap of thunder breaks overhead, followed by a light sprinkle. Ozzie yips in his crate. He hates thunder and lightning and wind. He actually hates all weather that isn't sun, which I think is the reason he has epic meltdowns whenever it rains in California. He feels betrayed.

"Hush." I lift him into the van and place him on the floor between the two middle-row captain's seats. "If you get us kicked off this van, I'm shipping you to Sheboygan." Ozzie turns away from me and stares out the open door to scream at the rain. "Good talk."

I riffle through my oversize purse to find his doggy cannabis treats. His barking escalates, which doesn't help things, considering my purse is more like a giant garbage disposal wrapped in faux leather. It contains everything from a few advance reader copies my publisher sent me to my traveling collection of crystals and lethal hand sanitizer.

"Where the hell are you?" I grumble under my breath.

"Right here."

I whip my head away from my purse so fast I smack it on the driver's seat in front of me. I know that voice. I know that voice the way I know my own. I look up, and there he is. Smith Mackenzie.

My ex-husband.

Chapter 2

I'm in the upside down.

That's the only thing that can possibly explain my current predicament. I, Penny Elsbeth Banks, have somehow managed to be sucked into a cruel alternate universe where kind and spicy romance authors are not only forced to attend Thanksgiving dinner as spinsters begging their family for money, but also forced to ride in cars with their ex-husbands. I'm basically one janky string of Christmas lights away from going full-on Winona Ryder.

"Smith?" My mouth goes dry. "Why are you standing in front of my rideshare?"

"*Your* rideshare?" He smirks in a way that I'm pretty sure most people would describe as charming. "I thought it was mine."

He taps on the leather mailbox-shaped carrier slung over his arm. A graying fuzzball of a Pomeranian pops her head out of the carrier and starts to pant. Instantly, my heart melts.

"Harriet!" I squeal. "Oh my god. I can't believe you still have her. Let her out. I need to hold her."

Harriet is Ozzie's littermate. We adopted them in what I now realize was a Hail Mary to distract ourselves from the fact that we had no business being married. We filed for divorce a few weeks later. Thankfully, the dogs lasted longer.

Smith slides into the captain's seat next to me and carefully pulls Harriet out of her carrier. Her little butt starts to wiggle a hundred miles an hour as he places her in my lap.

"Careful. She pees when she's happy," Smith warns me.

"So do I." I nestle into her as she showers my face with kisses. "I've missed you, little one. Both of us have. Ozzie, look. It's your sister."

I lower Harriet to Ozzie's crate, unsure of how the two will take to each other. Ozzie's a big, dopey goofball that loves everyone. Sometimes he loves them a little too much. He's a recovering excited humper. But, like me, Harriet might be less than thrilled with having relatives shoved in front of her snout after a plane ride.

She gives him a little sniff through the crate before launching into a complete love fest. They yip, whine, and piddle with delight. I open Ozzie's crate and watch as two old dogs become puppies all over again.

"Looks like they're all caught up." Smith's gaze shifts from the dogs to me. "I guess now it's our turn. How the hell have you been, Penny?"

"Uh. Fine?" I chuckle nervously, suddenly acutely aware that I'm sitting less than two feet away from my ex-husband.

He somehow looks the same way I remember him, but also so different. His chestnut brown hair is short, the way it was when we were in high school, minus the early 2000s frosted tips. There are a few streaks of gray around his temples and a little peppered into his beard. The beard is new. It changes his face in a way that isn't bad, just unfamiliar. It makes him look more serious and brings a hardness to his expression that doesn't exist in my memories. At least not the memories of Smith I choose to revisit. Smith always had this light in his eyes, a the-world-is-my-oyster and glasses-are-half-full sort of way about him. They lit up his whole face. That light's a little dimmer now than it is in my memories. I guess life has a way of doing that.

Part of me is curious what he's thinking about me. How closely do I match the memories of me that he's kept tucked away? My physical appearance isn't all that different. Same coppery red hair with a mind of its own. Same freckles that his mother used to say reminded her of constellations. Jeans and a flannel shirt like I wore all the time when it was just the two of us and I wasn't worried about trying to impress anyone. I'm sure I look the same to him on the outside, but if he could see me on the inside now, I'm not sure he'd recognize me.

"Geez, it's been what, ten years? Who would've thought after all this time we'd meet up like this?"

A romance author or the devil himself, would be my guess. Both get their kicks out of torturing folks, although romance authors at least have the common courtesy to promise a happy ending.

"Beats me," I reply.

"Where are you living now?"

"San Francisco," I say. "You?"

"Phoenix is home. Though I'm barely there."

It's the kind of statement that normally begs a follow-up question of *Why's that?* But I don't need to ask because I already know the answer. Smith's a nomad at heart. He could wake up in a new city every morning and be perfectly content. I'm the exact opposite. I need a home like a surfboard needs a wave.

"San Francisco is a great city. Expensive as hell. One of my clients lives there, and he told me he pays thirty grand a year for preschool."

"It costs a lot."

"Oh." He looks somewhat surprised. "Do you have kids?"

My stomach free-falls into my Birkenstocks. I didn't mean to imply that I had kids or that I had the slightest idea of the going rate for preschool. I meant that San Francisco in general is an expensive place to live.

"No." I shake my head. "No kids."

"Me neither."

We exchange awkward glances as if neither one of us is exactly sure where to take the conversation from here. Talking about kids felt a little too personal, at least for me. It's not like we're two old friends who fell out of touch. We chose not to be in each other's lives anymore. I don't hate Smith the way some exes do, but I also don't know that I want to spend the next twenty minutes catching up with him. What would be the point?

The van's back door slams shut, which unleashes the inner ankle-biting beasts deep within Ozzie and Harriet. They yip and howl with all the rage of a pair of Furbys, and I couldn't be happier for the disruption.

"Luggage is secured." Aidan eases into the driver's seat and adjusts the navigation system. "Let's get this show on the . . . hmm. That's odd. The navigation just added another twenty minutes to our drive."

"Why?" I pat Ozzie's back to help settle him. "Did the island move?"

"You're funny." Aidan chuckles as he shifts the van into drive. "It's just holiday traffic. I hope that doesn't throw too big of a wrench in your plans for the evening."

The real wrench in my plans is over six feet tall, with enough smolder to fill an entire Beverly Jenkins novel.

"That's no problem for me," Smith says. "It'll give us some time to catch up."

"Didn't we just do that?" I chuckle nervously. "You live in Phoenix. I live in San Francisco. No babies. I feel caught up."

Smith looks at me sideways, like he can't tell whether I'm joking.

"You two know each other?" Aidan asks. "Makes sense since the two of you are going to the same street. Pretty ritzy street at that. Did you guys grow up together or something?"

Great. Now the driver has questions. This rideshare is turning into *The View* very quickly.

"We were in rival gangs," I deadpan. "My family colors were plaid. His were floral. Twice a year we'd street fight with pool noodles, and the winner got to smash the loser's china piece by piece like they do in those mafia movies; except in the movies, they smash fingers instead of china. It was all very hard core."

"Uh." Aidan slow blinks at me in the rearview mirror. I'm not totally sure, but it kind of looks like he's signaling SOS in Morse code. "That's interesting."

"We're divorced," Smith says.

My breath catches in my chest. He said it so easily. Like it was no different than telling someone his eye color or his voting party.

Smith catches on to the fact that my eyeballs are now dangling outside my head. "You all right?"

"Are you going to tell him my bra size next? Maybe my social security number?" I lower my voice. "He's our driver, not Anderson Cooper."

"A divorce is public knowledge. You can google it." Smith shrugs. "What's the big deal?"

"It's not a big deal," I say defensively.

"Are you sure? Because your face is saying otherwise. You've got that little worry divot you always get when you're upset." He touches the spot in between his eyebrows where he thinks I have a *worry divot*, but I have a receipt for $500 worth of Botox that says otherwise. "I didn't mean to upset you."

"You didn't," I fire back.

"Good. I'm glad to hear it. I'd hate for us to have to settle this in the streets. I forgot my floral shirt and pool noodle."

I let the subject drop and focus my gaze out the window to catch my breath. I've been back in San Diego for an hour, and it already feels like a lifetime. I take my phone from my purse and summon the Smut Coven.

Penny: Houston, we have a problem.
Chelsey: Oh my god, did your dad say no already?
Jackie: Did you show him the Google Slides presentation I made for you?
Penny: Relax. I haven't talked to my dad yet.
Penny: I'm in my rideshare right now.
Penny: Sitting next to my ex-husband.

The van jerks to a halt, causing my seat belt to strangle me.

"Sorry about that," Aidan says over his shoulder. "You know what they say, nobody knows how to drive in the rain. Self included. So how long have you two been divorced?"

My entire body tenses at the word. I glare at him in the rearview mirror. "Aidan, your rating goes down half a star every time the word *divorce* is mentioned in here."

It's not that I'm embarrassed about being divorced. It's something that happened to me, like chicken pox when I was five and overplucked eyebrows when I was fifteen. It was unpleasant, but it didn't kill me, and most of the time, I don't even think about it happening at all. Divorce and my marriage are neatly tucked away in little boxes of emotion in the Old Penny filing system of my brain. I like keeping them there under lock and key. Smith bringing up our divorce screws up the whole system, which is the last thing I need before going home for the first time in a decade.

"What about marriage? I, myself, am recently engaged to my long-time girlfriend, Viktoria. We're meeting for the first time this Christmas. She lives in the Czech Republic, or at least I think that's where she's at. Her English isn't exactly great."

There's an entire *90 Day Fiancé* episode's worth of material I'd like to unpack with Aidan, and under normal circumstances, I would. But right now, I don't have the mental bandwidth to juggle his mail-order bride and my ex-husband.

"You take this one, or I'm going to make him stop at Target so I can buy a pool noodle and whack him with it," I say to Smith and open up my group chat again.

Chelsey: Shit. What are the odds?
Penny: Not in my favor.
Jackie: What does he look like? Is he still all dreamboaty?

I glance at Smith from the corner of my eye, as if I somehow need a reminder of the fact that he's aged quite well.

Penny: He looks fine.

Jackie: Fine?

Jackie: You're a USA Today bestselling romance author, and all you're going to give us is fine?

Chelsey: Never mind what he looks like. How do you feel about seeing him?

Jackie: Right. Feelings.

Jackie: Also, take his picture.

Penny: I don't know how I feel.

Penny: And I can't take his picture.

Jackie: Sure you can. Pretend you're taking a selfie.

Chelsey: Or take a minute to process your emotions.

Penny: That's weird.

Penny: The selfie fake out. Not the processing.

Penny: I'm not in the headspace to process feelings.

Jackie: Maybe taking his picture will help.

Chelsey: Jackie!

Jackie: What? You're not curious what he looks like now?

Chelsey: A little.

Penny: Fine. I'll take the damn picture.

Jackie: Thank you.

I turn on my camera, which is unfortunately on selfie mode. Nothing quite prepares you for seeing what you'd look like if Jabba the Hutt was your father. I flip the camera and steal a glance at Smith. Suddenly, my palms are all sweaty, and it feels like there might as well be a neon sign flashing above my head that reads *Peeping Tom*. The things I do for my friends. I lift my phone eye level and try to angle it so that it looks like I'm taking a selfie.

"Are you taking my picture?" Smith asks.

I fumble my phone. "No. I was taking a selfie."

"Really? You want a photo to commemorate your time in this rideshare?"

"That sounds awfully judgy coming from a man who made me take his photo with the Oscar Mayer Wienermobile on more than one occasion."

"Do not mock the Wienermobile." Smith holds out his hand. "Hand me your phone. I'll take the picture for you."

"As if," I say in my best Cher Horowitz voice. "The whole point of a selfie is that you don't need anyone to take it for you. Ask any Kardashian."

"True, but I'm pretty sure I could ask any Kardashian if they wanted their photo taken by an award-winning photographer and they'd jump at the chance."

"You're an award-winning photographer?"

"In the flesh."

"Have they called you to photograph the Wienermobile yet?"

"Not yet." He looks down at his hand. "The offer still stands."

"Fine." I quickly change my camera back to selfie mode and hand over my phone. "But make sure you get my good side. I don't have the Kardashian money to ensure that all of my sides are good."

"You never needed it, Pen."

Heat spreads across the apples of my cheeks, and I can't help but smile so big it hurts my face. He hands back my phone, and I instantly start to tuck it back in my purse.

"An award-winning photographer takes your picture, and you don't even bother to look." He shakes his head. "I'm insulted."

"Calm down, diva. Clearly the description *award-winning* doesn't extend to your personality." I open up my phone. Looking up from my screen isn't a picture of me. It's him.

"You can let Jackie know that you got the damn picture." He chuckles. "Her text popped up when you handed me the phone."

My cheeks go from heated to wildfire, and for the first time in a very long time, I'm speechless. I drop the picture in the group chat and tuck my phone away.

"By the way, what exactly is a Smut Coven?" He cocks an eyebrow.

"I'd tell you, but then I'd have to kill you, which I wouldn't mind doing, but it doesn't seem fair to make Aidan an accomplice."

Aidan slams on the brakes, and the van fishtails from side to side as we attempt to merge onto the 5. Ozzie and Harriet slide to the back of the van. I turn to reach for them, but Smith's arm holds me back like a human seat belt. He holds me like that until Aidan regains control of the van, and when Smith finally moves his arm, I think my heart might beat right out of my chest.

"I think he's trying to kill us both." My voice shakes.

"Sorry about that!" Aidan shouts over his shoulder. "You'd think on Thanksgiving, people would at least be willing to let you in. Won't be long until we're at the bridge, and then it should be smooth sailing. You two should be home in no time."

"Sounds good," Smith says.

Aidan lays on the horn. "One lane, buddy! You get one lane! Sorry about that, guys. It must be a full moon or something. All the weirdos are out."

"It's not," Smith and I say in unison.

We lock eyes, and suddenly it's like we're a couple of actors that have just broken the fourth wall. I reach for the smoky quartz necklace around my neck and run my fingers over its smooth surface. Fiona, Smith's mother, gave it to me. She taught me about moon phases, astrology, and crystals. She taught me a lifetime's worth of lessons. Smith never had much interest in that stuff when we were young. It was all too woo-woo for him, but I liked finding something to believe.

"There's a new moon in two days," Smith says.

"When did you start paying attention to the moon?"

"This summer." His face grows solemn. "Before Mom died."

My stomach plummets to my feet. "I had no idea. I didn't see anything in *Entertainment Weekly* or *Rolling Stone*." Smith's parents were famous musicians. Jasper and Fiona had a dozen number-one songs, a handful of multiplatinum albums, and enough songwriting credits to fill a museum. They were weird and eccentric, like all the best people are, and they loved bigger than the Pacific, like most people rarely do.

"She didn't want any of that."

"Smith, I'm so sorry." My throat tightens around my words. "She was an amazing woman. How are you doing? How's your sister?"

"We're all right," he says. "This is our first holiday since she passed, so we're just trying to figure out what normal looks like now. Mo's flying in tomorrow, and together we're going to get the house in order so we can sell it. No point in keeping it anymore."

"Right."

I offer a weak smile and put on a brave face, but on the inside, something is breaking. The thought of someone else living inside the Mackenzies' house hurts like a punch to the gut. It hurts more than the thought of my parents selling their home. Smith's house was my second home for years. It was the one place I could go and feel complete acceptance and zero judgment, because nobody there cared that I wasn't as accomplished as my sister, as poised as my mother, or as driven as my father. Most of all, I didn't have to pretend to care that I wasn't any of those things—I could just be me. I hate the idea of someone moving in and erasing that.

"Make a wish," Aidan calls over his shoulder as we cross onto the bridge. "My mother is very superstitious. She swore that if we didn't make a wish when crossing a bridge, the entire thing would collapse." He looks at us expectantly in the mirror. "So if you wouldn't mind."

"Got it," Smith says. "Two wishes coming up. Right, Penny?"

"Right." I nod.

I'd hate to be the reason a half-century-old bridge collapsed. My mother would never forgive me for making her seating arrangement uneven on Thanksgiving.

Chapter 3

Within minutes of crossing onto the Coronado Bridge, traffic comes to a dead stop. Turns out, one of us should've wished we'd actually make it off the bridge.

Smith and I listen to Aidan describe some of his mother's other superstitions. The most interesting of which involves never buying a book without reading the ending first. I thought it was some sort of *When Harry Met Sally* reference, but according to Aidan, his great-aunt Ina died in a hot-air balloon accident before she got to finish the final book in the Hunger Games series. A true disappointment.

The conversation takes a hard right turn when Aidan realizes that Smith's parents are Jasper and Fiona Mackenzie, and he's in the presence of rock and roll royalty. I can only listen to Smith talk about them for a few minutes before I start to feel weepy. Jasper died soon after Smith and I divorced, so I'm used to thinking about him in the past tense. Thinking about Fiona that way just feels wrong.

Penny: Smith's mom died.
Chelsey: Oh no. You two were close.
Penny: We used to be.
Penny: I'm feeling things.
Penny: I don't like it.

Jackie: After looking at that picture you sent, I'm feeling things too.

Jackie: Pants feelings. Big pants feelings.

Chelsey: Jackie, read the room.

Jackie: Sorry. I've been writing sex scenes all day.

Penny: It's fine.

Penny: It's just weird being here with him and knowing she's not around anymore.

Penny: Everything feels so weird.

I wait for my last text to send, but the message pops back undeliverable. The rain is coming down in buckets, and I wouldn't be surprised if it started hailing. I lean forward to check the navigation system for our ETA. It reads *Travel Time Not Found*.

"How long have we been stopped?" I ask Smith. "Do you have cell service?"

"Long enough for Aidan to go through my parents' entire discography." Smith takes his phone from his pocket. "I don't think so. I do have a traffic alert notification."

"Mind sharing that with me, boss?" Aidan asks.

"Sure. It looks like there are two separate accidents on the Coronado side of the bridge. No major injuries, but we should expect delays."

"For how long?" Aidan asks.

"It doesn't say."

"It doesn't say?" Aidan's voice tightens. "What kind of cockamamie traffic report doesn't bother to tell you how long to expect a delay?"

Smith and I shoot each other a look just as my phone rings. It's Phoebe, which is kind of like the first warning flare when it comes to my family's alert system. "Service might be sketchy, but it looks like it's back. I need to take this. Keep an eye on him."

"Where's he going to go?" Smith unbuckles his seat belt and moves to the front of the van.

"To hell in a minivan," I say over my shoulder as I climb into the back seat, which Ozzie and Harriet have unofficially claimed as their new home. "Hey, Phoebe—"

"Where the hell are you?" Phoebe snaps. Rarely does my sister raise her voice or fly off the handle—that's my thing—but right now I can tell she's dangerously close to losing it. "Just tell me that you are still coming, and that you didn't suddenly get hit by a bus or get bitten by a rabid squirrel and now you're foaming at the mouth."

I take it back. Phoebe has officially lost it.

"First, I would never be bitten by a rabid squirrel because small woodland creatures make me uncomfortable. I avoid them at all costs. Second, if you keep talking nonsense like that, I might strongly consider letting a moped run over my foot."

"I'm going to ignore everything you just said and just ask you to confirm that you're almost here."

"Well, I can't exactly do that."

"And why is that?"

"Because we're stuck on the bridge."

"Really, Penny?" She makes zero effort to hide the disbelief in her voice. "Is that the story you're going with now? *Penny can't make Thanksgiving because she can't cross the Coronado Bridge?*"

"It's not a story. Google it if you don't believe me," I reply defensively. "Why are you freaking out? You're Mom and Dad's favorite. You're always spending time with them. Are they giving you too many compliments or showering you with too many mentions in their will?"

"I'm not their favorite."

Phoebe is hands down my parents' favorite. She's the twin that did everything right. She's Beyoncé, and I'm Kelly Rowland. No disrespect to Kelly, of course. She's just no Beyoncé, and I am no Phoebe Banks.

"It's OK, you can say you're their favorite. I actually really like being first runner-up. There's so much less pressure. Plus, if you die first, I get the title anyway, so it all works out."

"Mom and Dad are the ones freaking out." She lowers her voice. "They've been trying to make sure everything is perfect for the return of their prodigal daughter, and now that you're running a little late, they're worried that you'll no-show on them."

There it is. Proof that I'm the black fly in their chardonnay. Proof that my presence, or lack thereof, throws off the entire family balance. But most of all, proof that they don't trust me.

"Tell them I'm going to be there, Phoebe. OK?"

"I will." She pauses, and I worry for a second that she still doesn't believe me. "There's something else."

"What?"

"Falon and I have some really big news." The excitement in her voice is palpable through the phone.

"If the news is that you're engaged, everyone already knows."

"It's not that. It's different. A little scary, but exciting. We want everyone to be here when we share it."

"I'll be there," I say. "I promise."

A clap of thunder breaks over the car, and Aidan lets out a yelp. Smith mouths *Help*, and I realize that Aidan's earlier freak-out is slowly morphing into an all-out panic meltdown. *Damn Mercury in retrograde.*

"I got to go," I say. "Smith needs my help."

"Smith?"

"Uh." I cringe, hating myself for bringing him into the conversation. "Yeah. Smith's in my rideshare."

"Your Smith?" Phoebe nearly chokes. "You're in a van with *your* Smith?"

"He isn't *my* Smith," I hiss. "But yes, Smith Mackenzie is in my van."

"I better cut Dad off now. When he finds out that Smith is in the same car with you, he's going to lose it."

A pit settles into my stomach. I've been so preoccupied with the chaos of being in a van with my ex-husband that I haven't had a chance to consider the potential anarchy that will happen if my dad sees Smith and me together. The two of them were never exactly BFFs when Smith and I were a couple, and I may have made Smith look less than favorable—read: a complete asshole—when I told them about the divorce. My father is usually a Southern gentleman, but I have a feeling that chivalry doesn't extend to ex-husbands. I think that's what ass whoopings are typically reserved for down south.

"He's not going to know." I lower my voice. "*You* weren't even supposed to know. Nobody has to know at all. OK?"

"If you say so." Her voice is laced with intrigue. "I am curious, though."

"About what?"

"You."

"What about me?"

"It's just . . . you know." I can practically see the wry smile that matches mine taking shape on her face. "You've never really gotten over him."

"That's not true." Heat rises across my skin. "Why would you say that? How could you possibly think that?"

"You just loved him so much. You'd talk about him for hours and go on and on about—"

The van makes an abrupt, sharp stop, jerking my body forward. My phone slips from my hands, and slides under the seat in front of me. I scramble to pick it up, my fingers fumbling over the screen, which is just out of reach.

"Sorry," Aidan says between rapid breaths. "My foot slipped."

"It's fine, Aidan. Maybe you should put in—"

"And how great the sex was." My sister's voice blares from underneath the seat. *Fuck. Fuck. Fuck.* I must've hit the damn speaker button. "I mean, he was never exactly my cup of tea for obvious reasons, but you worshipped his abs like some kind of—"

"Phoebe!" I shriek, shoving my face as far as it will go underneath the seat. "Stop talking!"

"Don't get me wrong. Martin seems great, and while I don't understand the appeal of a bulging—"

The van goes silent, and for a second, I wonder if it's possible I have just died of humiliation. There's a tap on my shoulder, which feels too informal a greeting for heaven or hell.

"It was a lot easier to get your phone from this side of the seat." Smith's lips are in a tight line that will likely break into a shit-eating grin at any moment. "I went ahead and hung up for you too."

"Thanks," I manage to squeak out. "I appreciate that."

"Anything else I can do for you down there?"

"No. I'm going to take a couple of minutes and wait for a lightning bolt to put me out of my suffering."

"The rubber in the tires might make that a hard wish to deliver. How about I go back up front and pretend I didn't hear anything?"

"Sounds lovely."

"If it makes you feel any better, you distracted Aidan from googling the odds of dying on a bridge in a hurricane."

"We're not in a hurricane," I mumble.

"We could be!" Aidan shouts. "And let me tell you, the odds are not looking good, folks."

"I'm going to go back up there." He lowers his mouth to my ear. "And I'm taking my abs with me."

"That's not pretending you didn't hear anything," I growl.

"I didn't mention a word about the great sex."

An icy shiver runs down my spine, tingling every hair on my body. I know that shiver. It's the kind of shiver that leads to feelings in areas of my body that have no business feeling anything about anyone in this van right now.

I grab my purse and hole up in the back seat with one of the advance reader copies my publisher sent me. My brain is a jumbled mess of emotions firing at breakneck speed, so I don't actually expect myself to focus on reading. I just need a physical barrier between me and Smith and his abs. I skim the front and back cover of the book. It's a regency romance, which isn't normally my vibe, but since our romance bookstore will carry all subgenres, I want to stretch my reading palate. I crack the book open and turn to the first page. *Sweat glistened like morning dew on the admiral's taut abdominals.* I close the book and chuck it back in my purse.

Maybe a romance novel isn't the best buffer. Maybe Aidan has a nice car manual he can loan me instead. There shouldn't be any mentions of abs or sex in a car manual, right? I need something to get me through the next two miles of this bridge, and I'm too scared to pick up my phone again. I always thought technology would be the downfall of society; I just didn't realize it was going to start with my phone subjecting me to public humiliation. Between the fog and the rain, you can barely see the bay through the window, which means counting sailboats isn't an option. I could try to sleep, but occasionally I talk in my sleep, and the last thing I need is for my subconscious to embarrass me further.

All of a sudden, all three of our cell phones emit an awful warning sound that makes it feel like the end of the world is upon us. Harriet and Ozzie take turns barking and whimpering, which is only slightly drowned out by Aidan's panicked breathing.

"It's just a storm update," Smith says calmly. "No need to panic."

"What does it say?" Aidan's face is about four shades paler than I remember it being at the start of our trip. "Does it say that we're in a hurricane? This feels like a hurricane to me, don't you agree?"

"We're not in a hurricane," Smith says. "The alert just says that there's a severe thunderstorm and we should expect travel delays."

"That's it?" Aidan's voice is shrill. "What incompetent institution is in charge of sending those alerts out? I could've looked out the window and told you that. How severe does it say the storm is? Like on a scale of one to ten, how close are we to dying in this thing?"

"We're not going to die, buddy." Smith pats Aidan's shoulder.

"But what if we do, and I never get to meet Viktoria in person? What if I end up dying before I ever get the chance to be married?

My mother's only wish is for me to get married." His foot slips off the brakes for a second, causing the van to lurch forward. "Sorry. Sorry. I . . . um . . . I think I just feel a little hot. Stuffy. Do you mind if I turn on the air-conditioning?"

Aidan fiddles with the temperature dial, positioning all the vents toward him at first and then away. He pulls at the collar of his button-down and dabs at the sweat beading down his face.

"Do you need a bottle of water or something?" I reach for the complimentary bottle in the cup holder next to me and hand it to Smith. "Also, it might not be a bad idea to put the car in park."

"Thanks." He takes the bottle, but he can't steady his hands enough to twist off the lid. "Um . . . I . . . uh . . ."

"I got you." Smith opens the bottle and holds it out for him. "Take a drink and put the car in park. We're not going anywhere right now."

He follows Smith's directions and leans back in his seat, closing his eyes as he slowly drinks.

"Have you ever had a panic attack?" Smith asks.

"Just once, when I was eleven." His chest heaves up and down a little faster. "I got stuck in an elevator for seven hours at Horton Plaza. I take the stairs now whenever possible. Do you think we're going to get stuck on this bridge for seven hours? If I can't take the bridge anymore, it's going to really limit my business."

"I can't imagine the storm lasting that long," Smith says. "You just focus on your breathing."

"I puked in that elevator," Aidan says. "Several times."

"If you could not puke in here, that would be much appreciated," I say. "Ozzie will probably try to eat it, and then I'll puke, and that will definitely limit your business."

"You're not as good at this comforting thing as he is." Aidan nods toward Smith.

"You're not the first person to tell me that."

And I have a feeling he won't be the last.

Chapter 4

"Do you have a paper bag, by chance?" Smith asks me. "We need to slow down his breathing before he hyperventilates."

All it takes is another big clap of thunder to finally push Aidan and the dogs over the edge. I think the dogs are more freaked out by Aidan freaking out than they are by the storm. I relocate them to the copilot's spot up front, while Smith convinces Aidan to lie down in the back seat.

"I actually might." I reach into my purse and feel around for Ozzie's cannabis dog cookies. "Will this work?"

Smith takes a look at the hand-stamped logo on the bag. It's a pink poodle and a marijuana leaf, which I think is the perfect blend of trashy and cute. A smile curls his lips as he pours the remaining cookies into the palm of his hand. He sniffs them and gives a nod of approval.

"Is that toffee I smell?" He hands the cookies to me.

"They're Ozzie's favorite. He's not great with flying, and they seem to keep him calm."

"Do they work on humans?" Smith tilts his head toward Aidan.

"Why don't we start with offering him a paper bag before we resort to drugging our driver."

"Good point."

Smith hands the paper bag to Aidan. He takes a series of rapid breaths, testing the elasticity of the bag to its limit. I have no idea if breathing into a bag actually makes anyone less anxious, but watching Aidan do it is giving me anxiety.

"Better?" I ask after he rests the bag on his chest.

"Now I'm just hungry." Aidan brushes some crumbs away from his beard. "I didn't eat lunch today. What if we're up here all night? I have low blood sugar."

"Are you diabetic?" Smith asks.

"I don't think so." A worried look crosses Aidan's face. "But food is my go-to when I'm stressed."

"Do you keep anything to eat in the car?" I ask.

"No. It's against company policy." Aidan's breathing starts to quicken again. "Also, if you could please leave this whole incident out of your review, I'd appreciate it. I really need this job. Viktoria won't marry me if I'm unemployed."

"Five stars are coming your way, buddy," Smith assures him. He turns to me. "Check our bags for anything that might be edible . . . other than the dog edibles in your purse."

"I'm on it."

My purse and Smith's man bag were moved up front when we turned the van into a triage unit for Aidan. I don't bother looking in my purse because I know that the closest things I have to food are some antique mints. Instead, I slide into the driver's seat with Smith's bag on my lap.

I almost can't bring myself to look through it. I'm the queen of snooping, but it feels wrong to riffle through my ex's belongings when he's just a few feet away. I run my index finger over the smooth, buttery leather. It reminds me of the leather jacket he always wore in high school. On cold nights, he'd let me borrow it, and I would breathe in the scent of his orange-spice cologne mixed with the earthiness of the leather. It was a little slice of heaven.

"Any luck?" Smith asks.

"Still looking," I reply.

I unclip the brass buckle and peer into his bag. It's neat and orderly, like I would expect it to be. There's a tablet secured in a matching leather cover. Two Montblanc pens and a stylus hang in leather loops on the interior of the bag next to his wallet. There's a paperback copy of the latest Stephen King novel and some sort of self-help book. Smith was always a reader, usually reading more books in a year than me, and there's something comforting in seeing that he still is.

A crack of thunder rattles the van, and Aidan lets out another yelp. I unzip the last compartment of Smith's bag, and to my relief, there's a pack of cinnamon gum.

"Here." I toss the pack to the back of the van. "This is all we've got."

I start to close Smith's bag, but something catches my eye. It's a small box in Tiffany blue. My heart sinks for reasons I don't fully understand. I steal a glance at the back seat. Smith and Aidan are locked in conversation. Apparently, Aidan has strong feelings about cinnamon-flavored gum. My fingers graze the edges of the box. It's too small to hold a bracelet, and the shape is all wrong for earrings.

"Peppermint soothes upset stomachs, not cinnamon," Aidan explains. "Don't you have any peppermint?"

"Penny, is there any peppermint gum in my bag?" Smith's voice is gruff.

"No," I reply, my gaze still fixed on the box. "Just cinnamon."

I close his bag and move back to the middle row before I have some sort of breakdown and open that ring box. I'm certain it has to be a ring box. The question is, what kind of ring is in it? Obviously, an engagement ring comes to mind. Not that it matters to me if it is. Smith and everything that has to do with him is going back in the Old Penny memory filing cabinet the minute this ride is over.

"Well, I'm running out of ideas," Smith says. "You got any?"

"I've got a worry stone in my pocket." I pull out the smooth amber-and-black stone. "It's tiger's eye."

"You want me to eat a rock?" Aidan wheezes.

"No. I'm going to want this stone back, and if you eat it, that's going to cause a problem. Tiger's eye is good for protection." I hold out the stone for him. "You can meditate on it. Sometimes people can get so relaxed when meditating with crystals that they fall asleep."

Aidan wrinkles his nose and makes a face. "Clearly it's not very good at protection. If it was, do you really think we'd be stuck on a bridge?"

"Well, the bridge hasn't collapsed yet, so it's kind of working, if you look at things from a glass-half-full point of view." I untuck my necklace from beneath my flannel. "This is smoky quartz. I wear it all the time when I'm traveling to help me feel safe."

Smith glances at my necklace. I can't tell whether he recognizes it as belonging to Fiona. There's a part of me that wants him to, though I'm not sure why. Maybe I just want a chance to talk about her with someone who loved her the way I did. Like a mother.

Aidan moans. "I don't think a magic rock is going to help me calm down."

"Not unless we hit him over the head with that rock repeatedly," Smith mutters before holding up what's left of Aidan's torn paper bag. "I think it's time to give the cookies a try."

A gust of wind whistles past the van, causing it to sway. Aidan braces himself with both arms on either side of the back seat as if he's preparing to be ejected into the eye of the storm.

"Do you think these winds are gale force?" Aidan winces as the van settles. "If they are, we're never going to make it. You know that, right?"

"I don't know what *gale force* means," I say. "My mother used to be friends with a Gayle, though. She was a jerk."

"Cookies." Smith motions toward my purse. "It's time for the cookies."

"I have no idea if these are going to work," I whisper. "I'm surprised you don't have something stronger."

"What's that supposed to mean?"

"Your parents used to grow weed the way my parents grow begonias. Don't you have a weed vape or something?"

"My parents would never vape weed." Smith shakes his head. "They were weed purists. It's rolled or nothing."

"We're suspended over the ocean on a giant tightrope, guys," Aidan continues, completely oblivious to Smith's and my conversation. "What if the bridge collapses? What if a tsunami hits us? What if the big one hits? What if—"

"You're right. Next time we get stuck in a van together, I'll make sure to pack a weed pen," Smith grumbles. "Now give me the cookies. They're our only hope."

"Fine." I take the bone-shaped cookies from my purse and thrust them into Smith's hand.

"Here you go, buddy." Smith shoves a cookie onto Aidan's lap. "We found something to eat. It's got a little CBD or THC or OPP in it that'll help calm you down."

"You want me to eat your dog's weed cookie?" Aidan makes a face. "Have you lost your mind?"

"It's totally safe," I say. "I buy them from this little boutique that sells artisan pet goods. They don't sell anything that isn't safe for human consumption. I promise."

"So, you've eaten these before?" Aidan points the dog biscuit at me.

"Well . . ." I stall and his confidence noticeably fades with each second of my silence. "No, but I suppose I would if I had to."

"Hand me one," Smith commands. "I'll have one with you, Aidan."

"I think I'd rather take my chances eating your magic rock."

Aidan tries to hand the cookie to me, but Smith intercepts it and takes a large bite. He chews it slowly at first. A weak smile flickers across his face. He nods and murmurs something that sounds like "Not bad" but could just as easily be "My bad." He motions for Aidan's bottle of water, and chases the bite down with three large gulps.

"There." Smith wipes his mouth with the back of his hand. He's not as pale as Aidan, but he's definitely a shade or two greener. "Now it's your turn. The both of you."

"Why me?" I ask.

"Because it's rude to bring food and not eat it." Smith lifts his brow and holds out his partially eaten cookie to me. "And solidarity."

"Fine."

Aidan and I cheers each other unenthusiastically. To my surprise, he takes a bite almost immediately. I, on the other hand, take a few extra moments to really allow the dread of eating dog food sink in. Smith clears his throat and gives me a look that I take to mean there will be no avoiding this cookie for the foreseeable future. I press it to my lips and gingerly take a bite.

The cookie turns into a paste on my tongue that remarkably manages to be both dry and gummy at the same time. The flavor isn't toffee as the smell of the baked good suggests. It's more like if toffee and garden soil had a love child. I assume the earthiness comes from the CBD or hemp or whatever marijuana-derived substance is legal to feed to a geriatric Pomeranian. The toffee flavoring tastes like it came from the same factory that makes cough medicine.

Aidan's watching me as if my reaction to consuming the cookie will directly affect his ability to keep eating his. I want nothing more than to roll down the window and spit the cookie glue now attaching itself to the roof of my mouth into the supposed gale-force winds that have caused Aidan's panic to escalate. But that's not an option. The only option if I want to restore any sense of calm in this van is to swallow. I force myself to do it, and Aidan follows suit.

"Are you feeling calmer?" Aidan asks.

"You know"—I take a long swig of water from one of the complimentary bottles tucked into the side-door pocket—"not really. I suspect it takes a little while, though. After all, it's a cookie, not a bong."

Not that I'm personally familiar with either.

"Have another bite." Smith smirks, fighting back laughter. "Both of you. Come on. Bottoms up."

"After you." I shove the cookie half an inch away from his face. "Solidarity. You said it yourself."

The van shakes from a sudden burst of wind. Rain smacks against the windows harder and faster, making it impossible to see anything but the faint glow of brake lights around us, the only reminder that we're not on this bridge alone. Aidan makes a whimpering sound, and in that moment, Smith and I both know what must be done.

"Bottoms up, boys." I grab the remaining two dog biscuits from my purse. "Bottoms up."

It takes ten minutes to finish our doggy weed cookies. Eleven minutes for me to regret suggesting that any human ever consume them, and, I suspect, a lifetime for me to ever get the god-awful taste of toffee-flavored dirt out of my mouth. For the record, I don't feel any calmer. I would venture to say my anxiety has actually increased since remembering one very crucial detail about Ozzie's experience with Barkie's Baked Goods for Dogs.

"I think these might have some laxative properties," I whisper to Smith as I struggle to read the ingredients on what's left of the paper bag. "Ozzie always seems to have to go after eating them."

We've claimed the front two seats of the van to give Aidan a little peace and quiet in the back. The dogs are snuggled into the space between our seats. A little elevator jazz à la Kenny G plays softly on the radio, and the AC is blowing cool air. If this combination doesn't put Aidan to sleep, it will surely knock me out, which at this point, might be preferable.

"I refuse to believe you're being serious." Smith fiddles with his phone, trying to force it to pick up service. "That just seems like a horrible design flaw. What good is a calm dog if he poops all over the place?"

"I didn't say he poops all over the place," I hiss. "I just mean that he always has to go afterward."

"I think the dog weed is making you paranoid."

"I'm not paranoid. I would just prefer to know whether we're all going to need to use the bathroom in the next hour or so."

"Hey, do you remember that Thanksgiving when we were in high school?" Smith's lips curl into a smile. "You stole that disgusting alcohol from your dad's liquor cabinet. What was that stuff?"

"Vermouth. Worst alcohol on the planet." I nod. "And yes, I remember that Thanksgiving." I remember it like it was yesterday.

"That stuff made me paranoid." He laughs. "To this day, I don't think I've ever been that drunk."

"You were always a lightweight."

"If I can survive that without getting sick, then I think I can survive eating dog food."

"Uh, you did get sick."

"Did I?"

"My parents wanted to burn down the tree house after you came down from there." The memory makes me smile. "Let's hope there isn't a repeat."

"Well, I've grown up a bit over the last two decades." He gazes out the windshield. "It went by fast, didn't it?"

"Some parts did," I whisper.

Other parts, particularly when I was in high school and college, seemed to go on forever.

Chapter 5

My girl Vermouth.

She's the first bottle I grab from my father's liquor cabinet in his office, and I instantly regret it. Vermouth tastes as if cold medicine, window cleaner, and a stale bag of black licorice had an orgy. I hate her from the first sip, but that doesn't stop me from taking another. And another.

"Pen, slow down." Smith grabs the bottle from my hand, splashing a little on my Abercrombie hoodie. He takes a drink and makes a face. "This shit is awful."

"Don't talk about Vermouth like that." I rest my head on his shoulder. "She's poetic, if you think about it. She's bold, but not necessarily in a good way. She's memorable. Also not necessarily in a good way. OK, fine. She's awful, but she's all we've got up here."

"Why exactly are we in your old tree house?" Smith takes another swig and shivers as it goes down. "My parents wouldn't care if you came over."

"Your parents don't celebrate Thanksgiving. They call it Colonizer's Day."

"True. But they are having a séance. They've also got normal booze like beer and those little bottles of fruity wine."

"Why are you so eager to abandon Vermouth?"

"Call me crazy, but I don't think she's going to help us get down from this tree if we keep partying with her."

In hindsight, the tree house is a less than ideal place to escape to. I haven't been up here since I was in middle school, and it's now home to a large community of dust bunnies, cobwebs, and probably a venomous spider or rabid opossum. My father has talked about tearing the thing down for years, but he's never gotten around to actually doing it. I bet if I started spending time in here again, he'd find the time to have it removed. He'd probably have someone here within a day to rip it out, along with the tree, just to make sure I didn't get any wild ideas about putting another one up in its place.

God, I can just hear him right now.

Tree houses are a distraction, Penelope. People who spend time in tree houses aren't the kind of people that get accepted into Princeton, and they're definitely not the kind of people who work for my company.

"I can't drink any more of this." Smith holds out the green bottle in front of me. "One more sip and your girl Vermouth is going to push me right out of this death trap."

"She would never."

"She would, and if the fall didn't kill me, your parents would."

"That would be a good distraction." I hold the bottle to my lips. "But I'm pretty sure once we cleared your body off the grass, my dad would still force me to sit down with Mr. Yates for my mock interview. Princeton waits for no one, not even death, you know."

"I had no idea how anticlimactic my death would be for your family."

"It's true." I force down another gulp of the putrid liquid. "But if it makes you feel any better, I'd really prefer you not to die. I'm pretty invested in us being together forever and having an epic honeymoon like Ashton Kutcher and Brittany Murphy did in *Just Married*."

"Their honeymoon was awful in that movie." Smith kisses the top of my head. The smell of vermouth on his breath is overwhelming. "Nothing goes right. They fight the whole time." He lowers his lips to my ear. "And they never have sex. How is that romantic?"

A warm smile takes shape over my slightly numb face. It won't be long now until my head goes foggy. After that, the fight with my parents this morning will seem like a distant memory. Hell, as strong as this stuff is hitting me, maybe I won't remember it at all.

"They see each other at their worst." A boozy hiccup escapes my lips. "And it doesn't scare them. At least not enough to stop loving each other."

"You should write that down in your notebook of story ideas." Smith chuckles. "Actually, you should write that down and give it to me. Fiona and Jasper could use some new material for their next album."

The patio door slams, causing a glitch in my mental journey from buzzed to drunk. I crawl across the rickety floor, no doubt covering the knees of my flared jeans in spiderwebs, and peer through the peephole in the center of a wooden plank. Marie, our maid, is standing on the backyard patio. She grabs a cigarette from the secret stash she keeps in her apron and lights it.

"Ms. Penelope!" she shouts in her beautiful French accent. "Ms. Penelope, the table is being seated!"

Marie takes a few puffs before putting the cigarette out on the sole of her black work shoe. She tosses the butt into the firepit before returning to the house. At least she can tell my parents she tried to find me. Of course, that also means it's only a matter of time before my mother comes tearing outside in one of her flowy caftans, looking for me.

"Last chance to run away to my mother's séance," Smith says.

"Who's Fiona trying to get a hold of today? Janis? Freddie?"

"Cobain." Smith shakes his head. "She's convinced this blue Fender she found in our attic is his. Swears he left it at our house when he came over for my dad's fiftieth birthday back in the nineties."

"Can't she just call Courtney and ask?"

"Where would be the fun in that?"

If I wasn't completely in love with Smith Mackenzie, I would hate his guts. His family is so ridiculously cool and easy to get along with. They always have the best parties. His parents invite over the most amazing and interesting people, and they do it for the simple pleasure of enjoying their company, not as a way to negotiate a deal or further benefit some aspect of their lives. Once, they spent eight hours locked in a game of Dungeons and Dragons with the guys from U2. They got so caught up in the game that they didn't have time to record a track for their next album together. But they didn't care. Jasper and Fiona never care about business more than people or family or fun. They're the polar opposite of my parents in every way imaginable. My parents never miss an opportunity for business.

Take today for example. Thanksgiving is supposed to be about family and friends and food. It's supposed to be about enjoying each other's company and being thankful for all that you have. It's the one day a year where you don't look at what your life is missing, because as long as you have the people that matter the most to you gathered around your table, you have everything you need. But that's not true for Carter Banks. For my dad, every day is a business day. Every day is an opportunity for a deal to be made, and every person a pawn to be used to further his own goals.

"He knows I'm not smart enough to go to Princeton," I mutter under my breath. "I'm not like Phoebe. I will never get grades like Phoebe."

"Huh? Are we still talking about Cobain?"

Smith is crouched over on his hands and knees. A tiny bead of sweat paints a trail from his gelled hairline to his smooth jaw. He's paler than I remember him being a few hours ago. Slightly green too, if I'm not mistaken, which I could be, seeing as how I'm pretty sure I'm drunk.

"I said my father knows I'm not smart. Phoebe is the smart one. I'm the creative one. Basically, Phoebe is the good daughter, and I'm the one that needs to be fixed."

Smith covers his ears like I've just blown an air horn in his face. "Why are you screaming at me?"

"I'm not."

"I can hear your voice in my eyeballs."

"Stop being so dramatic. Oh god. I sound like him now."

"Like who?"

"My father. I sound like my father."

Smith moves his hands from covering his ears to covering his mouth instead. "Your girl Vermouth is not settling well."

I pull myself up, grab a dusty plastic tub filled with a forgotten stash of CDs, and drop it next to Smith. "Puke in this."

"Penelope Banks!" My mother's voice echoes in my head like the voice of God. "Penelope, I know you're out there!"

I peek out the spy hole again just as my mother bends over to examine the remaining ash from Marie's cigarette on the patio.

"Shit." I brush off the dust and cobwebs from my jeans. "Looks like it's too late for me to make the séance."

Smith holds up one of my CDs from the tub. "Jessica Simpson? You seriously bought Jessica Simpson's debut?"

"She's highly underrated." I reach for the CD and miss it. The tree house is now swaying like a boat on ocean waves. "Plus, her vocals are angelic."

"You're uninvited from the—"

"Penelope, I see you up there!" My mother's voice grates like nails on a chalkboard. "Your father's friend has been waiting patiently for half an hour for you to make an appearance. Get your butt down here this instant." She pauses, and I swear I can hear her sniffing the air like a hound on the trail of a missing person. "Have you been drinking up there? Is that Smith's boot I see?"

"Yes, and I don't know." I grab the mostly empty green bottle and toss it in the CD tub with Jessica and the other late-nineties goddesses of pop. "Watch out. We're coming down."

"What do you mean you don't know?" she huffs. "You can't not know if you've been drinking, Penelope."

"I know, Mom. I have been drinking. I don't know if you can see Smith's boots or mine." I point to the rope ladder. Or at least, I think I'm pointing at the rope ladder. Everything is a little fuzzy. "You want to go down first, or should I? If you're still worried about falling to your death, my mother's down there now. She'll break your fall."

He lifts his gaze to meet mine. A big dopey grin takes shape across his lips for a moment, but it quickly fades. He grabs the CD tub and retches into it. Looks like any hope I had of a goddesses-of-pop karaoke night is long gone. He retches twice more before calling it quits and rolling to his side.

"You go down first," he groans. "I'll wait until after this tree house stops spinning."

I stumble my way down the rope ladder, using the pounding in my head as a guide. When I make it onto solid ground, it's as if the sun has suddenly decided to turn on its brights and point straight at me. I'm starting to think my girl Vermouth is actually out to get me.

"What are you wearing?" My mother tugs at the sleeve of my hoodie. "Where's the dress from Saks that I laid out for you?"

"I'm seventeen, Mom. I think I'm a little too old to be wearing the dresses my mommy lays out for me."

"You picked the dress out, Penelope!" She pulls something that resembles a tiny bird's nest from the topknot of curls piled on my head. "You look like you just crawled out of a gutter."

"Silvia!" my father shouts from the patio. *My god we do a lot of shouting in this family.* "Silvia, where is she?"

My mother and I lock eyes. The lines around her blue eyes soften, along with her painted-on brows, and for a moment, I almost think she feels bad for me. She knows as well as I do that I'm not cut out for Princeton. She's the one who signed me up for creative writing classes when I was in middle school instead of forcing me to do math tutoring. She's the one who always let me stop at the bookstore on the way home from school so I could check out the new release section. She knows how much I want to go to Berkeley, and yet here she is trying to force me into a stupid mock interview for a school I don't want to go to on a freaking holiday. Something inside me hardens, and I shoot her my best drunken death glare.

"I'm right here, Dad." I belch and don't even bother trying to hide it. "Is your friend ready to meet me?"

I brush past my mother, doing my best to put one foot in front of the other in a straight line, until I reach my father.

"What on earth?" My father eyes me warily, like I'm a feral cat. "Are you drunk, Penelope?"

"I'm not not drunk."

"Do you think this is funny?" He shakes his head the way he always does when I've disappointed him. Two shakes, followed by running one hand through his salt-and-pepper hair. "Do you know how many strings I had to pull to get Reginald Yates to join us for Thanksgiving? I flew him out from New Jersey. The man is incredibly influential at Princeton. He likely has hundreds of parents begging for him to practice their kids' college interviews with him, and yet here you are three sheets to the wind!"

"What exactly does that phrase mean?" I hiccup. "Does it mean bedsheets? Who has three bedsheets hanging out in the wind?"

"Silvia." My father motions for my mother, completely ignoring me. "Silvia, I need you to go inside and tell Reginald that Penelope is sick. We'll go ahead and have dinner. He'll be disappointed to miss out on the mock interview, but at least his dinner won't be spoiled."

"Hey, what if we pull a *Freaky Friday* and have Phoebe pretend to be me?" I ask. "Then your old pal Reginald won't be disappointed."

"He's already met your sister," my mother snips. "She had the decency to wear the dress she picked out and not get drunk with her boyfriend."

"Smith's here? I'll kill him," my father growls. "The only thing worse than that boy is his damn hippie-dippie parents."

"He's puked all over the tree house," my mother says. "We'll have to have the place condemned before we bulldoze it to the ground." She grabs my hood and pulls me toward the back door. "When we get inside, I want you to go directly to your bedroom. Do you understand? The last thing we need is for Reginald to see you like this and ruin any chance you have to make it into Princeton."

The ground starts to spin beneath my legs. I can't tell if I'm walking or floating. My girl Vermouth is taking turns between beating on my head like a bongo and whacking my belly like a piñata. "But I don't want to go to Princeton, Mom."

"You don't know what you want, Penelope."

She opens the door. A rush of Thanksgiving scents torpedoes my sense of smell, and a wave of nausea hits me like a brick to the face. My mouth turns on the waterworks, which means it's only a matter of seconds before my girl Vermouth makes her comeback.

"I think I'm going to be sick," I grumble. "Mom."

"Oh, Reginald." My mother jerks my hood like a puppeteer trying to stand a dummy to attention. "Reginald, I'm so sorry for the delay."

"Ah, this must be the famous Penelope." The man my mother called Reginald has one of those big, booming voices that would make a sports announcer jealous. "It's great to meet you. How are you?"

"Drunk." I turn my head just in time to miss covering Reginald Yates's shoes with vomit. My mother's caftan is less fortunate.

The last thing I remember before falling asleep is Phoebe gently keeping my hair out of my face while I dry heaved over the toilet. God, it would be so easy to hate Phoebe if she wasn't such a damn good sister. It's not her fault that she's naturally perfect. It's even less her fault that she got saddled with a twin who somehow ended up with all the worst traits in the family gene pool.

We don't have that twin thing where we can read each other's thoughts or anything, but Phoebe does know how to comfort me when nobody else in our family can.

"Everything will work out, Pen," Phoebe whispers as I drift to sleep. "Dad's friends with Mr. Yates. This will all get swept under the rug and forgotten in a few days. It always does."

She's right. If there's one thing my family does consistently well, it's pretending that everything is OK. Give it a few days, and things will be back to business as usual. Because Bankses are always business first and family second.

Chapter 6

The van is finally silent, minus the white noise of the rain drizzling on top of the van and Aidan's snoring. Harriet and Ozzie have migrated to the back seat and are curled up next to him, which is kind of adorable if you don't think about the fact that a semibuzzed complete stranger is spooning our dogs.

"I'm working on my review for Barkie's," I say. "Do you think I should take a picture of Aidan to include in it?"

"Not unless you want to be personally banned from their store."

"Good point." I slip my phone into my purse.

Smith drums his fingers on the steering wheel. "Now what do we do?"

"What do you mean, *What do we do?*"

"I mean now that Aidan's asleep and traffic isn't moving, what do we do?"

"Why do we need to do anything?"

"Because this." He motions to me and then him. "It's weird. Isn't it? I mean, I never come home. Never. And the one time I do, you're here. Don't you think that means something?"

I don't like where this is going. I just got Smith refiled in my system, and now here he goes trying to muck it all up again. "Uh. I don't know. I think it means we both use Dryver because it's cheap, and we both like to travel with our dogs. It's a coincidence. That's it."

"A coincidence." He rolls his eyes. "C'mon now, Pen."

Hearing him call me Pen softens me a little. "What do you want me to say? It's fate? It's written in the stars? Mercury is in retrograde?" Well, that part is true. "You don't believe in any of that stuff, or at least you didn't when we were kids."

"Maybe I do now." He lowers his voice, like he's speaking more to himself than me. "Ever since losing my mom, I've just started looking at my life differently. I don't like that we lost touch. I hate it, actually."

He looks directly at me with this intense longing in his eyes. It doesn't come across as romantic. I don't feel like Smith has been pining for me all these years. But it still catches me off guard.

I open my mouth to say something, but nothing comes out. I don't know what to say. Part of me wants to comfort Smith. Part of me even wants to tell him that I feel the same, but the thing is, I'm not sure that I do.

That clean break between us was a necessary step toward me being able to grow into the woman I am now. It taught me how to rely on myself. It taught me how to love myself and not compromise my own happiness for someone else's. If I didn't go cold turkey off Smith, I don't think I'd have two filing systems in my memory. There wouldn't be an Old Penny and a New Penny. There would just be a deeply unhappy woman.

"We were just kids, Smith," I finally say. "We did the best we could with what we knew at the time."

"I guess you're right." He pauses, mulling the idea over. "But what now?"

The question agitates me. Why is he so hell bent on pushing this? "What do you mean, *What now?* We eventually get off this bridge and then we go our separate ways."

"So you don't want to catch up? Or stay in touch?"

"I'm not saying that."

"Then what are you saying?"

"I'm saying I don't know, Smith," I snap. "This is the first time I've been home in ten years, and I was just getting over being scared out of my mind about that when you showed up. Give me a freaking minute to digest everything, OK?"

"OK."

I reach for my smoky quartz around my neck out of habit, and suddenly, I'm reminded of Fiona. My gaze drops to the emerald cut pendant and its delicate, inky swirls. I don't normally think of her when I wear this necklace. It's been so long that the necklace feels more mine than hers. But as I'm holding it right now, I can feel her energy. She was so kind and open and accepting. What would she say if she could see the two of us here now?

I look over at him. He's leaning against the wheel, likely avoiding eye contact with me. I don't blame him. He wasn't asking me to be his new best friend. He just wants to catch up with a friend he lost touch with, and maybe that's not too big an ask after all.

"Three questions," I say. "I ask you three. You ask me three. We see how that goes, and if it isn't too painful, we can keep catching up. How does that sound?"

"Like you're asking me to try out to be your friend," he replies. "It seems a little weird, considering I already had the job once before, and was promoted several times, if you remember."

"I do." I nod. "But I'm not asking you to try out, Smith. This is me seeing how comfortable I am being real in a place where I've always had to put on a front. It really is me, not you."

"You haven't been home in ten years?" He cocks an eyebrow.

"Is that your first question?"

"No." He laughs. "You go first. I need time to prep. If I only get three questions, I've got to make sure they're good."

My mind goes blank. Well, almost blank. Only one question bounces back and forth in the pinball machine that is my brain. I want to know why he's got a ring box, but I can't very well ask him about it without admitting that I slightly snooped in his bag. Half a snoop, really. I could ask him if he is in a relationship. That doesn't seem too forward, considering the fact that he's already asked me if I've procreated. Plus, I'm sure Jackie is going to want to know, and if I miss an opportunity to ask, she'll never shut up about it.

Oh, what the hell.

"My friend Jackie wants to know if you're single." I motion toward my purse. "She's the one who wanted me to text a picture of you."

"So this question is for Jackie, then, not you?" Smith smiles conspiratorially. "We're allowed to phone in questions?"

"The opportunity for phone-in questions has passed."

"Fine." The tiniest hint of heat splashes across his cheeks and neck. "You can tell Jackie that I'm in a relationship."

A pit forms in my stomach, and all of a sudden, I'm pissed. Not at Smith for being in a relationship. He's only been part of my life for the last two hours. He could have an entire harem of women, and I'd be fine with it. No, I'm pissed at myself for having a reaction. It's like my body and feelings are recruits revolting against my brain, which is very clearly trying to communicate to the rest of me that *we don't care if Smith is in a relationship.*

"Is it serious?" I blurt out. "Not that it matters to me."

"Right." He chuckles. "It's Jackie who's invested in this line of questioning."

"Obviously."

"It is serious. Quite serious if I'm being honest. She's actually flying here tomorrow. It'll be the first time she meets Mo."

My stomach twists and pulls in a way that is usually customary only after I've gone in too hard on a late-night Del Taco binge. My armpits have also joined the body revolution by turning into a swamp. This game is so fun.

"Have you two been together long?"

It's almost as if I literally can't stop myself from asking questions.

"Three months."

It's been three months and he's already carrying around a ring box. Three months? That's ninety days. Target gives you an entire year to return an air fryer and all that does is heat up chicken nuggets. I know this because it was the only way I was willing to commit to a kitchen appliance. How can he possibly be ready to marry someone he's only been dating for three months? We dated years before he proposed to me. Years!

We'd also been living together before he proposed to me, which is a crucial step on the path to marriage, in my opinion. Is he already living with this woman? Who moves in with someone that fast? Furthermore, how is it possible that out of the three people in this van, the romance writer is the only single person?

"Wow," I finally manage to say. "That's fast."

"When you know, you know. Right? You used to write romance. You get it. Oh, that's my first question." He smiles from ear to ear like he's enjoying this cruel, torturous game. "Are you an author?"

My phone buzzes before I can answer, and I practically dive into my purse to retrieve it. If there was ever a time that I needed the Smut Coven, it's now. Actually, it was five minutes ago, before I turned into a sweaty ball of anxiety with a stomachache.

"Ugh," I groan. "It's a text from my mother."

"Good to see the two of you getting along better," Smith says.

"Yep, we're basically besties."

My mother isn't much of a texter. She's not the sort of woman who communicates in brief and succinct messages, and with her Southern drawl, talk to text is completely out of the question. I cautiously open the message, and to my surprise, it's a photo. A photo of a very good-looking man to be exact.

Mom: This is Martin. He wanted to say hi.

I highly doubt this poor man wanted to say hello to me. Martin probably feels like he's in a hostage situation at this point, and he's not exactly wrong. My mother would set her own hair on fire before she'd let an eligible bachelor leave her home without meeting her spinster daughter.

I take a better look at the photo. Martin's leaning against our stone fireplace, head tilted back slightly, with a kind grin spread across his face. I'm not sure if it's the lighting or the questionable edibles, but he really does look like a Hemsworth.

Penny: Tell Martin I say hello too.
Mom: I'm going to tell him that you can't wait to get to know him better. 😏

I didn't think it was possible for anyone to have a more awkward Thanksgiving experience than me, but my mother has just confirmed that with minimal effort, things can always get more cringey. I open the picture once more, just to double-check that it's real.

"What does Silvia have to say?" Smith leans across the armrest before I have a chance to close out the photo. "Hey now. Your mom looks a hell of a lot different than I remember her."

"Well, she finally started shaving." I exit out of my phone and slide it back in my purse. "To answer your question, yes, I'm an author. Next question."

"That's weird."

"What's weird? My mother shaving?"

"I've just never seen your name attached to any books. I'd expect that to be the sort of thing good old Google would catch. Unless you've never been published."

"You've googled me?" I raise my eyebrow. "Why?"

"Why does anyone google somebody? Because I was curious. I also googled my mailman, if it makes you feel any better."

"Is he also your ex-wife?"

"Is that one of your questions?"

"No," I grumble. "Yes, I've been published. I'm actually a *USA Today* bestseller. I just don't publish under my own name. I use a pen name."

"What's your pen name?"

Nope. Not happening. My pen name is sacred like Peter Parker is to Spider-Man and Clark Kent is to Superman. The only people who know my pen name are the Smut Coven, my agent, and my publishing house.

"Veto."

"What do you mean, *veto?*"

"A veto is a veto." I shrug. "I didn't say we were required to answer every question."

"Can I ask why you're vetoing that question? And don't tell me it's because you don't want to answer it. That's implied."

"Is that an official question?"

"Yes, it is."

"Because my writing is just for me."

It's the *Reader's Digest* version of the truth, but it's the truth nonetheless. When I'm writing, I'm my most authentic self. My books are like little windows into my soul that nobody can judge or discredit. Other than reviewer_1987 on Goodreads. That woman hates everything I write, but it doesn't bother me. Writing is subjective, and I don't take bad reviews personally. What I would take personally, what would destroy the joy that writing brings me, is for my writing to disappoint my family.

I'm no Virginia Woolf or Harper Lee. I haven't penned the next great American novel, and I likely never will. I like to write about women falling in love and having great sex, even if I'm not experiencing either at the moment. Which I'm not. Not unless you count the stash of battery powered tools I keep next to my bed. The kind of books that I write aren't good enough for my parents. They aren't the sort of books they can brag about to their friends at the country club. They'd be embarrassed by them, and I've done enough on my own to give them a lifetime of embarrassment without adding to it.

"Who's Martin?" Smith asks. "That's my third question. I'm assuming he's the guy Phoebe was talking about on the phone earlier. The one with the body and—"

"I thought we mutually agreed not to talk about anything that you may or may not have overheard."

"I don't remember making that agreement."

"It's the dog weed. It's fried your brain just like all those 'Say no to drugs' commercials said it would."

Aidan stirs in the back seat, mumbling something about beavers and ducks. Ozzie and Harriet abandon their post at his side, which is probably for the best, considering we have no idea how Aidan feels about beavers or ducks.

"We need wood," he moans, his eyes still closed. "We need the beavers and the ducks to make a pact."

"I should probably go check on him," Smith says. "But don't think I'm going to forget about that last question, genie."

I fold my arms across my chest and nod in my best Barbara Eden impression.

While Smith attends to Aidan and his plan to unify the beaver and duck community, I summon the Smut Coven.

Penny: He's not single.

Penny: His girlfriend is flying in tomorrow.

Penny: Then he's going to make her his fiancée. After just 3 months of being together.

Jackie: 3 months? Who the hell gets married after 3 months?

Penny: EXACTLY!

Chelsey: How are you doing? Are you okay?

Penny: I don't know how I feel about any of it.

Chelsey: Well, of course you don't. He's the only man you've ever loved.

Penny: Is he? Is that really possible?

Jackie: It is. You've lusted for plenty.

Jackie: An entire football team's worth of lusting.

Penny: I get the point.

Chelsey: So he told you he's planning on proposing tomorrow?

Penny: Not exactly.

Jackie: Wait. Why do you think he is?

Penny: He has a box from Tiffany's in his bag.

Penny: It's ring shaped.

Penny: Why else would he carry a ring-shaped box from Tiffany's if he didn't plan on proposing? Rings aren't like condoms.

Chelsey: There's a lot to unpack here.

Aidan thrashes back and forth in the back seat.

"I think he's having a night terror or something. Any idea on how to snap him out of it?"

"Slap him?" I shrug.

"I'm not slapping our driver."

"He hasn't been our driver for the last thirty minutes that he's been unconscious."

"There's a bottle of water in the driver's side door. Hand that to me."

"You're going to waterboard the guy that's terrified of the rain? The man is literally trying to build an army of beavers and ducks."

Aidan throws a lazy haymaker in Smith's direction.

"Water. Now."

"Fine." I climb into the driver's seat and grab the bottle of water. I toss it to Smith. "If he ends up murdering you in his sleep, I promise to take good care of Harriet."

Smith rolls his eyes before turning his attention back to Aidan.

I go to move back to my seat, but my foot catches on the strap of Smith's bag, spilling half its contents onto the floorboard. "Shit. Sorry," I say. "I'll clean it up."

Smith waves over his shoulder. He's too busy baptizing the demons out of Aidan to pay any attention to me.

I scoop up his pens, gum, and other miscellaneous items—honestly, he carries more stuff around in his purse than I do—all the while keeping an eye on the jewelry box. This feels like a test from the universe. Like whether or not I open this box says something about the kind of person I am. Technically, Smith didn't tell me not to open it up. In fact, he's invited me into his bag twice since we've been stuck in this van from hell, and I am only a mere mortal. A mere mortal who won't be able to sleep unless she knows if her ex-husband is going to propose to someone he's only known for ninety days.

One look. That's it.

My heart pounds against my chest as I take the box in my hand. I peer into the back seat once more. Aidan looks like he's been born again. He's sitting upright, which means if I'm going to do this, it's got to be now. I press the small silver button, and before I can take it back, the box opens. I look down and my heart goes from pounding to an all-out flatline.

It's my ring.

My ex-husband is carrying around my engagement ring in his luggage. He's going to give the same ring that he gave to me to some woman he's known for three months. Three freaking months!

"Hey." Smith's voice startles me. I snap the ring box closed and place it back in his bag. "Look who's awake."

"Hi, Aidan." I give a curt wave.

"Looks like traffic is moving now too." Smith gestures toward the window. The cars in the lane next to us have started to inch forward. "We should be home in no time."

"Should I drive?" Aidan asks. "I don't think I'm fit to drive yet. Feels like I still need to sober up, ya know?"

"No problem." Smith makes his way back toward the front of the car, and I move back to my spot in the passenger seat. "I'll get us home."

He's smiling and giddy. It makes me want to kick him in the balls. How dare he be giddy to go home and give my ring to some woman he's known for less time than I've known my air fryer. That ring is a vintage, one-of-a-kind piece. It has no business being in a box from Tiffany's. It didn't come from Tiffany's. It came from a flea market in London. Why would his air-fryer girlfriend want a flea-market ring from London?

The cars in front of us start to move at a slow but steady clip. Smith puts the van in drive, which means in a matter of minutes I'll be home. Who would've thought I'd ever look forward to being home?

I don't think Clementine Street will be enough distance between Smith and me. I swear if he thinks about coming over with his young, naive fiancée I'm going to—

"So, who is Martin?" Smith asks. "That was my last question. Unless you're going to veto it, in which case—"

"He's my boyfriend," I say defiantly. "Martin is my boyfriend."

"Oh."

There's a hint of surprise in his voice. I'm not sure what his face looks like, because I personally don't think I can look at Smith without committing a felony. He probably wants to ask me more about Martin, but he's all out of questions. And our time together is thankfully almost finally over.

Chapter 7

The plan was simple. Impossible to screw up. One hundred percent fool-proof. Smith would drive Aidan's van to Clementine Street. He would park in front of his home—not mine—and Aidan would help me with my bags. I'd be in my house with the front door locked behind me before Smith even considered getting out of the driver's seat. Nobody in my parents' house, other than Phoebe and Falon, would ever know that I'd just spent the last two and a half hours stuck in a van with Smith Mackenzie, and if I played my cards right, I might be able to make it through the long weekend without anyone ever noticing he was staying across the street with his sister.

That was the plan.

But what transpired was an absolute nightmare.

"Why is my entire family gathered in the driveway?" I ask the universe as Smith pulls the van onto Clementine Street.

"This isn't the way they always welcome you home?" Smith, not the universe, replies. "I'm impressed that all of their umbrellas match."

"Silvia wouldn't be caught dead in a storm without matching rain gear. Drive slower," I command.

"Really? The neighborhood speed limit is fifteen miles an hour. If I go any slower, people are going to think we're part of a funeral procession."

Little does this man know how close he is to being the guest of honor in a funeral procession.

I reach for my phone and fire off a text to Phoebe.

Penny: WTF
Penny: Why is everyone outside?
Phoebe: Because we miss you?
Penny: Phoebe! Smith is with me.
Penny: I don't want Mom and Dad to see him. I especially
don't want Nana Rosie to see him.
Phoebe: Want me to blindfold them?
Penny: How much have you had to drink?
Phoebe: Enough to not be useful.
Phoebe: Tell the driver to step on it.
Phoebe: I'm freezing my tits off.

"Stop the car," I tell Smith. "Aidan needs to be driving. Aidan, rise and shine. It's time to get back on the horse."

"Pen, I'm not stopping the car. We're three houses away from your parents' place."

"Fine." I slump into my seat like a petulant child. "But don't say I didn't warn you."

"What are you talking about?"

"My family hates you."

"They hate me?" Smith hits the brakes, causing the van to lurch. "Why? I mean, I know they were never exactly my biggest fans, but I never thought they hated me."

He's not wrong. My parents have always had a healthy disdain for Smith and his family. They never liked the idea of us dating, but they tolerated it because on the list of questionable behaviors they'd witnessed from me, falling in love with the boy across the street with the hippie rock-star parents was a mild offense. When we moved in together, they were pissed. When we got engaged, they were disgruntled. And when they found out we eloped, they were furious.

But eventually my old-school, traditional parents came around to the idea that marriage would be good for me. It would settle me. Give me some direction. After we traveled around for a bit and realized we'd never be able to afford the kind of lifestyles we grew up with, my dad would take Smith under his wing and pull him into the family business. By our fifth wedding anniversary, we'd be the respectable sort of couple my parents dreamed of. The kind of couple they could invite to the country club for golf and a mimosa brunch with their friends. The kind of couple they'd brag about when we weren't around, instead of changing the subject whenever somebody asked about us.

Then we got divorced after less than a year of marriage, and any salvageable hope my parents had of turning me into the upstanding daughter they hoped for died with my marriage.

"Uh, probably because you divorced me," I say.

"It was a mutual decision, Penny."

"I may have made it seem not so mutual." Sweat prickles at the back of my neck. "I may have told them you called things off unexpectedly and then left me alone at LaGuardia."

"You told them I abandoned you?"

"A little."

"God, no wonder they hate me." He looks at me with this wounded expression, which feels rich coming from a guy who's about to reuse his ex-wife's engagement ring.

"Could you two stop arguing?" Aidan asks. "My parents used to argue, and it always made me feel nauseated. My mother still argues with my dad, but he's inside an urn now."

"Listen," I plead. "I couldn't handle disappointing them more than I already had, and since you weren't around, it just made it easier to blame you. It was a victimless crime."

"Until now." Smith eases off the brake. "What are the odds your dad takes a swing at me the second he sees me?"

"Just pull into your driveway and stay in the van. I'll get my bags, and if they ask any questions, I'll tell them that the driver got confused." I glance back at Aidan. "It's honestly not that hard of a story to sell."

"Great. I hide like I used to when I was a teenager sneaking out of your room. That's your big plan?"

"Yes." I hold my breath as we move closer to my parents' home. "Unless you've got a better idea."

"I do."

Smith stops the van directly in front of my family. It takes them a second to register that I'm sitting in the front seat instead of the back, and it takes my parents another half second to realize that the driver looks vaguely familiar. I put on the biggest, most enthusiastic smile my mouth can muster and swing open my door to greet them.

"I made it." I cover my head with my purse to keep the last few drops of rain from splattering across my face. "Better late than never, right? Mom? Dad? Anyone?"

Nobody has ever paid less attention to me in my life. I could light myself on fire, and I doubt that my parents would stop staring at Smith long enough to put out the flames.

"Is that Smith in the car?" Nana Rosie points with the hand that isn't holding her usual dirty martini. "I didn't realize he worked as a cabdriver now. I thought he made a boatload of money at that little magazine of his."

"He's not a cabdriver, Nana." I loop my arm around her. "It was just a weird coincidence."

"Well, are you going to explain this weird coincidence to us, Penelope?" my mother huffs. "Or will Smith fill us in when he fetches your bags?"

"He's not fetching my bags, Mom," I say.

"Is he the reason you're late? Your sister said you were stuck in traffic. Was that a lie?" my mom asks. "Were you two canoodling?"

Ew. Really?

"Didn't Phoebe show you the news? Everyone trying to get on the island was stuck." I suddenly realize that Phoebe and Falon are nowhere in sight. "Where is Phoebe?"

"She's inside with Falon and Martin." My mother's face falls. "Oh, poor Martin will be so upset. I can't believe you would do this to him, Penelope, and with Smith Mackenzie of all people. You told me you were taking one of those rideshares. I didn't realize that was some sort of code for a hookup."

"Mom, I haven't been flexible enough to hook up with anyone in a car since I was sixteen," I say. "I'm a writer, not a yoga instructor."

"You're not being funny, Penelope. None of this is funny at all." My mother turns to my father. "Carter, can you believe this?"

"No, I can't," my father says. He hands my mother their shared umbrella. "I'm going to go have a word with that jackass."

"Dad, stop." I tug at his arm. "This is all a misunderstanding. If we could just calm down and go inside, I could explain it to everyone."

The van door slams shut, quieting us all instantly. Smith's boots crunch on the gravelly road as he makes his way to the back of the van for my bag. Despite there being only a vehicle between us, Aidan's van might as well be a mountain. We don't move or say a word. We just wait with bated breath as Smith closes the back end of the van and then rounds the corner with my luggage and Ozzie in tow.

"Carter. Silvia. Nana Rosie." Smith nods to each of them. "It's nice to see all of you."

I stand with my family in pregnant silence, waiting to see who will be the first to address Smith. It's like being at the OK Corral if Wyatt Earp's brothers were all over seventy and smelled vaguely of gin and Chanel No. 5. If I'm the first to break the silence, there's bound to be an argument. My parents practically have their boxing gloves on, and I can't start the weekend with them pissed at me for no reason. That will diminish my chances of getting their help, which is the only reason I came home in the first place.

"Smith, my darling boy, it's so good to see you." Nana Rosie hands me her martini as she glides across the driveway to Smith. He leans down to hug her, and she kisses both his cheeks, branding them with her signature red lipstick. "It's been ages since we've seen you. How have you been?"

"I've been well," Smith says. "Thank you for asking."

"You certainly look well. Doesn't he look well, Silvia? Carter?"

Nana Rosie isn't a spring chicken, but she's still the sort of woman who likes to poke the bear, and while normally I find this part of her personality to be eccentric and fun, right now I find it terrifying. My dad may be in his seventies, but at six foot four, he's still a force to be reckoned with when he loses his temper. The same goes for my mother. She might be an old Southern belle in appearance and voice, but there's a fierce mama bear inside that tropical-print caftan.

"You've got a lot of nerve showing up with my daughter," my dad growls. "Especially after the way you treated her and this family."

"Dad," I interject. "Let's just calm down."

"Carter, I see that you're upset, but—"

"Stop calling me Carter. That's Mr. Banks to you, and don't you forget it." He takes a step toward Smith. "Now, get off my driveway, and don't—"

The van door slides open. A groggy Aidan pokes his head out, inspecting his surroundings like Punxsutawney Phil on Groundhog Day. He wipes a bit of crusted sleep from his eyes before slowly stepping out of the van.

"Wow," Aidan says. "You guys really do fight in the streets." He puts a hand on his hip and scratches the back of his head.

"Young man, who the hell are you?" my father asks.

"That's Aidan," I say gently. "He's our driver, or at least he was our driver until he overdosed on doggy drugs."

"Penelope Banks," my father snaps. "This is hardly the time for jokes."

"I'm not joking, Dad. Look, it's a long story, but the gist is that Smith's the reason we made it home at all."

My father's gray eyebrows furrow like a pair of dueling caterpillars atop his narrowed gaze. My mother appears equally perplexed. Her bright blue eyes dart between Smith and Aidan, trying to suss out who the liar is, since the usual suspect—me—is in the clear.

"Well, then I suppose we owe you a thank-you, Smith," Nana Rosie says. "Thank you so much for ensuring that our Penny made it home safely for her first Thanksgiving with us in far too long."

"It wasn't any trouble." Smith places Ozzie on the pavement, and he immediately runs to Nana Rosie with his tail wagging. "It's my first time home in a long time too, so I was just as eager to get here."

"I didn't think anyone was at your parents' place this weekend." Nana Rosie motions to the Mackenzies' home across the street. "By the way, I'm so sorry to hear about Fiona's passing. She was a lovely woman."

Am I the last one to know about her death? I know I'm not the best at staying in touch, but I would've thought somebody would've mentioned it to me.

"Thank you," Smith says softly. "She was something special."

"How about you join us for cocktail hour so we can have a drink in her honor." Nana Rosie turns to my parents, giving them one of those smiles that appears harmless, but anyone who knows my grandmother knows she means business. "Carter, why don't you tip the driver for the kids. Penny, you grab your bag and freshen up. Smith, I assume you have your own luggage too? You drop your bags off and come right over for drinks."

"Nana Rosie, I'm sure Smith is tired," I say, desperate to derail her plans. "I'm sure he just wants to go home, unpack, and—"

"Actually, I could go for a drink," Smith says.

"Really?" I choke. "Because we would totally understand if you weren't up to it. You know, after my parents were so rude to you and all."

"Penelope!" my mother snaps. "We weren't rude. We were confused."

"No, Silvia." My father clears his throat. "She's right. We misunderstood the transportation situation and reacted poorly. It's only good manners that we put our differences aside to host Smith for cocktails in his mother's honor, and as a thank-you for getting Penelope home safe. We'd be delighted to have you over, Smith."

"We would?" my mother and I ask in unison.

"Then it's settled." Nana Rosie claps. "Drinks in ten minutes for everyone. Well, minus the driver, of course. Tip the man, Carter."

Nana Rosie takes me by the arm and leads me up the curved driveway. Ozzie trails after us at our feet.

"This is going to be fun." Nana Rosie's tone is bubbly with excitement. "Two gentleman callers in one evening. That's one hell of a way to kick off a holiday if you ask me."

I gasp. "Oh shit."

With all the *West Side Story* street-battle chaos, I somehow managed to forget about my setup with Martin Butler. How the hell am I going to have cocktails with Martin and Smith together without Smith realizing that not only am I not Martin's girlfriend, but the two of us have never actually met?

"You going to finish that?" Nana Rosie nods at her martini still in my hand.

"Oh, absolutely." I tilt my head back and drain the rest of the drink down my throat. "And I'm going to need another."

"I can help with that."

Chapter 8

Smith Mackenzie should not be coming over for drinks. The name Smith Mackenzie shouldn't even be said in my house. It hasn't been for years. Saying the word Mackenzie has basically been the equivalent to saying Beetlejuice three times. We simply don't do it, because nothing good can come from a Banks discussing a Mackenzie. Nothing.

"We have a problem," I say, gasping for air. I haven't run up the winding staircase of my childhood home since I was a teenager, and it shows. I close the door to Phoebe's room behind me. "I'm fucked. Royally. Also, hi."

I rip off my clammy flannel and toss it onto the bed in between Phoebe and Falon. I'm about to unhook my bra, when I notice that Phoebe and Falon are eyeing me like some sort of carnival sideshow exhibit. Phoebe throws the flannel back at me.

"What the—"

"I'm just going to excuse myself," says an unfamiliar voice.

In my haste to get up the stairs and barricade myself in Phoebe's bedroom for all eternity, I neglected to notice that my sister and Falon weren't the only two people in her bedroom. Standing in the corner next to the window that overlooks the pool is the man that romance writers have been writing about since smut was nothing more than suggestive drawings on cave walls.

Martin Butler is all sharp jawline, defined muscles, and kind eyes. He's the type of man you do a double take for when you're walking on the street. The photo my mother texted me did not do him justice, but then again, I'm not sure even Michelangelo himself could do any better. Martin Butler isn't a Hemsworth. He's a category all his own.

"Oh shit," I say, holding my flannel against my chest. "I wasn't expecting anyone else up here."

"It's entirely my fault." Martin's eyes are glued to the floor, his cheeks flushed with heat. "Your sister was just giving me the tour of her bedroom . . . uh . . . I mean, she was showing me your parents' home and we ended up in her bedroom, with her fiancée of course, and then you came in and—"

"Gave him a tour of your tits," Phoebe deadpans. "OK, I think we're all caught up. Well, at least we will be once my sister puts her top back on."

"I'll give you your privacy."

There's something charming about how tongue-tied Martin is. It defuses my nerves in an unexpected but absolutely needed way. It's the juxtaposition of this tall, gorgeous man who has probably had bras given to him by adoring fans, or drunk barflies at the very least, suddenly behaving as meek and nervous as a high school band geek. I'm not even sure he'll be able to make it safely out of Phoebe's room without tripping over his words or feet. It would be a damn shame for him to start off a holiday weekend with an injury.

"This might be the fastest a man has ever left a room after seeing my boobs." I step aside from the door, still clutching my flannel. "Truly, a new personal best."

"Oh, I promise I didn't look." Martin's warm brown eyes lock with mine. "I mean, I did, but I looked away immediately after. It was an accident. I promise."

"Just to be clear, was the accident the part where you looked away?"

"Penny, leave him alone," Phoebe says. "The poor man has already had to endure an hour-long presentation of your baby pictures. I think he's suffered enough."

"We all have." Falon pushes her glasses back on the bridge of her nose. "I didn't know it was possible to actually hate a baby."

"Hey." Phoebe nudges her. "Half of those pictures could've been me. Mom could never tell us apart when we were babies."

"I'm just going to go downstairs." Martin holds up his copper mule mug. "I have a feeling I'm going to need a refill."

"Before you go." I turn around and quickly slip my flannel back over my head. "I was hoping I could ask you for a small favor."

"Uh, possibly?" The panicked look on his face reads anything but sure.

"I need you to pretend to be involved with me," I say, carefully choosing my words. "You see, my ex-husband is coming over for cocktails, and long story short, I may have led him to believe that we're an item."

"You may have?" Phoebe asks, visibly annoyed. "And since when is Smith coming over for happy hour?"

"Since Nana Rosie invited him." I wave my hand dismissively. "I don't have time to get into the details." I turn to Martin. "Are you in? Oh, and keep in mind that we'll need to look like we're not together for my parents."

"Let me see if I'm following." Martin swallows hard. "You want me to pretend to be involved with you in front of your ex-husband, while also pretending to not be interested in you when your parents are watching."

"I mean, you don't have to behave like you're uninterested. Just not too interested. We've only just met. I wouldn't want things to get weird, or at least not any weirder than you seeing me topless."

"Is it actually topless if your bra is still on?" Falon asks.

"Technically, yes," Phoebe replies.

"So, are you in?" I ask Martin. "I'm kind of on a tight deadline here."

"You're serious?" His expression shifts, as if he's finally understood the absurdity of my request. "You know your father is my boss. And I'm supposed to stay here for the weekend."

"Look, I promise I'm only asking for you to play the dual role of supportive-boyfriend-slash-brand-new-acquaintance tonight." I hold my fingers up in a peace sign. "Spice Girls honor."

"Is that a thing?"

"I'd trust Baby Spice over a Girl Scout any day of the week. Wouldn't you?"

Martin glances over at Phoebe and Falon, as if he's checking to see if I'm playing a practical joke on him or something. "I-I literally have no idea how to answer that."

"Are you a Capricorn?"

"Penelope!" Nana Rosie's voice blares through the vintage household intercom. "Are you almost ready? Smith will be here any minute."

"Almost," I shout.

"He looked good, didn't he?" Nana Rosie hiccups. A fair indicator that she's dipped into another martini. "Aged like a fine wine. Of course, that Martin fellow is no wet sandwich, if you ask me. He's a hot pastrami on rye if there ever was one."

Martin's face is so flushed it practically looks sunburned. He gestures toward the hallway and mouths something that is either *I'm going downstairs* or *I'm running away* before closing the door behind him.

"Nana, I'll be right down," I say.

"Whichever one you don't want, I get first dibs. Over and out."

The intercom goes silent.

I peel off the rest of my travel clothes and throw myself onto Phoebe's bed next to Falon. Phoebe's already in her closet looking for something suitable for me to wear. One of the benefits of being Phoebe's twin is getting to take advantage of her impeccable taste and a much more expensive wardrobe than my own.

"Don't get too cozy," Phoebe shouts from her closet. "You're going down there even if Martin's not willing to join in your ridiculous charade."

"But it's so nice." I bury my face into the soft comforter. "Just give me a pair of sweatpants and we'll call it a day."

"Can I ask why your ex-husband thinks you're in a relationship with Martin?" Falon asks.

"Because she's a liar." Phoebe holds up a black turtleneck sweater dress. "What about this?"

"I'm not a liar," I say, genuinely offended by the remark. "Phoebe, you have no idea what I had to deal with. I was trapped in a van with the last man who saw me naked before all my good parts started to go wonky. Also, that dress is giving me Diane Keaton vibes."

She ignores me. "I think the dress is a yes. Falon?" Falon nods in agreement. "Put this on."

"Are you just not going to acknowledge me?" I pull the dress over my head and shimmy it down my body. "That's it?"

"I couldn't ignore you if I tried, Penny, because you command the spotlight. No. *Command* is being too generous. You hog it."

"I do not."

"Really?" She rolls her eyes. "I tell you on the phone that Falon and I have big news to share, and you end up bringing your ex-husband over for cocktails and asking Martin to be your personal escort. You've completely stolen our thunder."

"Hun." Falon reaches for my sister's hand. "You're tired. It's been a long day." Falon turns to me. "She's just hangry."

"Don't apologize for me, babe," Phoebe says, pulling away. "I need to get this off my chest or it's just going to build up all weekend."

"Get what off your chest?" I laugh uneasily. "Are you seriously upset with me, Feeb?"

But I know the answer without her saying a word. The heaviness in her brows. The frustration in her eyes. The way her lips pull so tightly into a frown, they nearly lose all color. It's the same face I make when I've finally had enough.

"This is our first holiday being engaged," Phoebe says. "But all Mom and Dad care about is the fact that you're finally coming home. Now, I know you can't help that, and I was able to get past it, but then you got stuck in traffic."

"That wasn't my fault."

She holds up her hand and shushes me. "I know that. I get it. That's why I didn't mind entertaining Martin. He's actually a really nice guy. He's new to the office so I don't really know him, but what I know of him I like. He barely batted an eye when I downed an entire bottle of cabernet during Mom's photo presentation of your life from birth until high school graduation."

"Then what exactly have I done that has you upset with me?" I ask. "Because whatever it is, I'm sorry."

"Now Smith's staying over for drinks."

"Again, not my fault."

"I know." She sighs. "But now you're asking Martin to play along with one of your stories, and to be honest, it's exhausting."

"One of my stories?"

"Stories. Lies. Fictional retellings. Call it whatever you want. It's what you do whenever you come back home. You turn into this one-woman show and everyone else becomes some minor character whose only purpose is to support you. You've been doing it your whole life."

Normally, I would take being called a *one-woman show* as a compliment. But Phoebe doesn't mean it in a Carol Burnett kind of way. It's an insult.

Until this moment, I had no idea how deeply my sister's words could cut through me. Straight past my skin, muscles, and bones and right into my very soul. The corners of my eyes prickle with the threat of tears, which I blink back immediately. I don't cry, especially not here and now.

"Is that it?" I walk past Phoebe, our arms brushing up against each other. "Or are there any other opinions you'd like to share about me?" I pull out the chair of her vanity and plop myself down in front of her makeup bag and hair products. "I hope you don't mind me borrowing your stuff. If I were to go get mine, I'd have to go downstairs, and there might be people, which means there might be a chance that I'd steal your precious spotlight."

I catch a glimpse of her in the mirror tossing her head back in frustration before she exits the room, leaving Falon and me alone. Phoebe and I don't argue often. I used to think it was because we always got along so easily. She was the golden child. I was the class clown. I admired her, and she humored me. We complemented each other that way.

We grew apart after I dropped out of college. Nothing extreme. We never had a falling-out. We were just on different paths. She was on the one my parents wanted her to be on, and I went rogue. She went to grad school, got a big job followed by an even bigger promotion, and a few years later met the girl of her dreams. I got married, got divorced, moved to San Francisco, and started writing. Her whole life synced perfectly with everything my parents could've ever hoped for, and I cheered for her the entire way. It wasn't an in-person kind of cheer, but I was still proud of her, even from afar. I always have been. It hadn't occurred to me that she harbored resentment toward me.

"The holidays are hard on everyone." Falon places her hand on my shoulder. "She didn't mean what she said, Pen."

"Yes, she did," I say.

I undo my topknot and run my fingers through my messy curls. I don't bother trying to comb through them. What's the point? I smear on a little bit of blush and dab some concealer under my eyes.

"Try this." Falon hands me a tube of Chanel lipstick. "Phoebe always says this color would look better on you than her. I think it's your hair that makes the difference."

"Thanks." I take it. "Can I ask you something, Falon?"

"Sure."

"Do you agree with her? Do you think I'm some awful liar that sucks the life out of every room I enter?" My stomach drops to my feet as I brace myself for her answer.

"That's not what she said or meant." Falon pulls my hair back and ties it in a loose ponytail at the nape of my neck. "I think she just wants you to be you. She says it feels like you're putting on this front when you're around your parents, instead of just being yourself. They act differently too. I think she just wants everyone to be themselves and get along." She squeezes my shoulder. "Everything will be fine after she gets some food in her system. I promise."

Falon leaves me alone in Phoebe's room to finish getting ready, and all I can think about is whether the wooden trellis next to the window can still hold my weight after all this time. My parents had the trellis outside *my* room removed when I was fifteen. I snuck out to see a Kelly Clarkson concert with Smith and we ended up getting stranded in Malibu. My father didn't talk to me for weeks, and my mother seriously considered sending me to one of those wilderness survival schools for wayward teens.

I take one final look at myself in the mirror, and that's when I notice the picture of Phoebe and me tucked in the bottom of the frame. We're in our Princeton sweatshirts, sitting on beds opposite each other in our dorm. My hair is streaked with hideous highlights, and Phoebe's is freshly cut and dyed blond. Phoebe's hair color is the only way I know this photo is from our second year in college. Well, Phoebe's second year. My last.

This is probably the last picture my parents have of us both in college. Our family fell apart that Thanksgiving, and I'm not sure we were ever truly able to put it back together.

Chapter 9

Thanksgiving 2006:
The One with Naked Moon Dancing

"Just tell them the truth, Penny." Phoebe sighs as we collect our luggage from baggage claim. "Half the reason Mom and Dad get so upset is because you wait until the last possible minute to tell them what's going on at school and pretend everything is fine, which means they have to hear you're struggling from one of Dad's friends."

It's easy for Phoebe to tell my parents the truth. It always has been. Her truths are easy.

Mom, Dad, I got straight As again.

Mom, Dad, I got accepted into every Ivy League school I applied for.

Mom, Dad, I'm sorry I won't be able to come home for the summer. I've been offered an internship with Google. I hope you both understand.

If Phoebe's truths were my truths, I'd never have a problem telling them. Hell, I'd tattoo them across my face or pay a skywriter to broadcast them over Coronado Island. But my truths have never been remotely close to Phoebe's. Take the one I'm sitting on today for example.

I'm failing out of Princeton . . . again. This means for the second year in a row, my parents are going to have to hear: *Mom, Dad, I'm failing almost all of my business and engineering classes.* It also means that for the second year in a row, I'm going to have to sit through an awkward

Thanksgiving dinner with one of my dad's work colleagues telling us how lucky we are to have a guaranteed spot at the best—meaning wealthiest—international engineering firm in the world. I can hear his words now: *All you have to do is pass your classes, and you're guaranteed a lifetime of success.*

"Maybe." I grab both of our bags from the conveyor. "Just don't say anything if they ask you. Tell them that everything seems like it's been going better since I started tutoring."

Phoebe takes her bag, and we make our way to the escalator. "What if I just tell them to ask you, so I don't have to be caught in the middle?"

"If you say that, then they'll know something is wrong."

"Well, something *is* wrong. You're failing."

"Look, I'm going to handle this, Phoebe. I swear. I just need a little time so I can figure out how to do it in my own way. OK?"

"Fine," Phoebe groans in frustration. "But I'm not going along with any of your stories. I don't need Mom and Dad on my case because you've dragged me into your problems."

Her words sting, but I don't let on. She's doing me a favor, and lately getting Phoebe to do me a favor is like pulling teeth. She just fits in so well at Princeton, and I don't. It's like our roles in high school have been completely flip-flopped. She's the one involved in all the clubs and invited to all the parties, while I'm stuck in our dorm studying my ass off to no avail. When we walk down the hallway of our dorm together, it's Phoebe everyone wants to talk to. I'm just the tagalong sister. The sister who keeps failing. The sister who got into school because her father pulled every connection he had. I'm the twin that doesn't belong at Princeton, and if I'm honest, lately I've felt like I don't even belong with Phoebe.

"Hey." Phoebe points at a man three steps in front of us. "Is that Smith?"

I'd recognize that black leather jacket anywhere. His hair is longer. Not so gelled, and definitely without his signature frosted tips. We decided to "take a break" after we graduated two years ago. He was going to Berkeley, and I was moving across the country to try to make my parents happy. We used to call each other every week freshman year, but last summer, we lost touch. His parents were in London recording an album, and he tagged along to take a summer photography class at the Royal College of Art.

"Smith!" I shout over the airport din. "Over here!"

The couple in front of me grumbles something under their breath about manners and airport etiquette, but I don't care. Seeing Smith right now is the boost of serotonin I'm going to need just to get into the car my father arranged to take us home.

Smith looks from side to side before finally turning around. Our eyes meet, and he smiles at me like I'm the best news he's gotten in weeks. He waits for me at the bottom of the escalator, and I practically leap into his arms.

"Pen." His voice is muffled in our embrace. "God, I missed you."

I breathe in the smell of his cologne mixed with the aged leather of his jacket. "Not as much as I missed you."

"Ahem." Phoebe clears her throat.

"Phoebe. Good to see you too." Smith gives her a hug. "I like the haircut. The blond suits you."

A hint of a smile tugs at Phoebe's lips, which is a grand gesture when it comes to how she feels about Smith. It's not that they didn't get along or that they didn't like each other growing up. Smith changed the dynamic of our relationship. We went from being a duo to a trio, turning Phoebe into a third wheel.

"That's our car." Phoebe points at a driver holding a sign with our names written on it. "We should get going. Mom probably wants a break from Nana Rosie."

"Good old Nana Rosie." Smith chuckles. "I still remember that Thanksgiving a few years ago when she made all of those pies."

"Oh, yes." I nod. "The great pie fiasco of 2002."

"Why did she make so many pies?"

"Because the year before, she'd just had a hip replacement and couldn't bake. Our mom promised that she would bake Nana's famous lemon meringue and grasshopper pies, and she swore she'd follow Nana's recipes exactly."

"But she didn't." Phoebe chuckles softly. "She ruined every pie crust she touched and somehow managed to screw up canned pie filling."

"Mom ended up buying pies from the grocery store the morning of Thanksgiving, thinking Nana Rosie wouldn't be able to tell," I say. "Of course, she could and was immediately offended."

"That's putting it nicely," Phoebe says. "Nana Rosie had a complete meltdown. She said if she would've known that pies were going to be store bought, she would've baked them from her bed."

"The next year, she baked every pie she could think of. Hence, the great pie fiasco of 2002." I shake my head. "Mom got so pissed by the stunt. I'm surprised nobody ended up with a pie to the face that day. It wasn't until last year that Nana Rosie finally agreed to visit again for Thanksgiving."

"Well, I'm glad to hear she's back," Smith says.

"I doubt our mother is." Phoebe taps her watch. "We better get going."

"Do you have a ride, Smith?" I ask. "Because if you don't, you're welcome to ride with us. We're basically going to the same place."

"Are you sure?" he asks. "I told my folks I'd give them a call when I got to the airport, but I'd rather not spend the next half hour waiting for one of them to come get me."

"Totally," I say with a little more enthusiasm than planned. "Tell your parents you're on your way."

The car ride is mostly uneventful. Smith tells us about Berkeley and an art installation project he's working on for a local bar and music venue. Phoebe gives him the rundown of what life is like at Princeton— or at least what life is like for the people who do more than spend every waking hour in a classroom or being tutored. It kind of feels like old times. Maybe even better. I used to be the one with all the stories to share while Phoebe sat quietly. Now our roles are reversed, and to be honest, I don't mind it right now. In fact, having someone else do all the talking about Princeton is a huge relief. Phoebe looks happy. Smith looks happy. And I, for once, am happy to be in the same zip code as Smith Mackenzie again.

When our car turns onto Clementine Street, Smith's mother is sunning herself in a crocheted bathing suit and sarong on the front lawn. In her defense, it is an unseasonably warm fall. I smile just thinking about my mother losing her mind over the fact that our dining room has a clear view of the Mackenzies' front lawn. This is almost as good as the Easter that Fiona invited the entire Lilith Fair tour to sunrise yoga. Nobody was naked or anything, but according to my mother, she'd never seen so many unrestrained breasts and ungroomed armpits in all her life.

Fiona Mackenzie is a goddamn legend.

"Looks like your mom's taking advantage of global warming," I say.

"God, I want to look like her when I'm that age," Phoebe whispers.

"I'll get you her doctor's number, and you won't have to wait," Smith deadpans.

We pull to a stop in front of my childhood home, and immediately Fiona rushes over to greet us. She gives each of us one of her signature choke-hold hugs before looking us over as if we've just returned from war.

"Phoebe, you've never looked better. College suits you," Fiona says.

"It does." Phoebe blushes, tucking her blond bob behind her ear. "You look amazing too. It takes a lot of dedication to work on a tan in November."

"Oh, I'm not working on my tan, honey." Fiona adjusts her aviators and motions toward her yard. "I'm doing a twenty-four-hour charge on my crystals. It's a full moon in Gemini tonight."

Phoebe's eyes start to glaze over. "Oh. Right. Of course."

Phoebe's not exactly a fan of crystals and astrology. She's way too practical and logical for any of that, despite the fact that she's a triple Pisces like me. Smith's never been a fan of it either. I, on the other hand, can't get enough of it. I could listen to Fiona go on for hours about crystals, the moon, and birth charts.

"You girls should come over tonight when you're done with dinner. I'm doing a little moon ritual later, and with Mo and Jasper on safari, it'll be awfully lonely, just Smith and me," Fiona says. "Penny, you especially should come. I'll make moon water."

"Count me in," I say.

The driver brings our bags, and we say our goodbyes for now. Smith whispers something in my ear about how good it is to see me again, and I can't help but melt a little inside. I've dated a few guys at Princeton, but nothing even remotely serious. To be completely honest, only one made it to the second date, and that was mostly because he caught me trying to sneak out of his apartment early in the morning. It seemed rude not to accept his invitation for Starbucks. Otherwise, he would've definitely been a solid one-night stand.

It's not like I've been pining away for Smith or anything. Princeton just seems to be full of all the wrong guys. Guys who already have the next ten years of their lives planned out. Guys who know exactly what companies they want to work for and who they have to impress to get there. To be honest, I think most of the dates I've gotten are because of who my father is. Never in my life have I had so many dinner conversations about what it's like to be Carter Banks's daughter.

"There are my girls!" Nana Rosie calls from the front door. "Hurry up, you two, so I can get a look at you both."

Nana Rosie wraps me in her arms like a warm blanket on the coldest day. I miss this. I didn't realize until now how much I crave physical touch and connection with people who care about me. The only person I have a consistent relationship with at school besides Phoebe is my tutor, and I think he might fire me as a client if I ask him to hold me.

"You smell like pie, Nana," I say.

"And you smell like patchouli." Nana runs her delicate fingers through my wild curls. "I take it you stopped to visit with Smith's mother."

"She invited us to a moon ritual." Phoebe rolls her eyes.

"Really?" Nana Rosie hooks one arm with mine and the other with Phoebe's. We cross the threshold together. "You know, I'm pretty sure I participated in a moon ritual once."

"How was it?" I ask.

"Chilly. We were all naked, and if memory serves me, we were all the tiniest bit drunk." Nana Rosie chuckles. "Or were we high? I distinctly remember a suspicious mushroom in my salad."

"Sounds like an orgy, Nana," I say.

"Do me a favor and bring up the moon ritual again at dinner, Penny." Nana Rosie's eyes glisten with mischief. "I'd like to remind your parents that while I may be old, I'm not ancient enough to ship off to a nursing home."

"I don't think telling them about your wild teenage years will help," Phoebe says.

"Teenage years?" Nana Rosie shakes her head of tight gray curls. "Darling, that was last summer. That's another reason why I can't go to a home or move in with your parents. It'll cramp my style."

She guides us into the dining room, sharing a few other colorful details from her moon orgy that I highly doubt I will ever be able to erase from my memory. The moment Phoebe and I sit at the table across from each other, something feels off. Mom's in her usual spot opposite the head of the table, with her usual glass of white wine in hand, but she doesn't bother to get up to say hello or offer us each a hug.

"What can I get you both to drink, ladies?" Marie asks. The faint scent of cigarette smoke lingers on her uniform, further confirming the tension in the room.

"Club soda," I say.

"Me too." Phoebe adds, "Mom, where's Dad?"

"In his study," she replies. "Marie, after you get the girls their drinks, please bring out the first course."

"Without Dad?" I blurt out. "You can't start dinner without him. He'll riot."

She doesn't even look at me, much less acknowledge that I've said anything. How the hell can she be pissed when we've only just gotten here?

"Marie, will you let Carter know that we're starting dinner?" Mom asks. "Then bring out the first course exactly five minutes after you've alerted him."

Alerted him? Is my father one of Pavlov's dogs now?

I shoot a look at Phoebe across the table. She shrugs back at me. Maybe it's Fiona charging her crystals in her front yard? She's no longer sunning herself, from what I can see through the window, but her lawn chair is still there along with her crystal collection. My mother would definitely find that disturbing, but I doubt it'd be enough to make my father hide out in his study.

"Hey, Mom, do you have any plans tonight?" I wink across the table at Nana Rosie. "Because if you don't, there's a moon ritual happening—"

"Well, it's true." My father's voice booms from across the house. "You didn't want to believe me, Silvia, but it's official."

My mother's eyes double in size. She looks straight at me like a deer watching one of its deer buddies standing in the road, just seconds away from being run over.

"What's official? Is Dad pregnant?" I laugh nervously. "Did Maury Povich just confirm it?"

"Oh, Penelope." Mom shakes her head. "For once, spare us the jokes."

The soles of my father's loafers squeak on the marble floor as he comes to an abrupt stop. He's clenching a fax in his hand. The Princeton letterhead is visible from my seat, as is the disappointed look on my father's face. My stomach flip-flops.

"Penelope, do you know who I just got off the phone with?"

"I'm guessing not Maury?"

"Your counselor." He points at the fax. "When were you planning on telling us that you're failing all your courses? Just last week you told us that everything was going fine, and now I find out that you were lying to us again."

A wave of embarrassment flushes over me. All of a sudden, I'm a ten-year-old kid again, being chastised at the dinner table for hiding my report card. I can feel everyone's eyes on me, waiting for me to explain myself. Apparently, we can't go a single holiday dinner without me giving a *Sorry for being the family screw-up* speech. It might as well be a course on the menu at this point.

"Thanks for the warm introduction, Dad." I take a sip of the club soda Marie hands me, trying my best to play it cool. "It's good to see you too."

"Cut the crap, Penelope."

His tone is harsher than I ever remember it being. It stings like ice water to the face on a snowy day. The corners of my eyes prickle with tears.

"Calm down, Carter," Nana Rosie says. Her voice is calm but stern. "We're supposed to be sitting down to Thanksgiving dinner. Not a boxing match."

"We've talked on the phone every week this semester and never once did you mention you were struggling." His face is red with heat. He jabs at the fax with his index finger. "Why would you lie to us? If your mother and I knew you were in trouble, we would've found a way to help you. You promised that we would be a team this semester, Penelope. You swore it."

"Dad, she really did plan on telling you both today," Phoebe says.

"Have you been blowing off classes like you did last semester?" my mother asks. "What about the money we sent you for private tutoring? Where did that go?"

I roll my eyes. "Mostly to my cocaine dealer, Mother."

"Not funny," my mother snaps. "Why is everything a joke with you?"

"Genetics are a mysterious thing," I fire back. "Phoebe got the brains, and I got the jokes."

"I'm going to fly back to Princeton with you," my father says. "You and I are both going to meet with your counselor and whatever dean I can get a meeting with. I'll see if I can get your academic probation extended, and you'll go along with whatever option they give us. Do you understand, Penelope?"

I don't. That's the problem. And it's not just Princeton I don't understand. It's my parents. Why do they so desperately want me to fit in at a place I so clearly don't belong? And how do they not see that I don't belong there?

"I'm sorry, but I'm not cut out to be who you want me to be." My voice shakes despite my best efforts to steady it. "I wanted to go to school to major in creative writing."

"Writing is a hobby." My father shakes his head twice. "Do you have any idea how many students your age would kill to have the advantages you've been given? Do you know how many kids fresh out of college my company turns away? All you have to do is pass your classes, Penelope. That's all I—"

I push my seat away from the table and toss my napkin on the chair.

"Where are you going?" my mother asks frantically. "Penelope, sit down."

"I'm going across the street," I say over my shoulder.

My father growls. "Let me guess. That damn Mackenzie boy is back."

"You can't run away every time a conversation doesn't go your way, Penelope," my mother says.

"I'm not running away," I say. "I'm going to dance under the full moon with that damn Mackenzie boy's mother. Naked. Open the blinds tonight if you need to find me."

Chapter 10

Penny: I'm doing it again.

Jackie: Doing what?

Chelsey: Kegels?

Penny: Turning into the worst version of myself.

Penny: I swear, the minute I land back in this zip code, I go all Paris and Nicole from the early 'oos.

Jackie: I'm going to need you to be more specific.

Chelsey: At least you're not wearing a velour tracksuit with JUICY on your ass.

Penny: Honestly, it's too much to text.

Chelsey: Video chat?

Jackie: Maybe in the morning before I'm completely drunk with my NJ cousins?

Jackie: 10 AM?

Chelsey: I can make that work.

Penny: I'll try.

Chelsey: And Penny, just remember that we love you.

Chelsey: No matter what version of yourself you are.

Jackie: Seconded.

Those smut witches are the best humans on the planet, and I am simply not worthy of their friendship.

Penny: Love you hoes.

"Knock, knock." Martin pushes open the door warily. "I've been instructed to inform you that your guest has arrived."

"Thanks," I say dryly. I walk across the room to my purse and empty it out on Phoebe's bed. "I'll be down in a sec."

"I've, uh, considered your request." He clears his throat. "While I think it's the strangest favor anyone has ever asked of me, I'll do it. Under one condition."

"If you're hoping there's going to be a second peep show—"

"No. Believe it or not, I haven't asked a girl to show me her boobs since high school. And for the record, that was a dare."

"All right, then." I unclasp my necklace, which has gotten tangled in my hair and Diane Keaton dress. "What's your condition?"

"You help get me out of playing golf with your father on Friday."

"Not a golfer? You look like a golfer."

"What's that supposed to mean?" He quirks his brow. "It doesn't seem complimentary."

"That you look like a guy who likes to swing a stick around while smoking a cigar and riding in a little car?" I struggle to clasp my necklace over the turtleneck. "I don't know. I thought liking golf was a requirement at my father's office."

"Let me help you with that." He holds out his hand for the necklace. "I've got four sisters. I'm pretty good with clasps."

I turn around and hold my hair to the side and out of his way. "All right. I'll find a way to get you out of it. I can't promise that you'll like it more than golf, though."

"Virtually anything would be better." His hands hover above my shoulders, sending a thousand shivers across my skin. "There. You're all set. It's a beautiful necklace."

"Thanks." My cheeks flush with heat. "It's my favorite."

"So, we have a deal?" He holds out his hand for me to shake.

I shake his hand. "Deal."

He opens the door and presses his hand to my lower back. His touch is light, almost imperceptible, but to me it feels like a hot knife slicing through butter. It's been far too long since someone's touch has melted me, real or not, and I'd forgotten how exciting it is.

"After you," he says. "By the way, you look very nice tonight."

"Aw, I'm sure you say that to all the girls you fake date."

"Actually, you're my first."

He smiles at me devilishly, and I somehow manage to resist the urge to make a joke about virginity. No matter what performance Martin and I put on this evening, keeping my mouth closed right now is my Academy Award–winning moment.

We breeze down the hallway at a steady clip. I give him the abridged version of my history with Smith, and he gives me some basic details about his life. He's the youngest of five and the only son. He's originally from Kentucky, went to college at Yale, and moved to California a few months ago after my father hired him.

"Why not go back home for Thanksgiving?" I ask. "I mean, believe me, I understand not wanting to go home, but isn't staying with your boss's family just as stressful?"

"I don't know if you know this," he whispers as we round the corner to the dining room, "but your dad is a pretty cool guy."

"No one in my entire life has ever called my dad cool," I say. "Is your family the Donner Party?"

"They're actually gluten-free vegans."

"From Kentucky?"

"A rare breed."

"Somehow that seems worse."

"You have no idea."

I hold my breath as we cross the threshold into the dining room. My parents are on opposite ends of the table in their usual seats with their drinks. Scotch on the rocks for my dad. A glass of white wine for my mother. Phoebe and Falon are across from one another, each with an espresso martini, leaving two seats directly across from Smith open for Martin and me. If my anxiety was on the Richter scale, this would be the big one California's been waiting for.

Martin gives my lower back another little pat, only this time it doesn't make me go all melty inside. Not with Smith sitting at my dining room table with his leather bag slung across the back of his chair. Why would he bring that bag with my ring into my house? Is he worried that someone will break into his house and steal it, thus ruining his chances of proposing to his stupid air-fryer girlfriend?

"Look what the tugboat finally dragged in." Nana Rosie smiles. "Come have a drink with us before Smith thinks you're avoiding him."

"Well, we wouldn't want that," my father says dryly. "Penny, it looks like you and Martin have been introduced."

Smith quirks an eyebrow, and suddenly I'm frozen. Martin might not even need to put on a show at all. This whole ridiculous idea might unravel before we even take our seats.

"To Smith?" Martin pulls out my chair and then holds out his hand to Smith. "No, we haven't. Nice to meet you. I'm Martin Butler. I work for Carter."

"Oh, he's being modest," my mother interjects. "Martin's on the partner track at Carter's firm. He's an incredible engineer and formidable businessman. Isn't he, Carter?"

"Yes, he's a valuable asset to the firm," my father confirms. "Penelope, did you know that Martin attended Yale?"

"Of course I did, Dad." I drum my fingers on my thighs nervously. I swear I can feel Smith mentally poking holes in my charade. "You know what? I'm going to get us some drinks."

"If you wait a moment, Marie will be out with appetizers, and you can tell her what you'd like to drink," my mother says.

"No, I'm pretty parched." I stand and slide my chair back in. "What about you, Martin? Are you parched? You look parched."

"Very parched. A drink would be great, dear." The table falls silent. I don't know if Martin can feel everyone's eyeballs on him, but if he can, he doesn't let on. "So, Smith, what is it that you do?"

I spin on my heels and head toward my father's study before anyone has the chance to turn the conversation back to me and Martin. God, I wish I could disappear. We've been at the table for less than two minutes, and already I've practically sweat through my turtleneck dress. What kind of maniac invented turtlenecks? Diane Keaton must never sweat.

I pour a heavy-handed shot of tequila and down it while I google Martin. The last thing I want is for Smith to ask me a question that I can't answer and catch me with my pants down in another lie. The tequila goes down smooth—honestly, probably a little too smooth—so I pour another while I scroll through the many different Martin Butlers of the internet. He's not on any of the predictable socials. No Instagram, Facebook, or Twitter. But there is a TikTok result that catches my attention.

@KnotMartinButler

I click on the link, and within seconds a video of Martin Butler in a red-checkered flannel with rolled sleeves starts to play on my phone.

"The Hanson knot is a traditional Boy Scout knot," says Flannel Martin as he tugs on a piece of rope. "It has very little slip, and it can be used for all kinds of things outdoors."

Flannel Martin starts maneuvering the rope into a knot, but my gaze keeps honing in on his forearms. His muscles flex and pull with each delicate movement of his fingers. He tugs slow at first, and then fast and hard until he's left with what looks like a lasso. Maybe it's the tequila, but all I can think about is how amazing those hands would feel on my body.

"Chelsey and Jackie need to see this," I mutter to myself.

I send the link and contemplate pouring one more shot but decide against it. The goal is to keep a clear head, and two tequilas is already walking a fine line. Instead, I pour myself a glass of club soda and mix a quick Jack and Coke for Martin—a little heavy on the Jack because I am already two drinks ahead of him.

My phone pings with a text.

Chelsey: OMG. Who is this Greek god?
Jackie: This is what your mother set you up with for Thanksgiving? THIS!?
Chelsey: Can he tie me up? Please?
Chelsey: Tell him I've been naughty.
Penny: So I'm not crazy? There's something kinda hot about him, right?
Jackie: Kinda? No babe. There's something kinda hot about Henry Cavill.
Jackie: Harry Styles is kinda hot.
Jackie: This man is sex on a stick on fire.

"Ms. Penelope." Marie knocks on the doorway of the study. "Appetizers have been served."

"I'll be right there," I say, fumbling my phone.

I open up my TikTok app once more and do a quick scroll through his videos. There's got to be at least fifty. Martin tying knots wearing flannel in the forest. Martin tying knots on the beach in a tank top and trunks. Martin tying knots sitting in an office. I'm not going to pretend to understand why a guy like Martin makes videos like this. I write spicy sex for a living. To each their own. What I do know is that the nearly one hundred thousand subscribers on Martin's account are not all Boy Scouts.

"Penelope, I'm going to be dead by the time you come back here!" Nana Rosie yells.

"On my way, Nana." I tuck my phone away.

"Good!" she hollers back. "And then we're going to tie you to your seat for the rest of the night."

I nearly drop both drinks in the hallway. If only Nana Rosie knew exactly how capable Martin is for that exact job.

The mood feels lighter in the dining room. Smith and my father are locked in conversation about traveling overseas. Phoebe and Falon listen intently, occasionally smiling or laughing when the timing is right. Nana Rosie and my mother are eating, which is always a good sign. They're kind of like tigers in a zoo: loud and could possibly bite your head off if not fed at regular intervals. As for me, I'm pleasantly buzzed and allowing Martin Butler's TikToks to play rent-free in my head.

I set Martin's drink in front of him and take my seat next to him. He takes a sip and nearly gags trying to swallow it down.

"A little strong?" I whisper.

"Was your goal to poison me?" He dabs at his face with a linen napkin.

"Obviously. Didn't you pick up on the fact that we're modeling our relationship after Romeo and Juliet?"

"It all makes sense now."

"Well, you have to finish it." I start to fill my plate with the mini quiches and stuffed peppers Marie prepared. "Smith will know we're not madly in love if I don't know your drink of choice."

"Beer," he says. "For future reference, I'm a plain old beer kind of guy. Unless we're someplace fancy. Then I'll have a mule with whiskey."

An image of Martin in his flannel shirt in the woods flashes across my mind. I try to imagine how that version of Martin with the five-o'clock shadow and sun-kissed cheeks is the same man sitting next to me who looks like he fell off the pages of *GQ*. I'm buzzed enough to want to ask him about @KnotMartinButler but sober enough to know now is not the time to let the man doing me a huge favor know that I've cyberstalked him.

"I'll keep that in mind," I say.

"And that's how I ended up getting bucked off a camel in Cairo," Smith announces. "I've still got the scar on my knee to prove it."

Everyone, minus Martin and me, erupts in laughter, and for a moment, I think this terror of a day might actually end on a good note.

"I hope *National Geographic* paid you workman's comp." My father dabs at the tears streaming down his face. "That sure would've been an interesting claim."

"*National Geographic?*" I ask.

"Smith works for them as a traveling photojournalist," my father says. "Didn't he mention that to you on the drive home?"

"No, he didn't." I shake my head. "We were kind of busy with our driver."

"Whatever happened to that digital magazine the two of you got involved in?" Nana Rosie asks. "If I remember right, you ended up becoming a partner in the group?"

"Nana, Smith doesn't want to talk about work the whole time," I say.

The truth is that I don't want to hear Smith talk about work, particularly if that work involves *Digital Slap*, the online music magazine that played a key role in the demise of our marriage.

"I'm still involved with the company," Smith says. "But Penny's right. We don't need to focus on me. We could talk about the two—"

"Lovebirds at the table." I motion to Phoebe and Falon, desperate to turn the spotlight away from me. "Phoebe and Falon are newly engaged. It's all very exciting."

"It's true." Phoebe eyes me, like she knows exactly what I'm doing. "We're in love. We're engaged. Next subject."

My mind races trying to come up with something—anything—to talk about that can't possibly lead back to me and Martin. To my relief, Martin chimes in.

"Have any of you read Penny's latest novel?"

To my dismay, he's picked a landmine of a conversation starter. My family hasn't read any of my books. They know I write, and they know I'm successful enough to not have to sell my organs to make ends meet, but that's it.

"You know, I always thought I would have traveled more by this point in my life." My father interjects himself so quickly, it practically gives the table whiplash. "I just never seemed to find the time. The company always needed me. My family needed me. Now look at me, I'm in my seventies and there's so much of the world I've never seen."

Phoebe shoots me a *WTF* look from across the table. Our dad is a man of routine. He's up every day at five o'clock with the same three newspapers and a pot of coffee before work. He's eaten the same lunch at the same delicatessen across the street from his office since I was five. The man has a written inventory of his wardrobe so he knows when to buy the identical replacement pieces of clothing after they start to look too worn.

He's never once mentioned the desire to travel to exotic places. He barely tolerates traveling to local places. He's never even traveled to San Francisco to visit me. Of course, I've never extended an invite, but regardless, he wouldn't go. He doesn't go places. He likes his routines, and he likes the control he has over them.

"Well, now you've got Martin," Smith says. "I'm sure he could keep an eye on things while you and Silvia do a little traveling."

"Wouldn't mind at all," Martin says.

"I would love that, Carter," my mother says. "We could do that trip to Europe we've always talked about. Phoebe and Falon, the two of you could meet us on your honeymoon. Wouldn't that be fun?"

"I mean what girl doesn't dream about going on her honeymoon with her parents," Phoebe deadpans.

"To answer your question, Martin"—Smith clears his throat—"I haven't read any of Penny's books. Which would you recommend?"

"Phoebe, I think you're underestimating the benefits of traveling with a foursome. We'd get much better rates on travel with a good agent." My dad polishes off the last of his scotch. "Of course, a trip like that would take a couple of weeks to do properly. A lot of planning would need to go into it, and there'd still be some things I'd need to make myself available for. Smith, have you traveled to Europe recently?"

I can't believe it. It's as if my father's made a game out of avoiding any mention of me whatsoever, like I don't exist.

"Uh, well." Smith shoots me a confused look. "Yes, I was there this spring. I covered Glastonbury for *Digital Slap*. It was busy, but not as bad as during the summer."

"Glastonbury!" My father's eyes widen like saucers. "That's impressive. Isn't that impressive, Silvia?"

The man literally has no clue what Glastonbury is.

"Carter," Nana Rosie growls. "I believe you're monopolizing the conversation. Martin was asking Penny about her writing and you bulldozed right over it."

"I guess I must've missed that part of the conversation." My father stands, visibly shaky on his feet. He palms his empty glass. *How much has he had to drink?* "Can I get anybody else anything to drink while I'm up? Smith, your glass is looking dangerously close to empty."

"I'm good." Smith checks his watch. "I should actually call it a night. Harriet gets nervous when I'm out for too long anyway."

"Harriet? Is that your girlfriend?" My father sways, leaning against the table for support. "Wife?"

"It's his dog," I snap. "Ozzie's sister. We bought them together."

"I thought it was an odd name for a girlfriend." He shrugs, ignoring my tone completely. "Why don't you bring the dog over here? We're still just catching up."

Out of everything that's happened today, this moment right now is the most shocking of all. My father has never once asked Smith

Mackenzie to stay longer in his home. Never. In fact, he's been known for doing quite the opposite. Now, he's fangirling over him. He's a glass of scotch away from throwing his panties at the man.

"Gee, Dad, why don't you invite him for a sleepover?" I grab Martin's Jack and Coke and take a sip. It tastes like kerosene. "Maybe if you ask Mom nicely, you can go over to his house tomorrow."

"Penelope, stop it." My mother scowls. "Your father is just being polite. It's been a long time since we've seen Smith."

"Really? Remember when you saw him on the front lawn half an hour ago and wanted to deck him?" I fire back. "You called him a douchebag."

"I did no such thing," my father snarls. "I called him a jackass, and that was before he apologized to your mother and me."

"Apologized to you?" I stand, seething with anger and hurt. "What the hell does he have to apologize to you for?"

"Let's calm down now." My mother taps on the table, trying to regain some semblance of order. "It's been a long day for everyone. Why don't we retire to the living room for the evening and catch up on some television."

"Yes. We could have Marie prepare sandwiches and have a little picnic," Nana Rosie adds. "Martin, Smith, have either of you seen *The Bachelorette*? It's a fascinating program."

"He needed to apologize for leaving you in an airport." My father slurs his words. "For running out on his commitment to you. That's what he apologized for."

The room goes still. Frozen and icy cold. Nobody seems to have any idea where to look, other than not at me. The secondhand embarrassment is brutal.

"I need some air," I say quietly.

"I'll go with you." Martin takes my hand. "Smith, it was nice to meet you."

"Pen, wait." Smith starts to stand, but Martin waves him off.

"I've got her," he says. "She'll be OK."

Will she? I think as I make a beeline out of the dining room. I grab a coat off the hook and pause. An immediate feeling of déjà vu washes over me. Why am I always running out of this house? And why doesn't anyone in my family ever bother to stop me?

Chapter 11

The night air hits my face like pins and needles. I struggle to put the coat on, until I realize that it belongs to Falon and there's no way it's going to fit me.

As if on cue, Martin covers my shoulders with his jacket. His hand once again rests on my lower back, but I brush it off. I don't want comfort right now. I want to be pissed and mad and sad and full of the kind of angst that's common among emo teenagers and punks.

Those are the sort of feelings I'm used to having when I come home. I know how to deal with those feelings. They may not feel good, but they're familiar, and right now the only thing I want—other than Dorothy's red slippers to take me home—is for something to go as expected. And taking comfort from a man my mother probably paid to stay over for Thanksgiving isn't on that list.

"Do you want me to call a rideshare or something for you? My treat," I huff, keeping a solid two steps ahead of Martin. "I can have them pick you up on the street corner. You won't even have to show your face back in that house. I'll tell my parents you joined the witness protection program. I'm sure they'll understand, because apparently they can understand any human who isn't me."

"So I did that bad of a job?"

"Huh?" I slow my pace and look over my shoulder. "What are you talking about?"

"My performance as your boyfriend." Martin hurries his pace. "Personally, I didn't think it was that bad. In the scope of everything that transpired over drinks, it was actually a pretty minor role."

The corners of my lips tug with a smile that I one hundred percent am not consenting to. I force a frown and hang a left at the corner of Clementine Street.

"I don't know if you caught it, but I covered pretty nicely when Carter asked if we'd met. Then I slipped in that *dear*, which I definitely think Smith noticed."

"You lost it when you mentioned my books."

"I picked up on some tension around that subject, which was unexpected."

"Nobody in my family reads my books," I say. "We don't talk about it."

"Why? Did you pull a Christina Crawford and *Mommie Dearest* them?"

"Worse." I chuckle. "I write romance novels."

"I see." He cocks his head and smiles. "Can I read them?"

"Look"—I turn around and face him—"I appreciate what you're trying to do here. Really. It's kind and admirable, but you don't have to. This is the part of the evening where I wallow in my misery. It's the part where I realize that no matter what I do with my life, I'm always going to disappoint my parents. That's what this part of the evening is for. It's kind of like masturbation."

"Best done solo?"

"Exactly." I nod toward Orange Avenue. "Now, I'm going to head down that street, and you're not going to follow me."

"It's also illegal to do in public. Masturbation, that is." Martin closes the gap between us so that he's standing next to me. "So due to matters of public safety, I'm going to have to go with you."

I tilt my head back and let out a laugh so loud and unrestrained that it almost scares me. It throws me a little off-balance, and I lose my footing in the heels I stole out of Phoebe's closet. Just as I'm about to teeter off the curb, Martin wraps his arm around me and pulls me into him. He's warm and smells like Tom Ford's tobacco cologne. It's quite possibly my favorite scent in the world. I wear it all the time when I'm writing a particularly spicy scene because it always puts me in the right mood. The mood feels much more pleasant in Martin's arms than it does on paper.

Maybe he senses that he's holding me a beat too long. He starts to release his grip and mumbles some sort of apology, but I can't hear any of it over the pounding in my chest. I wrap my arms around his neck and pull him back, until both of his arms lock tightly around me. I nuzzle my face into his neck and breathe him in.

"For what it's worth," he whispers, hot breath against my ear, "I don't think you've disappointed anyone tonight. I think you're just human."

"Don't believe it for a second. You take off this dress and you'll find a zipper on this flesh suit."

"So you're an alien?"

"Absolutely."

"Can I ask you something?" He pulls away and places his thumb beneath my chin, tilting my head back. I nod. "Do you still have feelings for your ex?"

I shake my head no, and I mean it. Sure, Smith is still hot and, by all accounts, the same kind man I once loved, but there weren't any sparks flying between us in that van. And when I saw my old ring, it didn't make me miss him. If anything, it made me miss Fiona a little more, which was a problem in our marriage. I loved being a part of Smith's family more than I loved being his wife.

"No," I say. "Why?"

"Well." He leans in close, his lips just centimeters away from mine. "Because I think I'd like to kiss you right now."

"I think I'd like that too."

He presses his lips to mine and we kiss. Softly, but without hesitation. He glides his fingers through my curls, cupping my neck in his hand, and melting every one of my sharp edges. It's been a long time since I've been kissed like this, by someone I barely know. Even longer since I've let my guard down long enough for someone to see me so vulnerable.

I'm the first to pull away, and immediately I regret it. My body aches for more of him. His lips feel like fresh air in my lungs. His embrace like shelter from the cold sea air. The sensible thing to do would be to put on the brakes. Stop ourselves from further complicating things. But being sensible is overrated.

Martin brushes a curl away from my face. "Do you kiss all of your fake boyfriends on the first date?"

"I do," I say. "You should see what I do on the second fake date. Full-on praying mantis."

"You are an alien." He shivers. "Do you think we could be done with the wallowing portion of the evening?"

I suddenly realize that I'm not nearly as annoyed as I was before kissing Martin. Had I known sucking face with a gorgeous man was all it took to snap me out of a bad mood, I could've saved so much money on therapy.

"Sure," I say. "But fair warning, when we go back inside that house, we're going to have to watch *The Bachelorette* with Nana Rosie. There's no escaping it."

"Is that so?"

"Look, I can get you out of golf, but Nana's watch parties are like jury duty. She talks through most of the episode, and my mother asks a million questions because she can't ever seem to remember anything about the show. Phoebe always has a thousand opinions, and that means you're going to have to have at least half as many opinions, otherwise they'll think you're weak. You'll probably have a terrible time."

"Are you trying to scare me? I have four sisters. I'm an OG *Bachelorette* viewer. I'm talking Trista and Ryan."

"Those names mean virtually nothing to me."

"Then prepare to be impressed, Banks. Prepare to be impressed."

We make it back home in time for my family to forget that anything unpleasant happened over drinks. Marie's left out sandwiches, but it looks like everybody's already eaten. I'm not all that hungry anyway. Martin and I change into our pajamas—in our own separate rooms—and I send a quick update to the Smut Coven about the night's turn of events.

> **Chelsey: You kissed Knot Guy? My Thanksgiving is the worst compared to yours.**
> **Jackie: Speak for yourself. I just had to watch my mother fist a turkey.**
> **Penny: I mean it's not all kisses and sunshine. My dad and I had a small flare up during drinks.**
> **Chelsey: Over the bookstore?**
> **Penny: No. I'll fill you guys in tomorrow.**
> **Jackie: When are you planning on talking to your dad about it?**

A wave of guilt washes over me. The focus of this trip is supposed to be the bookstore. I can't let Smith or Martin distract me, and I definitely can't keep picking petty fights with my father the whole weekend.

> **Penny: Soon. I promise.**

The episode has just started when I finally make it into the living room, and to my relief Martin isn't here yet. He must still be changing, or he's chickened out entirely. Either way, I take my usual seat in the leather recliner in the corner, which means that if and when Martin does join the viewing party, he'll be stuck sitting with Phoebe and Falon on the couch.

"Explain how this works again." My mother reaches into the bowl of freshly popped popcorn. "How does one woman date all those men in an hour? Less with commercials, if you think about it."

"She doesn't date all of them, Silvia," Nana Rosie groans. "The goal of the first episode is for her to mingle with the guys to see who she connects with and then trim the fat. It's an incredibly efficient process."

"I can't believe I'm watching this again." Phoebe sighs from the end of the leather sectional. "Correction. I can't believe I'm watching this without a drink in my hand. Nana, why can't we watch something normal?"

"Oh, you mean like those crime documentaries you're so obsessed with?" Nana Rosie motions for my mother to pass her the popcorn. "What's normal about wanting to watch a woman poison her husband with oleander? Sounds awfully depressing if you ask me."

"Technically, they all have happy endings because they always catch the killer," Phoebe says.

"*The Bachelorette* is not so bad." Falon holds out an open bag of barbecue potato chips to Phoebe, which she snatches out of her hand like a hangry raccoon. "On second thought, Penny, now might be a good time for a bottle of wine."

"I'm on it," I say. "Anybody else have any requests?"

"A lobotomy," Phoebe grumbles, mouth full of chips.

"I'd love a beer," Nana Rosie says. "It goes better with popcorn in my opinion. In the can is fine."

My mother makes a face indicating that beer in the can is anything but fine, but she holds her tongue.

"Do you want me to pause it if you're not back before the ad break is over?" Falon asks.

"Not necessary," I say, knowing all too well that leaving this group without something to distract them for any length of time has the potential to end in a riot. "I'll be back in a flash."

I hurry into the kitchen, sliding across the marble floor in my fluffy socks. I feel a little like a kid back in high school again, lounging in my flannel pajamas and watching bad TV. It's the sort of thing I'd do all the time with Phoebe. During school breaks, we'd camp out in front of the

TV, watching our favorite movies. Phoebe would always pick something indie and edgy, while I wanted something romantic with Meg Ryan or Drew Barrymore. We'd devour bags of sour candy and tortilla chips with salsa, and we'd wash it down with Mountain Dews.

Life was so easy back when we were in high school. I never thought of us as being best friends back then, but now, I don't know what else we'd call it. Up until our senior year, Phoebe was the keeper of my secrets, and I kept hers. She came out to me when we were freshmen, years before she was ready to tell my parents. She was so afraid of being different from me. She was afraid I wouldn't know how to relate to her, but I wasn't. I'd been sneaking romance novels from the public library for years. If there's one thing I understood, it was attraction. I took her to her first Pride parade that summer, and I held her hand when she told Mom and Dad her junior year.

I can't remember the last time I held my sister's hand. I can't remember the last time she trusted me with her secrets, and I don't remember the last time I thought to tell her mine. That's the problem with coming back home, I guess. You realize how much you've missed since you've been gone.

"Penny! Where's the wine?" Phoebe shouts from the living room. "This kind of torture is illegal in some countries."

"Just a minute!" I call back.

I grab a bottle of chilled red from the wine fridge, along with two cans of beer—no glasses required—and three stemless wine glasses. I try to scoop everything into my arms to carry into the living room, but it's impossible to do in one trip. If living in San Francisco has taught me anything over the years, it's that making two trips is never an option. I eye Nana Rosie's gardening basket next to the back door.

Bingo.

I lift the top of the picnic-style basket, and a skunky, familiar odor hits me. I turn on the overhead light to get a better look inside.

"You've got to be shitting me." I hold up a sticky bud. "My grandma's a pothead."

The door that leads from the garage to the kitchen opens, and I snap the lid closed. Marijuana might be legal in California, but old habits die hard. In walks my father, followed by Martin. Both appear more surprised to see me than I am to find Nana Rosie's stash.

"Penelope." My father nods, wiping a layer of sweat above his upper lip. "Would you tell your mother to come see me in our bedroom? Please?"

"Is everything OK?"

"Perfectly fine."

He makes a quick exit down the hall to his bedroom before I can say anything more. I shift my attention to Martin and try to assess the situation. He's still in his clothes from before, which means whatever the two of them were doing occupied a fair chunk of time.

I narrow my gaze. "Why were you in the garage with my father? I thought you were changing."

"I didn't want you to find out like this, but your father cornered me on the way to my room and brought me into the garage so we could talk in private." He looks down at his feet. "Banks, your father has asked me if I would be willing to be his fake boyfriend at our company holiday party."

God, I love a man who can banter.

"Dammit." I sigh. "I mean, you did give an excellent performance."

"I was hoping you'd be willing to break it to your mother for me."

"As long as you're willing to hug her while she ugly cries."

"Deal." He makes his way across the kitchen, stopping next to my collection of beer and wine on the counter. "Is *The Bachelorette* viewing party a liquid-only event?"

"There's sandwiches and popcorn in the living room." I hold up Nana Rosie's basket and pull back the lid. "And Nana Rosie's special lettuce."

Martin peers into the basket and pulls out a bud, then lets it drop back in. "I've got so many questions."

"Penny!" Phoebe shouts. "Booze! Now!"

"Well, they'll have to wait." I close the lid and move the basket back to where I found it. "Right now, we have a party to attend."

"Lead the way."

Chapter 12

"The group dates are my favorite," Martin says in between bites of pizza.

Somewhere after the third or fourth episode, we ordered a round of emergency pizzas, and I'm glad we did, because as invested as everyone is in Kaitlyn's journey to find true love, we might end up pulling an all-nighter.

"If you ask me, I think the group dates are a complete waste of Kaitlyn's time," says Phoebe. "Half of these douches are just here for their fifteen minutes of fame, and she's having to carry them around like deadweight. This show would be so much better with lesbians."

"Hear! Hear!" Falon and I raise our drinks.

"I'm a fan of the group dates myself," Nana Rosie chimes in. "Back in my day, women were always throwing themselves at men. I like watching the tables turn."

"Shhh!" my mother hisses. "I'm going to turn on the subtitles if everyone can't pipe down, and you know how much I hate reading TV."

"Understood." Martin raises his hands in mock surrender before turning toward me from his spot on the floor. He motions for me to lean in from my perch on the recliner. "When are we going to ask your grandmother where she grows her pot?"

"Well, we could do it now," I whisper. "But then you'd have to sleep with one eye open tonight. She's nearly a hundred and isn't afraid of doing hard time."

"She's going to kill me over a question?"

"No. She'd probably just maim you a little for being nosy."

"Thanks for the warning, Banks."

He returns his attention to the TV, but this time rests his back against the recliner, positioning himself so that if I moved my leg even just a hair, we'd be touching. I like this level of closeness. The kiss earlier was a mistake, albeit an enjoyable mistake. It was my inner teen acting out because of what happened with my father over drinks. It was my way of distracting myself from my feelings instead of sitting with them like I've learned to do. I really do become the worst version of myself when I'm back home, and I don't want Martin to get caught in the crosshairs of the old me. I want him to get to know me as I am now.

My phone buzzes in my pocket.

Phoebe: You two look cozy.

I glance in my sister's direction. Both she and Falon have eyes on me like a mother chaperoning a school dance.

Falon: Very cozy.

This is the first time the three of us have ever been in a group chat together. I kind of feel like I've just been invited to sit at the cool kids' table. Naturally, I have to overcompensate.

Penny: Do you know Nana Rosie has a basket full of weed buds in the kitchen?

Phoebe nearly spits out her wine.

"Everything OK, Phoebe?" Mom asks.

"Went down the wrong pipe," Phoebe says.

Phoebe: Bullshit.

Falon: She told me she grows rare plants in that little greenhouse in the backyard.

Falon: I had no idea that's what she meant.

Penny: Go look if you don't believe me.

Falon: I think they're technically called nugs.

Penny: Noted.

Phoebe excuses herself from the living room with minimal disruption, and I wait with bated breath for her reaction to Nana Rosie's latest gardening endeavors. She shuffles back moments later with her jaw practically hanging to the floor. She grabs the remote from the coffee table and pauses the show.

"Why are we pausing?" Nana Rosie asks. "That man was about to disrobe. Give me that clicker."

Phoebe reaches into the pocket of her pajama pants and pulls out a nug. "You get the clicker once you explain why your basket is full of Mary Jane, Nana."

My mother leans forward in her recliner and squints. "What is that thing?"

"It's marijuana, Mom," Phoebe says.

"Where did it come from?" my mother asks.

"Give me that." Nana waves her hands frantically. "I never took you for a narc. Who gave you permission to rummage through an old woman's things?" Phoebe points at me like the snitch she is. "You? Why in the hell would you tell Ms. Goody Two-Shoes about—"

"I'm not a Goody Two-Shoes!" Phoebe plants her hands on her hips. "Falon, aren't you going to defend me? You're literally my lawyer."

"I thought she'd be cool, Nana," I say between fits of laughter. "I had no idea she'd air your dirty laundry like this."

Mom turns to Nana Rosie. "Is that what you've been growing in that greenhouse you ordered online? You said we couldn't go in there because you were growing carnivorous plants."

"It doesn't matter what I'm growing in my own greenhouse, OK?" Nana Rosie snatches the nug from Phoebe's hand. "I'm a ninety-six-year-old grandmother, not Pablo Escobar."

My mother wrings her hands together as she starts to pace. "This is illegal, isn't it?"

"Actually"—Martin holds up his phone—"according to Google, she hasn't technically committed a crime so long as she has six or fewer plants and isn't growing them outdoors. Of course, there are other rules, but those are the basics."

"How many plants do you have, Nana?" Phoebe asks.

"I plead the Fifth." She points to Falon. "And I call her as my lawyer if you decide to tip off the feds."

"You can't just call dibs," Phoebe says. "Tell her Falon."

Falon sinks back into the couch. "I plead the Fifth."

"It's past my bedtime, dears." Nana Rosie clicks her tongue. "C'mon, Ozzie. You can stay with me tonight and alert me if Judas over there comes to betray me again. And don't for one second think about sneaking into my greenhouse. I've got the place locked tight, and I sleep with the key hidden in between my bosoms."

"That's a mental image I didn't need," Martin mutters under his breath.

"Mother, we're going to need to have a discussion with Carter about this." Mom follows Nana Rosie and Ozzie out of the living room. "I don't think he's going to approve of any of it, legal or not."

"Fine, you tell my son about my greenhouse, and I'll tell him about those little nip and tuck procedures you've been trying to pass off as facials and expensive serums," Nana says.

"Rosamunde, you take that back!"

Their voices trail off as they head up the stairs, leaving the four of us cackling. I laugh until tears pour down my face and my belly hurts.

It's close to midnight, which we all agree is too late to attempt a raid on Nana Rosie's greenhouse. Tomorrow we'll get to the bottom of her backyard operation. With any luck, it could end up being the most relaxed Thanksgiving the Banks family has ever had.

Martin walks me to my bedroom, and I invite him in for a nightcap. Not because I want to revisit our kiss from earlier tonight, but because I enjoy having him around. And it feels a little lonely going to my room by myself. Phoebe has Falon to talk to until she falls asleep. Mom has Dad. Nana Rosie even took Ozzie, though I can't say that I blame him. He's probably getting a contact high from her right now.

I leave Martin with a bottle of wine at my desk, while I take my makeup off in the bathroom. Just as I splash water on my face, my phone buzzes with a text.

Phoebe: I'm sorry for what I said when I was hungry.
Phoebe: You don't make me feel like a side character.
Phoebe: And you're not a bitch.
Penny: You never called me a bitch.
Phoebe: I did. In my head. A LOT.
Penny: That's fair. Start over tomorrow? You, me, and Falon can do traditional Thanksgiving things like make pie and day drink?
Phoebe: Falon says yes.
Phoebe: Get some sleep.
Penny: I will.
Phoebe: And if you're going to sleep with Martin, please keep it down. I have a headache.
Penny: I'm not going to sleep with Martin. I barely know him. I don't even know if he carries condoms.
Phoebe: Reason #381 why I'm happy to be a lesbian.
Phoebe: Goodnight.

When I emerge from the bathroom, Martin is no longer at my desk. Instead, he's leaning against the wall, fiddling with a piece of nylon rope in his hands. The bottle of wine and two empty glasses remain untouched.

"You waited until now to murder me?" I point to the rope. "I mean, you had so many opportunities to do it earlier that would have been infinitely better."

"I tie knots." He holds up the cord. "It's a nervous tic of mine."

I desperately want to bring up his knot-tying TikTok channel but decide against it. His brows are slanted with worry, and I get the sense that admitting to stalking him would only add to his uneasiness. That's the problem with stalking people on the internet. There's rarely ever a good time to admit it.

"I hope you know I didn't plan for any of this to happen," he says.

"My grandmother secretly growing weed?" I chuckle. "Yeah, I didn't see that one coming either."

"Well, yes, that. But also this." He motions to me. "I'm having a good time with you. I'm actually having a good time with your whole family."

"Did my mother not send you the script?" I plop down on my bed and pull a chenille throw blanket over my legs. "I can let you borrow mine, if you like."

"Do you always use humor to defuse situations that make you uncomfortable?" He smirks.

"It's my version of knot tying." I point to the rope that he's tangled into what looks like a pretzel. "What's got you nervous?"

"The fact that I'm in my boss's daughter's bedroom, for one." He untangles the knot in one easy move of his hand. "Oh, and I made out with my boss's daughter. That's got me pretty nervous too."

My stomach flutters.

"I mean, he'll probably fire you once I tell him about that biting thing you did," I tease. Martin's cheeks flush with heat. "Unless you'd rather I keep that bit to myself."

"I'd consider it a big favor."

"All kidding aside"—I pat the bed—"you really don't need to be nervous. I think my parents would be thrilled if they knew I kissed a man they hand selected. You must come from excellent breeding stock."

"That's the thing." He starts to pace. "I don't. I'm from middle-of-nowhere Kentucky. I went to school on a track scholarship. My parents live in the same starter house that I grew up in, and the only thing remotely fancy about them is the Fancy Feast my mom insists on feeding her cats."

"I've seen those cat food commercials. They're very high class."

"I hate golf. I think the idea of spending thousands of dollars on a membership to a club is a ridiculous waste of money. I buy most of my work clothes from outlet stores, and if I'm being really honest, I lied about my address when your dad hired me." He pauses next to the wine bottle and palms the glass. "You were supposed to be different."

"I was?" I take the glass from him and hold it while he pours. "What exactly were you expecting?"

"Someone like Phoebe."

"A lesbian?"

"No." He pours himself a glass. "Phoebe is . . . well . . . look, I'm new and I don't work with her that much. She's in accounting, and I'm not. But the few interactions I have had with her have always been a little . . ."

"Mean? Cold? Aloof?"

"Exactly. I mean, she ratted out your grandmother, for crying out loud."

"Phoebe's a rule follower," I say. "She always has been."

"Can I ask you a serious question? Why didn't you want your ex-husband to know that you're single?"

The truth is, I wasn't really thinking when I said it. I was reacting impulsively, just like I was when I kissed Martin. Knowing that Smith had my old ring to propose to someone new made me question why I wasn't remarried. I mean, I know why I'm not married. You have to date someone seriously in order to get married, and all of my serious relationships post-Smith have been with the male characters I've created in my books. And all of that seemed OK. My life in San Francisco with Jackie and Chelsey and our future bookstore felt like more than enough because when I'm there, I'm not in competition with my family. I'm free to just be me.

"It's complicated," I say.

"I'm a smart guy."

"Some other time." I yawn. "It's past my bedtime."

Martin nods. "I'll let you get some sleep. Goodnight, Banks."

"Goodnight."

Chapter 13

When I wake up, I'm greeted by the not-so-subtle reminder that while I may be sleeping in my teenage bed, my body is definitely over thirty. My head throbs with what I can already tell will be a baby hangover, my mouth tastes like the bottom of a trash can, and my back feels like someone tried to twist it into a pretzel. I check the time, expecting it to be much later than the bright and early *7:00 a.m.* that's glaring at me on my phone screen.

I scroll through my phone, debating whether I should go back to sleep. Maybe the key to waking up refreshed like a teenager is to sleep past noon like a teenager.

There's a new text from an hour ago in my group chat with Phoebe and Falon.

Phoebe: We're doing a turkey trot 5K this morning. You're welcome to join!
Falon: You get a free t-shirt!

Ew. Why do people think that giving a run a cute name automatically makes the run fun? If gynos called it a turkey Pap and offered a free pair of underwear, would people be more willing to sign up? Just when I was starting to think that being in a group text with my sister and her future wife was cute, Phoebe had to ruin it with physical activity.

Penny: I don't turkey trot.
Penny: And I brought my own t-shirts.

I'm about to close my phone and go back to sleep when a text from an unknown number pops onto my screen.

Unknown: Hey, it's me. I got your number from your sister.

Apparently, Phoebe's had a much more productive morning than I have. I save Martin's number to my phone.

Penny: The snitch strikes again.
Martin: I wanted to see if you maybe wanted to grab some coffee this morning. There's someone I'd like you to meet.
Penny: Is it Dolly Parton? I've always wanted to meet Dolly.
Martin: Not exactly.
Penny: Fine. Starbucks?
Martin: They're open on Thanksgiving?
Penny: Starbucks and Cher never sleep.

I do the mental math of the amount of physical exertion it will take for me to make myself look presentable, which is challenging considering the fact my hangover is growing by the second.

"Penny!" Nana Rosie's voice bellows over the intercom. "Are you awake?"

I really need to figure out how to disassemble that thing. "Penny's not here."

"Then who, may I ask, am I speaking to?"

"Cher." I flip my hair for effect and don my best Cher voice. "Whoa."

"Excellent. Cher, please come downstairs so we can give you your to-do list."

"Whoa. Cher doesn't do lists. Cher lies in bed and waits to be served by men dressed in loincloths and bow ties."

"If Cher doesn't get her heinie down here right now, she's going to get *cleaning the turkey* added to her to-do list."

"Be down in ten," I groan. "And by ten, I mean twenty."

"Over and out."

I throw on a pair of jeans and pull a gray knitted sweater over my Jessica Simpson concert tee. I slip on my trusty Birkenstocks over a pair of white fluffy socks because according to Gen Z, socks and sandals are all the rage . . . and I'm also a giant wimp when the weather drops below seventy-five.

Ozzie scratches at the outside of my door, reminding me that he's yet to take his morning pee. Apparently, taking her bedmate out isn't on Nana Rosie's to-do list. You'd think that I could simply open the door to the backyard and let him out to do his business, but Ozzie is a city dog. City dogs only pee after they've had the chance to smell at least ten spots where other dogs have peed, and they'll only poop after twenty to thirty minutes of intense negotiation and threats. I buckle his tiny harness and leash, grab my phone, and sneak out through the garage before anyone has the chance to stop me. I don't "people" well before coffee, so really I'm doing everyone a favor.

I text Martin that I'm on my way. The closest Starbucks is just three blocks away, so it shouldn't take me long. I round the corner of Clementine Street and wait patiently as Ozzie sniffs three bushes and a fire hydrant before deciding to piss on the tire of a Prius. I think Ozzie was an oil tycoon in a past life.

We're halfway down Orange Avenue when I recognize my father walking straight toward us in a teal-blue tracksuit. "Dad?"

"Penelope." His eyes widen. "Good morning."

"Are you . . . exercising?"

My father doesn't exercise. Not unless you count getting out of a golf cart eighteen times to whack a tiny ball with a stick as exercise.

"I most certainly am." He pulls a napkin out of his pocket and pats his forehead as if to prove the point. "My doctor suggested that I try walking in the mornings to help get my heart rate up."

"Did he also suggest that you walk to Dunkin' Donuts?" I point to the napkin that has a dollop of jelly on the corner. "Because I feel like that might be counterproductive."

"No, I suppose I came up with that one all on my own." He shoves the napkin back in his pocket. "If you could not mention that part to your mother or grandmother, I'd appreciate it."

"My lips are sealed."

An awkward silence falls over us. Neither of us are quite sure what to do next. Do we acknowledge the argument from last night? Or do we sweep it under the rug like always? Historically, acknowledging an argument tends to lead to more arguing, and I never argue before coffee.

"Well, I guess I'll see you—"

"Penelope, I want to talk to you about last night." My father clears his throat. "Is now a good time?"

No. Now is the worst time. The only time more unpleasant would be later or sometime in the future.

"Well, I was going to grab some coffee," I say, hoping to convey that never would actually be the best time to have this talk. "And then Nana Rosie has some big to-do list for me to work on this morning, and if I don't get back in time, there's a chance I'm going to be stuck fondling a turkey, so . . ."

"I could use some coffee to wash down the doughnut. I'll go with you. My treat."

Is it?

I force a clenched smile. "Yay!"

We look at each other, as if neither of us are sure who should lead the way or quite literally take the first step. Ozzie tugs at his leash and sighs impatiently as if he, too, is in need of a shot of caffeine to make it through the morning. It's just enough of a gesture to get the two of us moving forward.

Dad points out some of the things that have changed around the neighborhood since I've been gone. Some businesses have closed, a few have modernized slightly, but the majority of the island—which is actually a peninsula—remains the same as it was when I left. I like that about Coronado. I've always liked the city. To be honest, if things were different with my family, I could see myself living here, raising a family, possibly along with Phoebe and Falon. I don't truly think that's in the cards for me, but it would be nice to get to a point where coming home for visits doesn't feel like pulling teeth. I doubt it could ever be easy, but god, it'd be nice if it wasn't so hard.

As we near Starbucks, I consider the possibility that my father might not bring up last night at all. Thanks to therapy, I know that sweeping things under the rug doesn't create healthy communication patterns, but if I don't screw up a little, my therapist will be out of a job. That would just be cruel. I resolve myself to not redirect the conversation.

"The weather is nice," I say. "Doesn't look like we should expect any more rain like yesterday."

"Oh, speaking of yesterday." My father taps his finger to his temple. "I wanted to talk about last night."

Well, shit.

"I wanted to apologize for my behavior, Penelope."

At first, I think I've misheard him. Maybe he was asking me to apologize for my behavior last night? Or maybe I'm way more hungover than I thought and am unable to follow the basics of a conversation. My dad doesn't apologize to me. Not ever. I mean, there was that one time when he was teaching me how to ride a bike and he pushed me down a big hill before teaching me how to brake. I ended up with five stitches in my knee. But even then his apology was followed by an addendum of *If you'd thrown yourself into the grass, this never would've happened.*

This apology doesn't seem like it has an addendum. If it has anything attached to it at all, I'd say it is a hint of remorse.

Maybe it's the bright morning light, but I'm shocked at how old he looks. His hair is almost completely white, except for a tiny sprinkling of pepper in his sideburns. The bags under his eyes are more pronounced, and there's a frailness to his gait that I've never noticed before. I've always had the oldest dad out of my friends, but he seemed strong and formidable. Like an elegant old lion always at the ready to defend his pride.

"I wasn't at my best," he says as we turn down Main Street. "I had a few too many scotches, not that that's excusable, and I acted poorly as a result."

"It's fine," I start to say, but he shakes his head no and cuts me off. "OK, it's not fine."

"Let me finish. There comes a point in a man's life when he realizes that he has more road behind him than ahead of him. It makes him look back at the life he's lived and the mistakes he's made versus the time he has left to make amends. Believe it or not, I carry a lot of guilt with me. A lot of regret."

The thing is, he's right. I don't believe it. My entire life, my dad has made his life—our whole family's life—look so intentional and engineered. My mother and Phoebe followed his plan perfectly. Mom volunteered for all the right charities. She used her Southern charm to win over international clients and their wives at the elaborate dinner parties she hosted. Phoebe graduated top of her class at Princeton and immediately went to work at his company, before pursuing her master's. I'm the only piece of the family puzzle that never quite fell into place.

Is my father going to tell me that he regrets the pressure he put on me when I so clearly wanted no part in the plans he imagined for me? Is he going to tell me that he wants us to build a better relationship or that he's proud of me for making it on my own for the last ten years? Are we going to have this long-awaited sentimental moment, all while I'm waiting for Ozzie to poop?

"I just felt like I needed to make things right with Smith," he says. "The way I treated him when he was just a kid was terrible. I never gave him a fair shot because of his parents."

OK. This isn't the direction I thought this conversation would take. Call me petty, but I kind of assumed that my position on the list of people to apologize to came before Smith's. Maybe he's structured this speech like an award show, starting with supporting actors and building up to leading roles?

We stop at the crosswalk opposite Starbucks. The line wraps around the front of the building and pours onto the sidewalk. I scan the crowd for Martin, but it's impossible to place anyone from this far away.

"I was proud to hear him talk about his accomplishments last night," he says. "He's carved out quite the life for himself, with very little help at all from his parents. It's not easy being self-made anymore. It's a hell of a lot harder now than it was when I was his age. He was right about that digital magazine. It's worth a hell of a lot of money."

The crosswalk signal flashes that it's safe to cross, but my body is wound so tight with anger that I can barely breathe, let alone walk. He's *proud* of Smith. The guy who's going to give my engagement ring to someone he barely knows?

My father moves ahead of me, likely still talking about Smith, but I'm no longer paying attention. Ozzie gives his leash a little tug, and somehow my legs start to move, despite my brain's efforts to completely disassociate from my body.

Maybe Smith is a genius businessman, but he's a garbage human if he thinks regifting his ex-wife's engagement ring is OK. And if we're talking about being self-made, I'm self-made. I made a life for myself alone in San Francisco after the divorce, and I didn't take a dime from my parents. I used the trust that Nana Rosie established for me to buy my home. I worked shitty hours in even shittier bars to make ends meet because I couldn't live off my trust forever. I worked in coffee shops that let me drink my weight in caffeine. I even worked two Christmases as a damn elf in a mall so I could buy myself a used computer after mine finally bit the dust.

I am self-made too, and it wasn't easy for me. Smith at least always had his family on his side. I had nobody. How does he not see that? Why doesn't he feel proud of and impressed by *me*? And why can't I say anything? Why can't I speak up? Why am I just letting him go on and on instead of telling him to listen to me?

"Penelope." My father's voice snaps me back into the present. "Did you hear me?"

"Huh?" I manage to say.

"I said there's Smith up ahead in line. He's waving to us."

Sure enough, there he is. Smith motions for us to join him. Cutting in front of a line of twenty-five caffeine-addicted folks looking for their morning fix sounds mutinous, but I don't think I can survive any more of my father's apologies. God, I'd give anything to have my hand shoved up a turkey butt right now.

"Why don't you go save a spot in line with him while I find a copy of the *Times* at that little newsstand on the corner?"

I'm on the verge of coming up with an excuse to go back home when it occurs to me that I wouldn't mind giving Smith a piece of my mind about him regifting my engagement ring.

"Hey, you made it." Smith scratches Ozzie behind the ears. "And you brought your dad."

"What do you mean?" I ask. "Were you waiting for me?"

"Um, yeah." He furrows his brow. "Because of our texts this morning."

"Oh shit. I didn't realize that was you."

"Who else would it be?"

"Oh my god, is that her, babe?" A woman with red curly hair pushes past Smith and locks me in the sort of hug that only seems appropriate for serious mud wrestlers. Ozzie yips, which is probably the only thing that keeps her from choking me out. "Penny, I'm so excited to finally meet you. I'm Sarah. Smith's girlfriend."

There's something a little familiar about her. I know that we've never met, but I can't seem to stop staring at her, which doesn't go unnoticed.

"You OK?" Smith rests his arm around her. "You look a little pale."

"She looks gorgeous." Sarah reaches for my hair like I'm a pony somebody dumped at a roadside petting zoo. She's lucky I haven't bitten anyone since I was three. "What products do you use? Your curls look amazing."

And it hits me. She looks like me. Actually, she looks like I did when I was her age, which, if I'm willing to guess, is probably in the neighborhood of twenty-two. Somehow, I liked her more when I thought she was an air fryer.

"Shampoo," I manage to say. "And conditioner." And to think I get paid to write dialogue for a living.

"Good tip." She smiles as she releases my hair, and I take a small step back for good measure. "It's working for you."

"Sarah just got in this morning," Smith says. "I caught her up on what happened yesterday."

"So brutal." She makes a pouty face. "Here I thought I had a hard time getting in from China, but what you guys had to go through sounds a million times worse than navigating Beijing."

"Did someone say Beijing?" My father stands next to me, his newspaper rolled up under his arm. "I've always wanted to go to Beijing. I've got international partners there."

Smith introduces my father to Sarah, the amateur mud wrestler and former air fryer. Within seconds, the three of them are locked in another rousing conversation about international travel, and I'm stuck as the odd one out, all because I didn't stay in bed. I could slowly walk away and I don't think they'd even notice. I take another step back. I could—

"Your grandmother wanted me to let you know that Cher was supposed to be in the kitchen ten minutes ago." Martin's breath blows warm against my ear, sending a tiny jolt of heat down my back. "Your sister said I would find you here."

The relief I feel when I turn around and see him standing behind me with two cups of caffeine is indescribable.

"How did you get those?" I take one of the cups and breathe in the familiar minty aroma. Peppermint chai latte, my favorite. "And how did you know what to get me? Are you a wizard?"

"I ordered ahead." He smiles. "And I asked your sister."

"You *are* a wizard."

"What's all that?" He nods toward my father, Smith, and Sarah. "Are you being held hostage? Blink twice if you need me to rescue you."

"Martin," my father says. "It's good to see you this morning. Were you able to take care of that bit of business from last night?"

"I was."

"Excellent." My father nods. "Well, you should join us this morning for coffee."

"Actually, I just came here to get Penny. Her presence is requested in the kitchen."

"I'll catch you at home, Dad." I wave. "Sarah, it was great to meet you. I'm sorry we didn't have longer to get to know each other."

But at least we will always be connected by the same ring.

"Actually, Penelope, Smith was just telling me that his sister had to leave this morning for some sort of business emergency. He and Sarah don't have anywhere to go tonight for Thanksgiving, and they've graciously accepted my invitation to our dinner tonight."

"Unless you're not OK with it," Smith says. "It's last minute, and if you want some time alone with your family, I totally understand."

At this point, not only would I prefer to fist the turkey, but I'd be willing to stick my entire head up its ass if it got me out of this moment.

"What do you say, Penny?" Sarah smiles at me like she's in a toothpaste commercial. "Oh, and you must be Martin! You're Penny's—"

"Dinner's at seven!" I blurt out. "See you then!"

I drag Martin and Ozzie away before my father decides to adopt Sarah and Smith.

Chapter 14

"We should smoke some of Nana Rosie's pot," I say to Martin as we stroll through the neighborhood. We've decided to take the long way home, or actually, I have. I'm not sure Martin knows his way around yet. "We should sneak into her cannabis casita and smoke with a big bong and pet the grass until it's time for me to get on a plane back to San Francisco."

"Why do I have a feeling you've never come close to smoking anything at all?"

"What gave me away?"

"The *big bong*."

"What can I say." I sip my chai. "I took that DARE program very seriously."

"I can tell."

We walk in comfortable silence for a few blocks, allowing Ozzie to smell every fence, tree, and fuel-efficient car. I've only known Martin Butler for a handful of hours, and already I feel more comfortable walking with him than I did with my father earlier. I'm not sure if that says more about me or Martin, but either way, I like spending time with him.

I like the way he walks next to Ozzie, creating a human barrier, whenever a bigger dog passes us. I like the way he takes pictures of the old houses in the neighborhood because he likes the Victorian architecture. At least, I think that's why he keeps taking those pictures. If there's a string of burglaries here next week, I guess I'll finally get the chance to call in to one of those crime tip lines.

I like that he dresses like a normal person. It doesn't feel like having money has changed him, and that's refreshing and a little unexpected for Southern California. Despite the suburban feel of Coronado, it's still in a very monied area of SoCal, which means the people here aren't just trying to keep up with the Joneses. They're trying to outdo them. As far as I can tell, Martin doesn't seem to care about the Joneses. Maybe that's the blessing of being an outsider from the start, instead of growing up an outsider in a family of natural insiders.

"So, I guess we've got another dinner to get through with me being your fake boyfriend," Martin says as we round the corner of Naval Street. "I hope my second performance is as good as the first."

"Ugh." I roll my eyes. "You know, it's your fault that this is happening."

He lifts his brow. "I'm afraid you're going to have to help me fill in the blanks on that one."

"You were supposed to be at Starbucks." I inhale the rest of my drink and chuck the empty cup into an open garbage can. "You told me you wanted to meet for coffee and had someone you wanted me to meet. I asked if it was Dolly Parton. At the time it made sense since you're both from Kentucky."

"Ma'am"—Martin wags his finger at me—"Dolly is from Tennessee."

"Close enough." I shrug. "I take Ozzie to meet you and your mystery guest, and I end up running into my dad and meeting Smith and his shiny new girlfriend instead. That's why this is all your fault."

"Well, when you put it like that, I guess it is." He clears his throat. "Seeing as how you have Smith's number, maybe you can tell him you're not comfortable with them coming to dinner. He did say that it was up to you."

"People don't mean that when they say it, at least not in my experience. Plus, if my dad found out I revoked his invitation, he'd be upset with me because *a Banks never goes back on their word.* I need a solid twenty-four-hour stretch without fighting with my dad if I have any hope of getting a loan for the Smut Coven."

He quirks his brow. "Listen, you can't use the phrase Smut Coven without giving me some details."

I give Martin the details. In the time that it takes us to walk around my neighborhood block twice, I fill Martin in on everything. I tell him about the girls and the books they write. I tell him about the night we found the perfect building with the big sunny windows that were practically begging to have someone sit next to them and read. I tell him how Jackie helped us build a business plan. She's a Virgo, so numbers are her thing. Chelsey's a Cancer, so she'll make sure the place is beautiful and homey. It'll be the kind of store people will want to spend hours in and tell their friends about.

For the first time since I boarded the plane back home, I feel excited about the store again. It's the same sort of electric buzz I get when a new book idea hits me and demands my attention. It's the kind of passion I need to convey when I'm talking to my father about the loan we need to make this dream a reality. But how the hell do I do that when my father won't stop talking about Smith Mackenzie and his exotic international travels?

"Why only romance books?" Martin asks. "Wouldn't it make sense to carry all types of books to appeal to more readers?"

"Because then we'd be like every other bookstore," I reply. "Romance is the most read genre. It's the backbone of the publishing industry. But it's not given half the respect or shelf space that other genres receive. Do you know how many independent bookstores I've visited that don't even have a dedicated romance shelf, let alone a section? A shit ton. But you bet your ass they have a huge travel book section that nobody touches."

I'm practically levitating. I've got so much fiery passion coursing through my veins that I could do nine rounds with a prizefighter and never break a sweat.

"It's like McDonald's." Martin taps his chin thoughtfully. "Nobody likes to admit it's what they ate for dinner, yet they're selling millions of burgers every hour across the globe."

"Exactly!" I give Martin's shoulder what I think is a playful punch, but seeing how he winces, I may have overdone it. "And we don't want there to be any shame or guilt associated with romance books. We want our booksellers to be knowledgeable and proud of the books we sell, and we want our readers to feel safe. No judgment. Just guilt-free pleasure."

"How do you think your dad's going to react to your pitch?"

"I hadn't really thought about it," I say. "I guess I've been so caught up in finding an opportunity to make the pitch that I haven't had time to think about how he'll react or what he'll ultimately decide. I mean, the man has never been proud of what I do for a living."

"That's not true." Martin shakes his head. "Not by a long shot."

"Were we at the same table last night?"

"He's got this picture of you on his desk. It's not a professional shot or anything. Just a candid of you sitting in a leather chair with your legs curled up underneath. You've got a book in your lap and this little smirk tugging at the corner of your mouth, and your curls are piled on top of your head."

"You sound like you've spent a fair amount of time with my picture." I lift an eyebrow.

"I'm in his office a lot." Is he blushing? "Anyway, one day he caught me looking at it, so he told me about you."

I rack my brain trying to place this picture he's describing, but for the life of me, I can't. It doesn't sound like my dad to have such a candid photo in his office on display. A professionally painted portrait of his family? Yes. That's my dad. School pictures rotating out of metal picture frames every year. That's Carter Banks. Posed and poised is what my dad prefers, or at least that's what the Carter Banks I knew did.

"What did he say?"

"He said, *That's my Penelope. She's an author.*"

My Penelope.

He used to call me that when I was little. He's never called me Penny. Both he and my mother hated the idea of me being named after pocket change. *My Penelope* was the closest I ever got to having a nickname with him and, god, did I love it. Even now, my breath catches in my chest just thinking about him calling me that. Hearing him say it had felt like a warm hug, and more often than not, it was the closest my father could ever come to an actual hug.

"Then he told me all about how hard it is to get a book published," Martin went on. "He made it very clear that you did it all on your own. He said, *Penelope is like Jane Austen or Emily Dickinson. She makes her own rules. She doesn't need anyone to be happy.* After that, I couldn't wait to meet you."

"My writing is nothing like Austen or Dickinson," I say. "Neither of them ever wrote a good orgasm, as far as I can remember."

"I think he meant their drive and will, and not their ability to articulate a woman's climax."

"They also ended up dying alone. What about that sounded appealing to you?" I ask. "Have you always had the hots for Gilded Age spinsters?"

"I'm not even sure I know what a Gilded Age spinster is, Banks. I just know that I hadn't ever heard your dad talk about someone the way he talked about you, and if you could impress Carter Banks, then you must be something special."

"I wish I knew him the way you do. The person you're describing couldn't be more different than the father I grew up with."

"Maybe he's not the same father anymore." He takes my hand, and something about it just feels right. "You're not the same daughter.

Maybe you both need a reintroduction, and maybe this business venture of yours is the way to go about it. You'd get to see him in his element, and he'd see you in yours."

"I'm asking for a loan," I say. "Not a business partner."

"Your dad isn't the silent-partner kind of guy, Banks. If you want his money, he comes with it. That's a good thing. You want a guy like your dad in your corner. Anybody can give you money to run a business, but your dad can show you how to make a business thrive."

We stop in front of my house, and I make a point not to look at the Mackenzies' place. Poor Ozzie's panting so hard, I think he's syncopated his breaths to say *Help me, help me.* My heart rate is up too, only I'm pretty sure mine has to do with the idea of my father being my business partner. Of course he'd want to be a part of it! I was an idiot not to realize that on my own.

"My dad can't be my business partner," I say. "He's not even a part of the Smut Coven."

"Let me help you come up with your pitch and plan." Martin rests his hands on my shoulders. "I know how your dad thinks about business. I can help you position yourself so that you feel safe and stay in charge."

"OK." I glance over my shoulder at my parents' front door. "Any chance you want to come inside with me and defile a turkey?"

"You're into some kinky shit, Banks." He gives my shoulders a squeeze. "I'm actually going to keep walking a little longer. I do my best thinking when I'm walking, or when I'm in the shower."

"You must get really excited when it rains."

"Not nearly as excited as my neighbors get." He raises his eyebrows. "Be gentle with that turkey. It's had a rough go."

"I can relate."

I hurry into the kitchen and wash my hands, dragging out the process like I'm a surgeon prepping for the OR. Diced onions and garlic sizzle in a cast iron frying pan, filling the kitchen with their salty, sweet scent. Phoebe pushes them back and forth in the pan with a wooden spoon while Falon rips apart a loaf of French bread. They're side by side in matching turkey aprons, lost in conversation. Meanwhile, my mother is at the helm of her standup mixer with Nana Rosie barking orders in between sips of her mimosa.

"Where's my coffee?" Phoebe glares at me. "Martin promised me coffee."

"I drank it." I smile. "And it was delicious."

"You are the worst sister in the world. You know that, right?"

"Obviously. I keep the certificate over my bed, and once a year, the town throws a parade in honor of all the worst siblings, and I always get to sit in the lead float. It's a real honor."

"Here. Grate this." Falon sets a cutting board and a bag of carrots next to me. "And if you accidentally cut off your fingernail, do not simply continue grating."

"Oh my god, that was one time, Falon, and you weren't even in the family yet." I throw a carrot at Phoebe's back. "I can't believe you told her about that."

"She's never been able to trust carrot cake since." Phoebe kisses Falon's cheek. "She's counting on you to not screw it up this time."

I grab a strainer from the cabinet and throw the bag of carrots in it. I rinse them in the sink and cut off the tops, hoping that Nana Rosie will continue to micromanage my mother's cooking instead of mine.

"Silvia, if you put any more sugar in that batter, we're going to have to stick a candle in the cornbread and sing it 'Happy Birthday.'" Nana Rosie takes a sip of her mimosa. "Cornbread is a savory dish, not a diabetic coma."

"I'm following your recipe exactly." My mother wipes a bit of sweat from her brow. "You specifically call for a cup of sugar."

"Let me see that thing."

My mother hands Nana Rosie the yellowing index card from her recipe box. Nana Rosie puts on her glasses and inspects the card closely.

Odds are that my mother is right and Nana Rosie is wrong, but the thing about being in your late nineties is that you have the luxury of not giving a shit and never having to admit your mistakes.

"That says half a cup, Silvia. You should really consider getting your eyes checked."

"Thank you, Rosamunde." Her lips pull from a thin line into a crooked smile. "I'd hate to have glaucoma and not realize it. Although, I have heard that the marijuana plant can be used for medicinal purposes when it comes to eye disease. Would you happen to know anything about that?"

"Shots fired." Phoebe waves finger guns over her head.

"Can it, or I write you out of my will, blondie," Nana Rosie grumbles. "We are not discussing my garden right now. We're making dinner."

"Do we get to discuss it after dinner?" Phoebe begs.

"Tread lightly." Nana Rosie takes another sip of her mimosa. "I could write you out of the will today and die tomorrow."

"You always ruin the fun when you threaten us with death," Phoebe says.

"Hardly a threat when she's been promising it for forty years," my mother mutters under her breath.

"Penelope, come over here and finish the cornbread for your mother," Nana Rosie says. "It looks like she's exhausted all of her cooking talents and once again come up short."

"I'm going to lie down and have a look at nursing homes." My mother unties her apron. "I hear that in the nice ones, they even let the residents help out with the cooking."

"Those are prisons, dear." Nana Rosie smiles, unfazed by the threat. "And I'm fairly certain that they ration sugar there better than what you've managed to accomplish here."

My mother throws her hands in the air and sighs as she leaves the kitchen. Some things never change, and I, for one, enjoy this tradition.

"I thought I was in charge of the turkey," I say, putting aside the carrots.

"That's cute, dear." Nana Rosie pours me a mimosa. "Marie came over early this morning to get the turkey in the oven."

"To think I did all of that stalling for nothing."

"Is that what you call walking three times around the block with Martin Butler? Back in my day, we called that flirting." Nana Rosie bats her long fake eyelashes. "You like this man, don't you?"

"You know, Nana, this recipe does call for half a cup of sugar." I hold up the card, desperate to drive this conversation as fast and far in the other direction as possible. "I'm just going to have to double this batch so we don't have to throw it all out."

"Good idea." Nana Rosie polishes off the last of her mimosa. "Now, let's get to more important matters: Do you intend on sleeping with Martin at all during your visit? I only ask because I'd like to know whether or not my granddaughter is up-to-date on safe-sex practices."

"Nana!"

"What? I'm on the internet. I read things."

"Nana, I'm not sleeping with Martin." I crack an egg on the side of the bowl and watch it slide into the gooey cornmeal batter. "In fact, I'm not sleeping with anyone within one hundred feet of this house."

"I guess that rules out Smith. Pity. For a minute, I thought there was a chance for us to play *The Bachelorette* right here. It was quite nice to see him last night."

"Well, brace yourself, because you're about to see plenty more of him this evening. Dad invited him and his girlfriend over for dinner."

"You've got to be kidding me," Phoebe groans from across the kitchen. "Is it too much to ask that Falon and I get a tiny bit of attention this holiday so we can share our news and have our moment? It's like that Thanksgiving before Oxford all over again."

"What is that supposed to mean?" I ask.

"What's the news?" Nana Rosie asks.

"We want to wait and tell everyone at the same time." Falon takes the whisk and bowl from me and starts mixing. "Maybe we'll just have to wait until tomorrow morning when it's just family. We could do it over brunch."

"I don't want to wait until Friday morning." Phoebe glares at me while she pours herself a glass of prosecco and adds a tiny bit of orange juice. "This is dinner-worthy news, not brunch."

"Can we get back to the part where you said this is like the Thanksgiving before Oxford?" I rest my hands on my hips. "Or as I like to remember it, the Thanksgiving that you ran me out of my own house?"

"I didn't run you out. That was a choice you made all on your own. You were behaving completely unreasonably because for once the moment wasn't about you and—" Phoebe pauses and unties her apron. "You know what, it's not worth it."

"Phoebe, where are you going?" Nana Rosie asks. "There's still so much food we need to make. Surely you two can call a truce for the time being."

"I need some air, Nana." Phoebe makes her way to the back door. "And don't worry about dinner. I'm the one who always comes back to make sure everything is taken care of."

I don't know how to describe what I'm feeling. It's some unfamiliar combination of surprise and hurt and anger. I can't control who Dad invites to his home for dinner. How was I supposed to know that Phoebe made plans to make this big announcement tonight? What if I wanted to use tonight's dinner to talk about my bookstore? That's dinner worthy, isn't it? I thought we'd squashed everything last night. We've been getting along so well. I've got the group chat between us to prove it.

"She's just stressed, Penny," Falon tries to reassure me.

"I get that, but why does she keep taking it out on me?"

I realize the answer before Falon has a chance to reply. I'm the source of her stress. Me being here has thrown everything off for her. If I wasn't here, Smith wouldn't have come over last night, and he wouldn't be coming over again this evening. It would just be another normal holiday. I've taken that away from her.

"Maybe we should go talk to her together?" Falon suggests. She's an excellent Switzerland, which is great considering how often the Banks family is on the cusp of nuclear war. "We can both assure her that tonight can still be just as special as she planned, despite a few extra guests."

"You go ahead," I say.

The only way Phoebe's going to feel assured of anything is if I leave, and I'm not doing that again. I don't want to invalidate her feelings, but I can't make her happy at the expense of the store. Chelsey and Jackie are counting on me to pull through on this.

I also can't sacrifice my own happiness for Phoebe, or anyone else for that matter. Despite all logic and reason, I'm a little happy right now, even with Smith and his Penny knockoff coming to dinner tonight. It's not a big happy—nothing to shoot off confetti cannons over—but it's happier than I expected. And I don't want to give that up just yet. I want to hold on to it, and see if it's possible for this little happy to grow roots and bloom.

Chapter 15

I balance my ancient laptop on my knees, praying to all things holy that my battery doesn't die, while Smith navigates through the sludge that is the 5 on Thanksgiving Day. The *Berkeley Gazette* doesn't loan laptops to low-level journalists, and as the official curator of the obituaries, there truly isn't anyone less important. This means I'm forced to use my old college laptop, which likes to play a fun game of roulette whenever it's time to save a document. To save the file or to completely obliterate it along with three other files is the question my laptop asks every time it runs out of battery, and I can't stomach the idea of one more thing letting Irene Steadman down.

"Poor Irene." I bite at my cuticles nervously. "I think I might've found someone whose family is worse than mine."

Smith takes a drink of his third gas station coffee in the last eight hours. "I'm intrigued. Go on."

"Irene Steadman died alone in her home. The official date of her death is unknown, but her body was discovered on November 13 by her downstairs neighbor. Irene is survived by her six cats. No memorial or funeral services are to be expected. Irene was seventy-four years old."

"Is that what her family sent over or one of the six cats?"

"Family. She actually has two kids and a few grandkids, but her son, Eddie, asked that personal family information not be included."

"What an asshole." Smith drops his hand from the gearshift of his old Mustang and squeezes my hand. "You know that's never going to be you, right?"

The midday sun catches the moonstone on my engagement ring, setting off a shower of iridescent lights across Smith's face. He's too busy dodging traffic to notice the colorful display, but I can't stop staring and thinking to myself, *I get to marry Smith Mackenzie. I get to marry my best friend. I get to be a Mackenzie.*

And because I get to be a Mackenzie, I will never end up like Irene Steadman.

"I know." I tilt my head onto his shoulder. "I'm allergic to cats."

"Do you think they ate her?"

"Her cats? No. Her family? Possibly."

We pull onto the bridge and my stomach churns. Not because of the bridge itself, but because of what the bridge means. In less than ten minutes, I'll be home for the first time since I dropped out of Princeton and moved to Berkeley to be with Smith. It's our first holiday as an engaged couple, which means today should be an exciting day. There should be a champagne toast before my father carves the turkey, and my mother should have a stack of bridal magazines that she insists I look over with her. Everyone should be happy and excited, and Smith's family should be joining us too because being engaged is something to be celebrated.

But none of that is happening.

My parents don't even know that we're engaged, and even if they did, my parents would rather spend Thanksgiving deworming livestock than with Smith's parents. I think the only reason they're OK with Smith stepping foot on our property is because I refused to come home without him. The way my parents see it, the Mackenzies are the reason for my undoing.

I gaze out the window as we hit the midpoint of the bridge. Smith's Mustang is so low to the ground that if you tilt your head back, all you see is sky. It's like taking a roller coaster to the clouds. "I wish your parents weren't out of town. I feel like I haven't seen your mom in ages."

"I think they're really digging the expat life in Thailand," Smith says. "It might end up being a permanent thing. Even my sister says she likes it there. She says it's given her an opportunity to completely reinvent herself after the split with Noah."

"Sometimes I think that's what I want."

"To break up with Noah?" Smith squeezes my hand. "I heard he's kind of a dick when it comes to giving your stuff back."

"I'll keep that in mind." My body tenses as the car slowly descends over the bridge and the island comes into view. "We should move to Thailand with your parents. Imagine the kinds of photos you could take there. We could live on their compound to keep our expenses down, and I could write. We'd all be together, and the two of us wouldn't ever have to deal with my parents except for through postcards and email."

"I thought you liked our little place in Berkeley. Just last week you said that you couldn't hear the upstairs neighbors having sex at all hours of the night and the moldy smell in the hallway was distinctly less moldy."

"Those are all positives, but we also barely see each other. I'm up at the crack of dawn to work at the coffee shop, and then I spend all afternoon at the paper. You work practically every night and weekend. I'm always alone, and sometimes I think it would be nice to have your mom and dad around to talk to. They're so easy to talk to. You really lucked out with them."

We pull onto Clementine Street, and my heart starts to beat a little faster. My mouth goes dry, but I don't risk drinking any more coffee than I've already consumed. The last thing my heart rate needs is a jolt of caffeine.

I focus my attention back on Irene Steadman, specifically, the email that her son, Eddie, sent in. Maybe there's something in here that I've missed. Most children prefer to write their deceased parents' obituaries, which means it's usually my job to proofread, but occasionally the Eddies of the world submit a few random facts and request that a staff writer create the final rendering.

> *Dear Ms. Banks,*
>
> *My mother, Irene Steadman, had six cats. We don't know when she died because nobody noticed right away. Her neighbor smelled a bad odor and called the cops to investigate on the thirteenth. She was 76, I think. My sister and I would prefer our families not be mentioned in the obituary. Irene wasn't exactly a good mom.*
> *Thanks.*
> *PS You can add that last line if you want.*
> *PPS We're not having a memorial or funeral because, honestly, who would come?*

I guess I could include the fact that she was a mother.

The car slows, and Smith parks in the driveway of my house. I save Irene's rough draft and gingerly place my laptop into its musty carrying case. I'd normally leave it in the car since I won't be doing any work today, but the carrying case has the *Berkeley Gazette* logo on it, which gives my whole *I'm a real paid writer* argument a tiny bit of proof. Of course, my parents don't know that I get paid to write about dead people.

"I'm going to run to my place for a minute and turn the heat on, so I don't freeze tonight." Smith leans over and kisses me. "You going to wear your ring, or were you planning on waiting to tell them the big news until after all the knives have been removed from the dinner table?"

"You're sleeping at your parents' place?"

"Is that a problem?"

It annoys me slightly that he doesn't see the inherent problem, but considering the fact that we've spent the last eight hours stuck in a car together, I'm willing to bet I'm being a little overly sensitive. And by *overly*, I mean a lot.

"Um. Well, I guess not. I just sort of assumed you'd stay over at my place since we're engaged now and we already live together."

"I didn't think your parents would be exactly thrilled with the idea of me staying over." Smith cups my face and kisses me again. "Plus, I thought you and your sister might want a girls' night or something. You two barely talk anymore."

He's right, which isn't helpful, because I really prefer it when he's wrong.

Phoebe and I stayed in touch pretty regularly while she was at Princeton after I left, but once she graduated, she started working for our father and our weekly calls became infrequent at best. She got busy, and I . . . well . . . I got tired of hearing her talk about the place our father always wanted us to work at together.

"Fine." I kiss Smith slowly, savoring every second his lips are on mine. "But if shit hits the fan, you better come get me out of the tree house. Got it?"

"I'll be there with your girl Vermouth. Promise."

⌒⊚

Stepping into my parents' home is like opening a window to an alternate reality where nothing changes. The same food that we've eaten at Thanksgiving for as long as I can remember is arranged on the buffet table like always. Tiny place cards with our names on them mark the same seats we've sat in since my sister and I were old enough to not be in high chairs. Even the flower arrangements—a medley of red roses, chrysanthemums, and sunflowers—stay the same. It kind of feels like the only thing that's different is me.

"There's my lucky Penny!" Nana Rosie's voice echoes through the foyer. "Put those bags down and let me get a look at you, darling girl."

I set my bags down carefully and make a beeline for my grandmother. Like the house, she doesn't change, but with her, I don't mind it one bit. In fact, I prefer it. I stretch out my arms to hug her. "I've missed you, Nana."

"Wait one minute now." Nana's eyes narrow. "What is that I see on your finger, my dear?"

Shit.

"Nothing." I shove both hands in the pockets of my cardigan like a child who's just been caught stealing candy from the store counter. "Nothing at all."

Nana Rosie's green eyes twinkle with mischief. She gently tugs at my left sleeve until I finally take my hand out and show her my ring.

"This is not nothing, my love." She holds my hand up to the light, admiring the setting of the simple solitaire. "It's beautiful."

"It was Fiona's ring," I say proudly.

It's simple: a gold band and a moonstone solitaire. Nothing flashy like what you might expect from a prolific rock star, but then again, Fiona isn't a typical woman. Jasper bought her the ring at a London flea market when they were teenagers backpacking through Europe. It's what the ring symbolizes that I care about. This ring is a part of the Mackenzie family history, and they trusted me with it because Smith chose me.

"I take it your parents don't know."

"Not exactly."

"But you plan on telling them today?"

"Telling who what?" Phoebe's voice startles me.

I whip around just as she throws her arms around my neck. We hold each other for a moment until our breathing syncs and I can feel her heartbeat against my chest. We used to do this all the time when we were in kindergarten. Phoebe was terrified to go to school. She cried day after day, until finally the teacher asked me if I could figure out a way to settle her. Distractions didn't work but holding her did. My mother thinks it's what we must've done when we were in the womb. Maybe we did. But I also think that sometimes Phoebe needs to fall apart a little, and she trusts me enough to let her do that.

"I missed you," I whisper softly. A lump of emotion forms in my throat. "A lot."

"Me too." She pulls back. Her hazel eyes are misty like mine. "So, what's the big secret?"

"This." I hold up my hand. "I'm engaged."

I'm not sure what reaction I expected from my sister. She's always been a little indifferent when it came to me talking about boyfriends and such. I chalked it up to her not being interested in men. She was supportive of me getting back together with Smith but still indifferent. But telling her I'm engaged isn't the same as telling her I'm back with Smith. An engagement is supposed to be a big deal. It's the sort of thing that elicits a big reaction, good or bad. Phoebe doesn't do either. She simply looks at my ring, then looks at me with the blankest of blank stares plastered across her face.

"Oh." She blinks away the last hint of emotion from her eyes. "Nice."

Nice?

She turns her attention to Nana Rosie. "Nana, Mom and Dad want to have drinks by the firepit while we wait to eat."

Nana Rosie groans. "I guess it won't really matter if I have to take my medication late. What do doctors know about blood sugar anyway?"

"First, why do we have to wait? Smith's across the street. He'll be here any minute. And two, did you completely miss the part where I just told you that I'm engaged?"

"I'm going to excuse myself to the kitchen, girls," Nana Rosie says. "Maybe there's a garnish or two back there that Marie forgot to use that can stave off my diabetic coma."

She saunters off to the kitchen like a cat ready to dip its paw into a bucket of cream.

"Since when did Nana Rosie become diabetic?" I ask.

"She's not." Phoebe tucks a short lock of blond hair behind her ear. "She's just dramatic."

I wait for Phoebe to acknowledge my questions, but she doesn't. Instead she busies herself with rolled silverware on the buffet table, unrolling perfectly fine rolls only to reroll them again. My frustration grows with every second that goes by and with each rolling and unrolling of cutlery. Why is she being so weird about this? Scratch that. Why is she being so rude? She likes Smith. He's a great guy, and he makes me happy. After the hell I went through at Princeton and with disappointing Mom and Dad, she of all people should want me to be happy.

When she starts rearranging the flowers, my anger moves from a simmer to a full-out boil. "Phoebe, did my engagement ring do something to piss you off?"

"Great. More drama," she deadpans. "No, Penny. I'm not mad that you're getting engaged."

"Then what's the problem?"

Phoebe plucks a dying chrysanthemum from the arrangement. She eyes the dead flower in her hand, as if she's deep in thought and carefully considering her words. It's like she's not sure whether she wants to tell me what's gotten her so worked up, and it's in that moment that I realize exactly how far apart we've grown.

"Just say it, Phoebe." I rest my hand on top of hers and the dead flower. "I don't want to spend this weekend fighting."

"I invited a friend." She clears her throat, eyes still focused on the flower. "A colleague, actually."

"A colleague?" I waggle my eyebrows. "Oh my god, are you dating someone? Why didn't you tell me? Is it serious? Who is she? Tell me—"

"Penny, stop!" she snaps at me. It catches me off guard. Phoebe's plenty moody, but she's not the type to raise her voice without reason. "It's a colleague, OK. I don't have time to date or look for a relationship. I've got a career and a life that I'm trying to build for myself, and I don't need you causing a scene at another Thanksgiving that will derail all of it."

"What are you talking about?"

"The woman I've invited over is Caroline Winston. She's the dean of admissions of one of the most exclusive business cohorts and master's programs at Oxford."

Now it's my turn to stare blankly. "So?"

"So, you have to be invited to join the program, and I want to make a good impression on her." She sighs in exasperation. "Dad didn't set this up for me. I did. I'm the one who found out she'd be doing a lecture series at UCLA in November, and I'm the one who invited her over when I realized she wasn't flying out until Friday. Everything that happens at this dinner table today is a reflection of me, not Dad."

My blood has moved from boiling to scorched earth. "And you think that me getting engaged will make you look bad?"

"No." She pinches the bridge of her nose like she's trying to stave off the giant headache that this conversation is bound to give her. "I'm just saying it's very likely that Mom and Dad are going to say something about your engagement that will upset you, even if they don't mean to. You'll overreact, which will inevitably lead to an argument. You'll storm out like you always do, and the rest of the meal will be painfully awkward, which is going to be the lasting impression Caroline Winston has of me."

I don't know what to say, and I don't think I've ever been speechless with Phoebe. She's embarrassed of me. *Me.* Not Dad and his obsession with business and status. Not Mom and her unrelenting need to play matchmaker. Hell, I don't even think Nana Rosie's naked moon dancing would embarrass Phoebe the way she's worried I will.

"Look"—her eyes soften a little—"I love you, and I'm happy for you and Smith. Really, I am. I'm also just really stressed."

"I can tell."

"Would you mind not telling Mom and Dad until after dinner? Or at least until after Caroline leaves? You could just stick your ring in your pocket, and then when the coast is clear, you can scream it from the rooftops. OK?"

"No." The word shoots out of my mouth like an arrow. "Absolutely not."

"Seriously?"

"I'm not taking off my ring, Phoebe. I'll hold off telling Mom and Dad, but I'm not going to hide my engagement because you're worried it might hypothetically lead to an argument that will embarrass you."

"You think they won't notice? Have you met our parents?" She points the dead flower at my face like a baton. "And it's not a hypothetical argument. You guys always argue. It's your thing. And you argue double on holidays!"

"It's not my fault!" I wave the flower away.

"Of course it's not!" She smacks the flower on the buffet table. "Nothing ever is."

"What the hell is that supposed to mean?"

"I've never asked you for anything, Penny. Never. And the fact that the one time I ask you to do something important to me, you flat out refuse is bullshit." She dumps the flower in the bin next to the buffet table. "It's bullshit, and you're too selfish to realize it."

"Well, I'm sorry my engagement is such an inconvenience to you."

The doorbell rings like a buzzer signaling the end of a round in a boxing match. Both of us start and stop awkwardly toward the door, neither of us knowing how to proceed. It's not like we haven't fought before. It's just never felt this personal. Thankfully, Marie sweeps in to answer the door.

Smith breezes into the dining room, blissfully unaware of the battle that just took place. "Hey, is someone else coming to dinner? A black SUV just pulled up."

Phoebe and I stare at each other blankly. Every fiber of my body is telling me to leave. I could grab my bags and be out the door before my parents noticed. I could wave at Caroline Winston on my way to Smith's house, and Phoebe could tell her I was just a neighbor stopping by to say hello. My family could have a nice, quiet Thanksgiving completely drama-free. I don't even think Phoebe would try to stop me. I'd be doing her a favor.

"Are you two OK?" Smith rests his hand on my shoulder.

"We're fine," I lie. "But I just got a call from my editor. Apparently, Irene Steadman's family wants me to meet them in person tomorrow to go over her obituary. We should probably drive back."

"I thought her family hated her," Smith says.

"I guess they had a change of heart. Families are funny like that sometimes." I hold Phoebe's gaze. "One minute you think you know how they feel about you, the next you don't."

I give Phoebe a brisk hug and collect my bags. She doesn't try to stop me.

Chapter 16

I am going to take up space.

I deserve to be here for this Thanksgiving just as much as my sister does, and my news is just as worthy to be shared over Thanksgiving dinner. Unless of course they're announcing that they're having a baby, in which case, fine, I'll move my news to the port course of tonight's menu. But I don't think Phoebe's news is a baby. Phoebe is afraid of babies, and babies are afraid of her.

If I had to bet money, Phoebe's news is academic driven. Maybe she's getting another degree. Or the big news could be that they've finally set a wedding date. That would be exciting news, but it's not giving me main-course energy. That news feels decidedly dessert-course energy. That is, of course, if there's even going to be a dessert course.

Nana Rosie left me with her famous lemon meringue pie recipe card and a pat on the back before she retired for her traditional pre-Thanksgiving nap. Shockingly, I have never made a pie. The closest I've ever come to baking a pie is ordering one from the McDonald's drive-through. But I am nothing if not resourceful.

I set up my laptop in the kitchen, along with all the piemaking essentials, and videoconference in the Smut Coven.

"I thought this was supposed to be a business call." Jackie glares at me through my computer screen. "We are in the book business. Not the Betty Crocker business."

"I thought we were catching up to talk about Smith," Chelsey says in between sit-ups. The woman is a human workout Barbie. "Or Knot Guy. I forget who we're rooting for you to bang at this point."

"First, this *is* a business call." I pour myself another mimosa, which seems like the perfect first step when it comes to starting a business call or baking a pie. "This pie is vitally important to our business in ways that I will soon explain. And second, we are not rooting for me to bang anyone."

"Explain to me how this pie is going to help us secure a loan," Jackie says.

"Maybe she's going to poison someone with it?" Chelsey adjusts her blond ponytail before starting another round of crunches. "Because that actually sounds a little on brand for you. Or at least for your food."

I choose to ignore that last comment because it's not entirely wrong. I've subjected my roommates to an array of poorly cooked meals. Jackie even bought me an apron for my birthday a few years back that says *If you see me wearing this, say you already ate.* I catch the girls up on what's transpired over the last twenty-four hours, including the part where my father invited my ex-husband over for dinner with his new girlfriend.

"And you're sure that was your ring you saw?" Chelsey has switched from sit-ups to spiked sparkling water, as one does when there's hot tea being spilled. "Maybe he just had something made to look like your old ring?"

"How would that be any less creepy?" Jackie throws her hands in the air. "I mean, what kind of juice box would pull that ducking spit?"

Jackie's six-year-old niece Aubree has joined the chat, so our swearing is extra creative.

"It was definitely my ring. It's an art deco solitaire. The stone isn't even a diamond. It's a moonstone, which will probably mean nothing to Sarah, but it meant everything to me. It was his mother's ring, which is why I gave it back in the first place." I take a heavy breath. "I guess it never occurred to me that he'd someday give that ring to someone else."

"Maybe you can ask him to give you your ring back," Aubree suggests in between bites of pumpkin bread.

Jackie mouths *Sorry*, but I don't mind. There's something kind of sweet about having a kindergartner help troubleshoot my problems. Maybe if I'm lucky, she'll be able to tell me how to bake a pie.

"I can't, sweetie." I smile. "It doesn't belong to me anymore."

"Maybe you can ask his mom to give you another ring."

"Oh." A wave of emotion catches me off guard. Maybe it's muscle memory, but without thinking, my head turns toward the dining room window and I allow myself to look at Smith's house. "I wish I could, but she passed away."

"That happened to my hamster," Aubree commiserates. "I accidentally fed her too much chocolate and she died."

"That's how I'd like to go," Chelsey says. "Or in bed with a guy built like a—"

"Shut up, Chelsey," Jackie mutters.

The front door creaks open. Ozzie gives a half-hearted bark from his spot under the breakfast table. My father's voice carries through the house, and I can make out the tail end of a conversation about Madagascar.

"Fudgesicle. I've got company," I say. "Looks like I'm going to need to cut this meeting short."

"You're going to be fine," Chelsey says. "Even if the pie sucks, I know you're going to be able to get your dad on board. I can feel it."

"But to be clear, *on board* does not mean your dad is going to be the unofficial fourth member of the Smut Coven." Jackie points her finger at the screen. "Foursomes never work. Look at Destiny's Child."

"What's Destiny's Child?" Aubree asks.

"Good lord, educate the children, Jackie." Chelsey sighs.

"I'll check in with you guys later." I wave before signing off.

"Something smells good." My father's voice booms from the living room. "Are you in need of any taste testers?"

"You've already had a jelly doughnut this morning," I say as he shuffles into the kitchen.

"That was supposed to be our secret, Penelope."

"I promised I wouldn't tell Mom, and if you'll notice, Mom's not here."

"I'm actually noticing that nobody's here. Where is everyone?"

"Strip club." I shrug. "Nana's really into that whole Thunder from Down Under group. I'm in charge of making the pie."

He points at my laptop. "What's that for?"

"YouTube," I reply. "I can learn how to do anything on YouTube."

"Oh, no, you can't do that." My father rolls up the sleeves of his tracksuit. "My mother knows exactly what her pie is supposed to taste like. It's a recipe that's been passed down for over one hundred years."

I watch in semi-shock as my father collects flour, shortening, and vinegar. He asks me for a cup of ice water, an egg, and measuring spoons, commanding the kitchen as if he's done it every day of his life. To be clear, he hasn't. To be crystal clear, I've only ever seen my father make toast and the occasional sandwich.

"What's going on?" Martin takes a seat at the breakfast bar. "I didn't realize your dad moonlighted as a chef."

"Not as a chef." My father chuckles. "But when I was putting myself through school, I spent a little time working in a B and B as a baker."

"Wait. If you're a baker, then why does Grandma make the pies every year?" I ask.

"I might be the baker, but she's the executive chef." He scans the kitchen counter. "Penelope, can you get me the pastry blender?"

"Sure," I say. "First, just tell me what a pastry blender is."

"I've got it." Martin strides across the kitchen and grabs a wire contraption with a wooden handle that looks like a torture device. "I'll flour the countertop for you too."

"Whoa now." I hold up my hands. "You bake too? Is this some secret skill set that all engineers possess?"

"I grew up eating a lot of potpies." Martin takes a handful of flour and dusts a small section of the counter with it. "The key to a good potpie is the crust."

"I haven't had a good potpie in years," my father says. With a big smile on his face, he slices into the flour and shortening with the pastry cutter. "I've forgotten how good it feels to work with your hands."

He beats an egg with a fork and drizzles it over the flour and shortening. With a spoon, he ladles the ice water and vinegar into the dough along with a teaspoon of salt. He stirs the dough by hand and then separates it into two balls. I watch the whole thing like it's a carefully choreographed show, completely in awe. I'm not necessarily amazed that my father can make pie dough. I'm amazed that he seems to be enjoying doing it.

Right now, in this moment, he's not Carter Banks, the CEO of United International Engineering. Right now, he's just a dad on Thanksgiving. For the first time, possibly ever, he's family first, not business.

"Stick these in a couple of plastic bags and put them in the freezer for fifteen minutes." My father dries his hands on a hand towel. "Martin, I trust I can leave you in charge of the lemon filling? Penelope, you can handle the meringue?"

"Not without YouTube."

"Looks like the entire weight of dessert rests on your shoulders, Martin," my dad says, slightly out of breath. "I'm going to lie down for a bit. Try not to burn the place down."

I consider taking a page out of Nana Rosie's book and getting in a little pre-Thanksgiving nap too. I wash my hands and grab my mimosa.

"Good luck," I say over my shoulder.

"Where do you think you're going?" Martin asks.

"Probably hell, but I'm OK with it."

"Banks, we've got work to do," Martin says. He grabs a handful of lemons and lines them up next to the sink. "Let's work on that pitch,

OK? I can help you structure the arrangement with your father, but you've got to sell him on the heart of your business. Do you have anything tangible to show him?"

"I have an email with a presentation," I say. "Does that count?"

"You tell me." He rolls up his sleeves, revealing forearms that look more perfect now than they did in his TikTok videos. "Does your dad strike you as a PowerPoint kind of guy?"

"Technically, it's Google Slides."

"Is there a difference?" He slices a lemon in half. "Never mind that. You know, you do a very good job at avoiding direct questions."

"It's a gift."

"Pretend I'm your dad." He squeezes the lemon into a bowl, straining the seeds with his fingers. "I'll give you honest feedback, and if you're able to sell me on the idea, I'll even let you zest my lemons."

I really don't want to imagine Martin as my dad, but it doesn't look like there's any way out of this little role-playing exercise. And truthfully, I need the practice. If I'm going to take up space, I'm going to be sure to make the most of it.

"OK, so the whole idea is—"

"No." Martin slices another lemon in half. "Not a chance in hell."

"I haven't even started my pitch," I say defensively. "You can't hate an idea you haven't heard."

"And you can't pitch a business idea to a man like Carter Banks by saying *The whole idea is.*" He makes his voice soft and breathy when he repeats my words. "You also can't do it sitting at a counter with a half-empty mimosa in front of you."

"So, one, I don't sound like that, and two"—I down the rest of my mimosa—"my drink was half-full."

"You need to take this seriously, Banks. I don't offer the opportunity for someone to zest my lemons to just anyone. Try it again, but this time make me want to read more. You're a writer. Tell me a story that I don't want to put down."

"You're making me nervous." I push in my barstool. "And if you're making me nervous, how the hell am I going to be able to do this in front of my father?"

Martin puts the lemon down and rinses his hands. He strides over to the breakfast table and takes a seat at the head of it.

"What are you doing?" I ask. "We're supposed to be making pie."

"No pie is being made until you pitch me." He folds his arms across his chest. "Your dream is more important than any pie."

"You greatly underestimate how Southern my family is."

"You wouldn't have come here in the first place if you didn't think you at least had a shot," he says. "You're scared, and I get it. Your dad is a force to be reckoned with, but so are you. So pitch me. Pitch me, and if it stinks, I'll tell you."

My pitch might stink, but the concept doesn't. The concept is solid. I might not have the brains for business like Phoebe does, but we've done our research. Between Jackie, Chelsey, and me, we're going to make this bookstore happen. In fact, we're going to do more than make sure it happens. We're going to make it succeed.

"Tell me the three places you spend the most time in, other than your home." I take my place at the end of the table opposite Martin.

An intrigued smile takes shape on his lips. "Let's see . . . I go to the gym a few times a week. There's a sports bar not far from my place that I get dinner at most nights, and I visit a local camping store by my office at least three or four times a month."

"OK. So, you go to the gym to work out, and the sports bar to eat. Right?"

"That's right, Sherlock."

"Does that mean you go to the camping store three or four times a month because you camp that frequently?"

"No." A puzzled look forms on his face. "I don't have the time to camp that often."

"Why go, then?"

"Uh, well, I guess it's because I like it there. I like to see what new stuff they've gotten in since my last visit. I like talking to the store manager and a couple of the clerks. It's got a good atmosphere." His eyes lock with mine. The light bulb inside his head starts to burn a little brighter as he follows the mental breadcrumbs I've left in front of him. "I go there because it's the one place I can talk to other people who are into camping the way I am."

"And even though big box stores carry camping supplies at a cheaper price, you probably would still rather go to the locally owned place because it feels like—"

"Home." His eyes light up. "I go there because I'm not just buying a product. I'm part of a community."

"And if this locally owned place had events from time to time, would you go to them?" I bite back a smile. "For instance, if there was a knot-tying class, would you sign up?"

"Ma'am, I wouldn't sign up for it. I'd teach it."

"And share it on your TikTok? Or whatever other social media you might have to help market the class and get the word out?"

"Banks, have you been stalking me?" His voice is low and gravelly and makes me feel a little melty inside.

"I'm in the middle of a pitch, Butler." I lean across the table. "Please save your personal questions for the end of the presentation."

"All right. Continue."

"Creating an intimate place where people can gather to connect over a shared interest is the goal of our bookstore. Just like your local camping store is a place that you look forward to visiting regardless of whether you plan on camping anytime soon, our bookstore will be the same for hundreds, if not thousands, of romance readers and writers. In addition to offering a wide selection of books and bookish merch, we'll also feature guest authors, book clubs, and classes for romance writers to take to improve their craft. We won't just be in the business of selling books. We'll be in the business of building a community." I pause, my heart racing. "Because that's what books are made for. They're made to connect you to people, real or fictional, even when you feel like you're completely alone."

"Wow," Martin says softly. "That was really something, Banks." He stands, pushes in his chair, and makes his way to my side of the table. "If you pitch your father like that, there's no way he won't back you."

"We'll see." I shrug. "Because if he doesn't, then my only options are crowdfunding or prostitution."

"It's always good to have a backup plan." He cups my cheek. "But I don't think you need one." He leans forward, and for a moment I think he's going to pull me into a kiss. Instead, he reaches into his pocket and hands me a lemon. "You will, however, need a zester."

"You're into some kinky shit, Butler."

"Just wait until I show you how to whip a stiff peak."

I've never written a foodie romance, but suddenly I'm feeling incredibly inspired.

Chapter 17

"I've got big news to share tonight too," I say to Phoebe and Falon.

We're in Phoebe's room in various stages of getting ready. Falon has been ready for the last thirty minutes, Phoebe just needs to put the finishing touches on her hair, and I look like a raccoon that's been living inside a dumpster behind a Ross Dress for Less.

We haven't talked about what happened earlier today in the kitchen. Instead, we've decided to pretend like it never happened. Actually, it was Phoebe who decided to pretend like nothing happened. She was the one who came sauntering into the kitchen after all the work was done, carrying a grocery store pie and acting as if she'd purposely gone out to buy a pie and not to get away from me. She was the one who invited Martin and me to watch the football game with her and Falon in the living room, even though she knows that I don't understand football. And finally, she was the one who insisted the three of us all get ready together in her room like one happy family.

"Obviously, I want you guys to have an opportunity to share your news too." I hold up one of Phoebe's fitted work suits against me and look at it in the mirror. If we're going to pretend that everything is fine, that includes me calling dibs on her wardrobe. "I don't think there's any reason we can't both share good news tonight."

"Two questions." Phoebe slicks back her pixie cut with a little sculpting gel. "First, why are you hell bent on stealing my clothes?

Second, and arguably more important, since when did you decide to have news to share?"

"I didn't bring anything nice to wear," I lie. I do have a cute dress and a nice fall cardigan that I could wear, but that doesn't exactly scream serious businesswoman. I need to look the part if I want my dad to fully buy into my vision. "And I've actually had news to share this whole time. I just didn't have the guts to bring it up until now."

"Well, isn't that convenient." Phoebe shoves a gold hairpin rather aggressively into place. "You do realize that we already have to contend with your ex-husband and his girlfriend tonight, right?"

"What's the big deal? We've shared a birthday for over thirty years, why can't we both share something exciting at dinner? In fact, why can't you just tell me what your news is, and I'll tell you mine? You used to tell me everything."

"Penny." She looks at me incredulously. "You're acting like we're close, and we're not. That birthday we share? How many times have you ever called or texted me on it?"

"We always talk on our birthday."

"Because I call you or I text you. I'm always the one who initiates contact."

I'm shuffling through my mental Rolodex of our last thirtysome-thing birthdays, trying desperately to find an example of me reaching out to Phoebe. I need there to be at least one time that it was me who called her and reminded her that she was technically the younger twin by four minutes, because if there's not, then I'm an even bigger jerk than I ever thought possible.

"Maybe we can work something out." Falon rests her hand on Phoebe's shoulder. "I'm sure your parents are going to be happy for all of us. There's plenty of love to go around, right?"

"You don't get it." Phoebe shakes her head. "I'm not worried that there's not enough love or appreciation to go around. Our news, while very exciting to us, has the potential to ruffle some feathers. I don't want to risk Mom or Dad getting upset and making a scene in front of Smith and some stranger."

"Are you telling them that you've decided to re-pierce your nipples?" I try to lighten the mood. "Because that probably will be a shock."

"I don't want to joke, Penny. Everything is always a joke to you."

"OK. I'm sorry."

"I planned how I wanted tonight to go for over a month, and then less than a week ago, I find out that you're coming home. Why you decided that this was the holiday you finally wanted to springboard back into our lives, I have no idea. But I adjust. Then Mom says Martin is coming, and I adjust again. Now Smith is going to be here, and just when I think I can salvage our plan for tonight, you want me to adjust again."

She's never looked at me like this before. Like she resents me. Like she can't stand the sight of me. All of a sudden, the room feels too cold. It's like the house itself is telling me I'm not wanted here. That I don't belong here now, just like I didn't all those years ago.

Ten years ago, I would've run. I would've bolted through the front door just like I did when Smith and I got engaged. But I'm not running this time. I don't want to be at odds with my sister. I want to be able to take up space and be in the group chat and deal with problems instead of letting them fester.

"I don't think this has to be this difficult. I don't know why we can't compromise."

"I've tried to compromise with you, Penny. You're incapable of it. Anytime you don't get your way, you take it as a personal offense and then disappear."

"That's because your compromises are completely unfair!" I raise my voice. "I wanted to tell my family that I was engaged, and your idea of a compromise was for me to take off my engagement ring and pretend it never happened."

"Are you serious?" Her mouth hangs open. "I asked you to hold off on dropping a bombshell that was going to piss Mom and Dad off and make a huge scene in front of Professor Winston. I told you to wait until later that night, but instead you ran away. Do you have any idea how much drama you caused when you left? Do you think for a second Mom or Dad believed that you had an emergency obituary that needed your attention?"

"They knew I was writing the obituaries?"

"Of course they did. Do you think they're idiots, Penny? Our parents might be old, but even back then, they knew how to google a byline. Mom and Dad blamed me for you spending the holidays with Smith's family after that."

"That's ridiculous. It wasn't your fault that I stopped coming here. I mean, sure, I was mad at you, but I got over it. I liked being with the Mackenzies. They made me feel like I belonged."

"Well, that would've been really nice to know. Maybe the next time you decide to disappear for a decade, you could call or send a text and let us all know that it's not just one of us you don't want to be around. It's all of us."

She sprays a cloud of hair spray on her already perfect hair and leaves without so much as a backward glance my way. Falon follows her this time. She doesn't attempt an apology or encouraging word. There aren't any. I think, for once, Phoebe said everything she needed to.

I hang her suit back in the closet. It doesn't feel right to wear it tonight. I can be just as convincing in my floral dress. I don't need to be my sister to be taken seriously in this family. I put on my usual makeup but decide to go with a red lip. I never felt comfortable wearing red lipstick when I was in high school. Something I read in one of those terrible women's magazines convinced me that redheads couldn't wear red lipstick. Fiona was the one who convinced me to start wearing it. She always wore red lipstick on stage because it made her feel powerful. I want to feel powerful tonight. But as I hold the gold tube of red lipstick, I hesitate to bring it to my lips. I want to feel powerful, but maybe tonight isn't the right time to command attention.

I don't agree with all of my sister's grievances, but I can't deny the hurt that she feels. I'm not even sure when or why I got so dead set on bringing up the bookstore tonight. There's nothing wrong with tomorrow night. In fact, tomorrow would be better. It's a new moon.

"Knock, knock." Martin taps on the door. "Can I come in?"

"Only if you have alcohol."

"I don't but I know where to get some," he says. "Also, you look beautiful. Almost as beautiful as my lemon meringue pie."

I offer a half smile. It's all I can muster, and even that takes effort. He looks just as gorgeous as ever, dressed in a pair of gray slacks and a black button-up shirt, rolled at the sleeves. There's the tiniest bit of blond scruff on his jawline, reminding me of the outdoorsy flannel-clad version of him on TikTok.

"You feeling OK?" He closes the door behind him. "We can go over your pitch before we go downstairs. Marie is putting out appetizers and drinks, and Smith and his girlfriend have just arrived. They probably won't even notice we're gone if—"

"I don't think I can do the pitch tonight, Martin," I say.

"Why? You were so good earlier."

I see the disappointment in his face. I hear it in his voice. The combination results in a familiar sinking feeling in my stomach, only this time instead of feeling guilty or ashamed, I'm agitated. Why does he care whether I pitch the store to my father? He doesn't know me. He doesn't have any investment in me or the store.

"I'm going to do it tomorrow," I say firmly. I grab my smoky quartz necklace and drape it around my neck. "It's a new moon tomorrow, and that's important to me."

"The moon is important to you?" He lifts his brow and smirks. "I've never heard that one before."

"What's that supposed to mean?" I struggle with the clasp of my necklace. "The phases of the moon are important to me. I'm not making an excuse."

"OK." The tone in his voice irks me. The man ties knots to calm down and posts videos of it on TikTok, but I'm the crazy one for caring about the moon. "Let me help you with your necklace."

"I'm fine," I say.

"It's OK to have cold feet, you know."

"I don't have cold feet, and even if I did, it's not any of your concern."

"Whoa. Did I do something to offend you? None of this is making any sense to me."

"I'm not offended, and I'm not obligated to make sense to you." I pull on my cardigan and stuff my necklace into my pocket. "Let's just drop the subject."

"Come here." He pulls me in close to hold me, but I step back. He holds his hands up in mock surrender. "I just want to give you a hug and tell you that everything's going to be all right. Penny, I like you. I think you're brilliant, and I hate to see you self-destruct."

I don't want him to "hate to see me self-destruct." It's too much pressure, because inevitably I will self-destruct, just as I always do when I'm home, and when that happens, I'll have let him down too. Then he'll look at me the way my parents and Phoebe do. He'll look at me and think, *What a shame. She had so much potential. If only she could've followed through.* I can't have Martin look at me that way. I won't allow it.

"You're a nice guy, Martin," I force myself to say. "But I'm not looking for someone to comfort me or hug me or kiss me. I'm not self-destructing, and if I do at some point, it's not your problem. I don't need you to worry or even care about me. I just need you to be my fake boyfriend for one more night."

I leave before I can take it all back.

ᦂ

I pour myself a glass of red wine in my father's den before anyone notices me. My goal isn't to get drunk. I just need to take the edge off. I need to blend in. Maybe I'll have a glass and then ask Nana Rosie to take me on a tour of her greenhouse.

I pop my head into the foyer to see if I can spot Nana without blowing my cover, but the minute I do, Smith eyes me. Stupid Smith Mackenzie with his mud-wrestling air fryer of a girlfriend. I duck back into the den, but it's too late. He's standing in the doorframe within seconds, and to add insult to injury, slung over his shoulder is his leather travel bag. The same bag that had my engagement ring in it yesterday. Why the hell would he bring it here?

"I hope this isn't too weird," he says. "Sarah and me coming over, that is."

As if I needed the clarification.

I open my mouth with the intent of saying *It's fine* because that's really the only appropriate response to a question like that. Anything else would make things awkward and uncomfortable, and my whole life, I've been trained to not make people feel uncomfortable when in my home. I've been taught that if anyone is to feel awkward or uncomfortable, it should be me.

I don't want to do that anymore. I want to tell Smith exactly how much undue stress his invasion of our Thanksgiving has caused my family. I don't need to be rude about it or uncivil. I just need to communicate the facts.

"You're an asshole, Smith."

Not exactly a fact and not necessarily civil, but it's a vast improvement over some of the choice phrases running through my head.

"Huh?" He lifts his brow and leans forward as if he's somehow misheard me. "Did you just call me an asshole?"

"Yes, I did." I stand a little taller. "You're an asshole, and I think you should leave."

"You want me to leave?"

"Right now."

His initial expression of confusion shifts into something in between wounded and annoyed. "I asked you this morning if you were OK with us coming over. You told us dinner was at seven. You remember that, don't you?"

"Yes, I remember that." I reach for the wine bottle and top off my mostly untouched glass. "And now I've changed my mind."

"What am I supposed to tell Sarah? You want me to interrupt her talking to your sister and tell her that you've changed your mind and now we need to leave? That's not right. You can't just take back an invite after you've already given it, Penny."

He adjusts the strap of his bag on his shoulder, and something inside me pops like a champagne flute shattering on concrete.

"Why not? People take back things they give all the time." I press my finger into his chest. "In fact, some people not only take things back, but they also give them away to new people. That, Smith Mackenzie, is not right."

"What are you talking about?" He pushes my hand away. "You're not making any sense at all."

"I'm making perfect sense." I lower my voice to a growl. "What isn't making sense is you and that air fryer sitting in my dining room."

"Are you drunk?"

"There you two are," my mother says. She's standing in the hallway holding a glass of something bubbly. "I've been looking all over for you guys."

She glides across the den in her silk chiffon caftan. Her hair is done up in one of those big, sweeping updos that Southern women come out of the womb knowing how to do. Her makeup is bold and dramatic, which makes her look a little like a love child between Blanche Devereaux and a drag queen.

"Honey, did you forget to finish your makeup?" She grabs my chin. "Your lips are naked."

"My lips are fine," I say through gritted teeth.

"If you say so." She turns her attention to Smith. "Carter is looking for you. He has another travel question. I swear the man thinks he's Indiana Jones or something now. You can find him in the living room."

Smith's gaze darts between my mother and me like a child unsure of which parent is the one he should actually be listening to.

"Smith, is everything OK?" my mother asks slowly. "You do remember your way around the house, don't you?"

"Sorry." He shakes his head. "Must've had a brain fart. I'm going to go into the living room because you told me to, Silvia."

He backs out of the den cautiously, keeping eye contact with me as if at any moment I might tackle him to the ground.

"*Brain fart?*" My mother crinkles her nose. "I hope he doesn't say that at the dinner table."

"Would you prefer he say *brain flatulence?*"

"I'm going to ignore that."

"I think that's what Emily Post recommends."

"So, what do you think of Martin?" She runs her fingers through my hair. "You two seem to be getting along nicely."

"Yep."

"That's it?"

"It is."

"Knock, knock!" A voice sends a chill down my neck. "Oh my gosh, are we wearing the same dress, Penny?"

Sarah leans against the doorframe, and for a moment, I wonder whether I'm in an episode of *The Twilight Zone*. Not only is she in the same floral dress as me, but our shoes are shockingly similar and our hair is styled almost identically. The woman full-out *Parent Trap*ped me.

"Everyone's in the living room listening to Smith talk about traveling." She rolls her eyes as if nothing in the world could be more boring. "I'm trying to round everyone up so we can eat. I've got a ridiculously early flight tomorrow."

"Well, we'd hate to keep you late," my mother says in her best "bless your heart" voice. "I'll go get Marie."

My mother leaves me alone with the air fryer, which feels a million times more offensive than the time she accidentally left me at the grocery store. At least at the grocery store I could scream at the top of my lungs and cry and people would come and help me. If I do that now, they're probably just going to have me committed.

Sarah leans back and forth on her heels, like she's waiting for me to say something. I probably should say something, but my brain is in a state of anarchy. I don't know how to make small talk with this woman, and I don't want to. But I also don't feel like I can be mean to her, because the truth is that none of this is her fault. It's my idiot ex and her future idiot husband's fault.

"Thanks for being so cool about us coming over," she says. "Smith was really bummed when his sister had to leave, especially with this being the first holiday since their mom's death. He says you guys are the next closest thing to family that he has."

Well, that's a stretch.

"It's no trouble," I force myself to say. "My parents always have a ton of food, and they enjoy entertaining."

A warm smile spreads across her face. "If you think about it, we're kind of like family now."

I imagine my jaw falling to the ground like a cartoon character and me physically having to crank it back into place. Maybe I misheard her. Maybe she's new to life and isn't sure how families work.

"I need a drink," I say.

"Oh, do you not like your wine?" She points to the still-full glass that I'm holding. "I love a good red."

This woman is like a stray cat. I give her an ounce of attention and now she wants to eat my food, drink my wine, and become my sister.

"Here you go." I hand her the glass. "I'm going to go to the kitchen and get something stronger."

"I'll go with you."

"I'm going to go to the bathroom before I go to the kitchen, and that's definitely a one-person job."

"OK," she says cheerfully. *So fucking cheerful.* "I'll see you at the table."

I'd honestly be happier to see the electric chair at this point.

Chapter 18

On my way to the bathroom, I slip out the back door, pull out my phone, and summon the Smut Coven.

> **Penny: Smith's girlfriend is Lindsay Lohan-ing me.**
> **Jackie: You'll need to be more specific.**
> **Chelsey: Lindsay is thriving now, but I don't think that's what you mean.**
> **Penny: She's in my house, wearing my clothes, and basically saying we're sisters.**
> **Chelsey: She's your twin?**
> **Jackie: I'm going to need pictures.**

I pass the firepit and sneak around to the living room, where everyone is still congregating because nobody in this house is in any hurry to get this night over with other than me. Using the cover of my mother's azalea bush, I try to snag a few pictures, but it's hard to get anything decent without a flash.

> **Penny: Can't send a picture now without blowing my cover.**

I'm about to try another angle when there's a tap on the window. I whip my head up to find Martin staring at me. He mouths *What are you doing?* and in return I stick my tongue out because I don't owe Martin Butler an explanation.

He mouths for me to stay there, which I do, but not because he told me to. My cardigan is stuck in the azalea bush, which means I'm stuck in the azalea bush.

The back door opens and shuts. Martin's footsteps are quick and heavy on the patio as he sprints over to me, which seems a little unnecessary. I'm stuck in a bush, not a well.

"What are you doing?" he asks.

"Playing hide-and-seek," I deadpan.

"Does your family usually play hide-and-seek before dinner?" Martin holds out his hand. "Because if they do, they're not very good at it. You're definitely winning the game right now."

Something in his tone is off. It doesn't have that usual cheeky air to it when we banter. It's oddly serious. I choose to ignore it.

"Help me. My cardigan is stuck."

Martin turns on the flashlight on his cell phone and shines it at me, temporarily blinding me. I feel his hand on my shoulder, and a moment later, I'm free from the dumb bush.

"Can we go inside now?" Martin asks. "I'm really hungry."

"I can't go in there with her," I scoff. "Did you see what she's wearing? And her hair? She looks more like my twin than Phoebe does right now."

"You could be triplets," he says with the same strange tone as before. Maybe it's nerves? "Hey, do you think we're going to have Twinkies tonight? I could really go for a fried one. Have you ever had a fried Twinkie?"

"You're being weird." I smack his arm playfully. "I'm not worried about food. I'm worried about the girl who thinks we're part of the same family now."

"Ooh, like a sister wife. Do you think she cooks?"

"You are not helping."

"I just saved you from the bush."

I go to smack him again, but my foot gets caught on a paver and I end up falling into Martin. He catches me and holds me just long enough to catch a whiff of a familiar odor on his jacket.

"You've gotten into Nana Rosie's gardening basket." I turn on my cell phone flashlight and point it at Martin's face. "You're high!"

"Shhh!" He giggles. Not a chuckle. It's an actual giggle. "I got it from Falon. She and your sister and I took a few hits in the bathroom."

"That's not fair." I stamp my foot like a child. "I have barely had a sip of wine and you guys are hotboxing yourselves in the bathroom. What the hell?"

"Isn't that your Nana's greenhouse?" Martin points to the spot where the tree house used to be. In its place is a small structure with opaque plastic walls. "Let's go straight to the source. Maybe she has Twinkies in there."

Martin takes my hand and pulls me behind him as we sprint across the backyard. A smile breaks out across my face, and I feel like a senior in high school all over again. We stop at the greenhouse door, and I double over to catch my breath.

"Is there a lock?" I ask.

"Yeah." Martin palms a silver bike lock. "But it's not actually locked."

"Oh, Nana Rosie." I shake my head. "She still thinks she lives in Mayberry, where there's no crime and no need to lock your doors."

"I don't think there was weed in Mayberry." Martin pushes open the door. "I don't think Andy Griffith would've allowed it."

It's dark inside, even with both our cell phone flashlights, but the layout is pretty straightforward. There's a single aisle with waist-high counters on both sides. At first, I'm a little disappointed because the only green stuff I see are actual plants, but as we make our way back, Martin spots our target.

"Looks like Nana Rosie is within state code." Martin counts a total of six marijuana plants in black nursery pots. "It also looks like she partakes."

Martin hands me a clear glass bong, which brings the total number of bongs I've ever held in my life to one.

"Are you seriously suggesting that Nana uses this to get high?" I ask.

"Well, she's not using it to eat Twinkies," Martin grumbles.

"What do I do with this?" I hold it like it's a bomb or a baby. "I told you I took that DARE program very seriously."

Martin takes it back and places it on the counter. "Hold up both of the flashlights."

I do, and I watch as Martin maneuvers through the steps of bong prep as effortlessly as a Starbucks barista making their fiftieth Frappuccino of the day. Much like when I watch my latte being made at Starbucks, I'm clueless as to what he's actually doing. There's water from a bottle of Evian on the counter and there's some ground up weed. That's about all I can distinctly make out.

"Here ya go." Martin holds the bong in front of me. "You're going to cover this hole with your finger, and I'm going to light the bowl for you. Press your face to the mouthpiece and inhale. Got it?"

"That's too many directions. You do it first."

"Are you serious?"

"I'm a visual learner, Martin."

"I'm not going to be able to make it through dinner at this rate."

"I'll save you a piece of pie."

"Twinkie pie?" His eyes widen. "God, why hasn't anyone ever thought of that? It's a freaking genius idea. I'm calling Hostess myself just as soon as—"

"Focus, Martin."

"Right."

Martin lights something and the bong starts bubbling like a beaker in a mad scientist's lab. The smell is what gets to me. It's so potent and rank that it makes my eyes start to water and my stomach churn. Just as Martin presses his face to it, I abandon ship. Senior year me would be so embarrassed of thirtysomething me. I make it out of the greenhouse just as Marie opens the back patio door.

"Ms. Penelope, your family is waiting for you," Marie says. "Have you seen Mr. Butler by chance?"

"Holy shit, this stuff is strong!" Martin announces from inside the greenhouse.

Marie and I lock eyes.

"I'll let Mr. Butler know it's time to eat."

"Mr. Butler?" He giggles. "When did my dad get here?"

"I'll let your father know that you'll need a minute." Marie nods before slowly backing into the house.

꙳

By the time I convince Martin that his father is not hiding in my parents' backyard and lure him back into the house with the promise of cornbread and pie, dinner is already underway. I plop Martin down at the end of the table as far away from my father as possible, and I take the spot next to him.

My phone buzzes with a text the moment I sit down, and the name Martin flashes across my screen. Of course, I know that this text isn't actually from Martin. It's from Smith, whose number I mislabeled, but Martin, who happens to be looking over my shoulder, does not.

"Holy shit," Martin announces during an unfortunate lull in the conversation. He points at my phone screen. "How did I do that?"

He garners a few curious looks from around the table, but none quite as obvious as Smith's.

"Eat your cornbread," I whisper through a clenched smile.

I hold my phone underneath the table and open the text.

Martin: We need to talk.
Penny: Now isn't a good time.

Martin: Before dessert?

Penny: IDK

I make a show of putting my phone on silent and turning it face-down on the table as Marie brings out the salad course. I shovel a few bites into my mouth and keep an eye on Martin to make sure he eats something too. My understanding of how marijuana affects the body is limited at best, but at least if Martin is eating, he isn't talking.

A walnut flies across the table and hits me on the cheek. Across the table, Phoebe points at my phone and motions for me to turn it over. She's about as subtle as a mime on acid, but my parents don't notice. They're too busy listening to my doppelgänger to realize that a quarter of the table is completely stoned.

I grab my phone and once again make sure to keep it out of Martin's view.

Phoebe: R U hi 2?

Oh, Phoebe. I only wish I could record this moment and savor it later on when I'm not in charge of stopping a grown man from making an ass out of himself in front of his boss.

Penny: No

"Do you smell that, Silvia?" My father lifts his nose in the air like a bloodhound trying to catch a scent. "I think that skunk is back again. You know, we've had the worst time with skunks lately."

My mother's face turns as red as a brick. "No, Carter. I don't smell anything."

It's the worst lie ever. The dead can smell the weed on Martin's jacket.

"Really? You don't smell anything?" My father appears utterly befuddled. "Mother, what about you?"

Half the table shifts their attention to Nana Rosie.

"Oh, it's definitely a skunk," Nana Rosie replies without breaking a sweat. "I was talking with Alice next door, and she thinks there's a family of them squatting in the neighborhood."

"Do skunks normally travel with their families?" My mother shoots Nana Rosie a sideways look. "They always seemed like solitary animals to me."

"Of course they have families," Nana Rosie fires back. "Do you think baby skunks just fall from the sky?"

"Like ninjas," Martin says with a mouthful of cornbread.

"What was that, Martin?" my father asks.

"Skunks are ninjas," Martin replies.

"They certainly are. Every time I go out there, the little bastards completely vanish. If it wasn't for that god-awful smell, I'd never even know they existed."

"You should do a stakeout." Martin smacks the table enthusiastically. "You could set up a tent and wait for them to show themselves, or if you're afraid to sleep outside, you could put up some cameras. You should probably have some cameras in the backyard anyway to make sure nobody breaks into Nana Rosie's weed house."

"Weed house?" my father asks slowly.

"He means seed house," Falon blurts out. "Nana Rosie keeps heirloom seeds in there. They're very valuable."

My phone screen lights up with a text.

Nana Rosie: Penny, dear, please change the subject before I write you and your sister out of my will and leave my remaining fortune to build a skunk sanctuary by the beach. Love, Nana.

I'm not built for this kind of pressure. I'm not the person you call to make sure that a dinner party doesn't go off the rails. I'm the one who does the derailing.

I scan the table for a lifeline. I just need someone I can volley a question to and change the subject. Phoebe and Falon are out. Phoebe can barely keep her eyes open, and Falon looks like she's afraid of her own shadow. Martin's useless, and I'd rather talk about skunk ninjas than listen to Smith right now. Mom and Nana Rosie are eyeing each other like rival mob bosses, which means my only real lifeline here is Sarah.

Oh, goody.

"So, Sarah, you mentioned you had an early flight tomorrow," I say. "Where are you going?"

She drops her fork and puts her hand to her chest as if I just called her name from the podium of the Golden Globes. "A couple of places," she says excitedly. "First I'm going to Denver to attend this big expo for work."

"What do you do for work?" Look at me asking a follow-up question. I'm basically Barbara Walters.

"I'm a baby-name consultant."

"A what?" My father scratches his head. "Did you say you're a name consultant?"

"That's right." She nods. "I help expecting parents come up with names for their new babies and fur babies."

"Fur babies?" Nana Rosie asks. "Honey, do you mean dogs and cats?"

"Among other furry and even scaly family members."

"I'm struggling to follow this conversation," Martin whispers in my ear. "Is it because I'm high?"

"Nope." I shake my head.

"What does that mean?" my mother asks. "I mean, what exactly is it that you do?"

Sarah informs us that for a fee of anywhere between $50 and $300, she provides parents-to-be with a curated list of baby names to choose from. People message her through her social media platforms and provide her with a list of their likes and dislikes when it comes to names. She then scours social security records and vintage yearbooks to build a list of possible names. Depending on the level of service paid for, Sarah will continue to meet with the new parents until the perfect name has been selected.

"And you support yourself doing this kind of work?" my mother asks.

"Oh, yes," Sarah replies. "It started out as a hobby, but it quickly turned into a full-time job. I was just named to *Forbes* 30 Under 30. Can you believe it?"

No.

I can't believe any of this. She's young, smart, and rich. She's also freakishly unjaded by having to spend a holiday with her boyfriend's ex-wife and her family. I want to hate this woman with every fiber of my being, but she's making it damn near impossible.

"That sounds absolutely fascinating," my father says. "And where will you be off to after that?"

"Dubai."

My heart stops.

"Smith's family has been going there for years for the holidays." She rests her head on his shoulder. "Since I wasn't able to meet his sister here, we're going to spend Christmas with her in Dubai. I've never been before, but Smith says the beaches are brilliant."

"They are," I say so softly that only Martin can hear me.

If there is any place that Sarah would ever be completely within her rights to describe as magical, it's Dubai. Dubai was my magic place, and now just like my old engagement ring, it's going to be hers.

Chapter 19

Thanksgiving 2011:
The One with Fruit Salad

This year is different.

This year I'm eight thousand miles away from Marie's Thanksgiving buffet, Nana Rosie's famous pies, and my parents' infamous judgment. This year it's not even really Thanksgiving at all because this year my husband and I are in Dubai with his family, which is now my family. Our family. This year, we're with our family, and I've never been happier.

Fiona peels the leathery rind from a mango and begins to slice it into chunks. She lets the mango fall from its seed into a glass bowl filled with pineapple, oranges, and other vibrant fruits. It's become part of our morning tradition over the past few weeks. Fiona and I wake up early before Smith, Jasper, and Mo. We do our morning meditation and yoga on the beach, followed by tea on the balcony. Then we make a fruit salad with a spicy ginger-lemon dressing for breakfast before everyone wakes.

This little ritual of ours is my favorite part of the day. It's the first time I've ever had a morning ritual that didn't involve three alarms, rush hour traffic, and four hundred caffeine-deprived customers telling me how to make their perfect cup of coffee before six a.m. This—the routine, Dubai, and Fiona—all of it makes me feel alive. I've written more words in the past three weeks than I wrote all of last year, and I think I've finally figured out why.

"This fruit salad is magic," I say between mouthfuls. "If I wasn't the one making it, I'd swear you were lacing it with psychedelics or hallucinogenics. Is there a difference between the two?"

"In my experience, no." Fiona grates a little lemon zest on her fruit salad. "Of course, Smith's godfather, Willie, might have a different opinion. I can call him if you'd like."

"That's OK."

"How's the book coming? Have you figured out yet if your heroine ends up with the broody old flame or the newcomer that's great in the sack? That reminds me, have you worked up your character's birth charts yet?"

Fiona's the first person I've ever shared my writing with, and there's something exhilarating about being able to talk about my characters with someone who knows them. Not to mention the fact that Fiona is an incredible writer herself. Of course, songwriting isn't the same as writing a novel, but Fiona's storyteller. She knows what it takes to pour your heart and soul onto a page and create something that will transport the listener or reader to another world. She's the queen of details, hence the birth charts, and she's an expert at sniffing out inauthenticity. That was my biggest problem when she first read my work.

Fiona could tell from the first chapter of my original draft that I was playing it safe. Last Christmas, we spent the holiday with them in Dubai. I'd been stuck for months in the worst writing slump and had convinced myself that I would never finish it. When Fiona asked to read my writing, I was scared shitless. Letting Fiona Mackenzie read your book is like letting Julia Child eat your microwave dinner. As scared as I was, I let her read it, and the advice she gave me completely changed the way I approach writing.

Your main character has no depth, she told me. *You've made her so perfect, she's boring. People don't read books about perfect people. Perfection doesn't speak to the soul. Perfection is the antithesis of soul. If you're going to write, you must write fearlessly. You have to let yourself go. Be willing to be ugly and unfinished. Lay your soul naked and bare. Anything less is a waste of time.*

Immediately, I tossed my old draft, gave up the idea of birthing the next great literary fiction piece, and decided to write what I wanted to read. Romance. Unabashedly sexy, sultry, and heartfelt romance. It's the best decision I've ever made. Second best, actually. Eloping with Smith last month was the best.

"Nothing is set in stone for the heroine." I sprinkle a little raw coconut on my fruit salad. "But I'm leaning toward the new guy who's great in bed. He's a Scorpio. The old flame is a Capricorn. Hence the moodiness."

"I love a Scorpio in the bedroom." Fiona carries her bowl to the table on the balcony. "Jasper is a Leo, but his Venus is in Scorpio, which gives the best of both worlds, in my opinion. He's an excellent lover. You know, when Smith was conceived—"

"Stop right there." Smith covers his ears as he stumbles from the hallway in his pajamas. "The last thing a man wants to wake up to is his wife and his mother discussing his conception." He's shirtless and in a pair of gray sweatpants, which is an ideal male wardrobe for all occasions as far as millions of romance readers are concerned. Myself included.

"Typical Capricorn," Fiona teases. "I'm going to go wake up Monroe and Jasper. We may not be celebrating the colonizers' holiday, but we can still gather around the table and have a meal together with good, deep conversation."

"More conversation?" Smith pours himself a cup of mint tea. "All we do is have deep conversation. Can't we talk about something light and fun?"

"Your father and I could share what we've been learning through our recent study of tantric sex."

Smith groans. "Deep conversation it is."

"Fine." She pushes her thick gray curls into a bun on top of her head. "But I highly recommend the book we're studying, especially for two young people with such good knees." She kisses his cheek, leaving a coral lip print behind, before heading upstairs to wake Jasper and Mo. *God, I love that woman.*

Smith joins me outside on the balcony. This—him with his tea and me with my fruit salad watching the gentle Persian Gulf waves—has become another one of my favorite rituals. Eventually, we'll both bring our laptops out here and spend half the day working and talking about work and life. We've spent more time together on this balcony than we do most months back in our new apartment in LA.

"Good morning, wife." Smith kisses my forehead. "Want to run away with me for a couple of minutes before this non-Thanksgiving breakfast gets started? I've got something I want to discuss with you."

I spear a piece of pineapple with my fork and feed it to him. "Is this about your call last night with the concert promoter?"

"It is."

"Good news or bad?"

I hold my breath. Last month, Smith applied for a director of digital photography position at a music magazine. It's a start-up and swears that paper magazines are on the way out and digital is the way of the future. I'm not sure if I buy into that, but what I do buy into is my husband no longer being gone every night to photograph concerts at dive bars for nothing pay. This job would let him work from anywhere, even Dubai if we wanted to. And, god, do I want to stay here in Dubai.

"Amazing news." He pulls me out of my seat and drapes his arms around my waist. "They want to hire me, Pen."

"Oh my god!" I kiss him, savoring the hint of pineapple on his lips. "I don't want to talk about this on the beach. We should talk about it here with everyone. You finally have a job that won't require you working every weekend and crazy late nights. We need champagne!"

"Hold it on the bubbly." He lifts my chin to meet his gaze. "I said they want to hire me."

"Yeah, I got that part. Hence the bubbly."

"But it's not for the director of photography."

"OK," I say slowly. "Then what do they want to hire you for?"

"That's where the walk on the beach comes in."

Suddenly, this walk on the beach sounds a hell of a lot like walking the plank. He's excited. I can see it in his eyes and the way his smile won't stop. But he's nervous. That's why he keeps shifting his weight from side to side. That's the problem with marrying someone you've known since you were a kid. You know all their tells without them having to say a word.

But why is he uneasy? Any job has to be better than the one he's got.

"I'm making you nervous," he says. "You keep biting your lip."

I guess he knows all my tells too. "I just want you to tell me what the job is here. Is that OK?"

"Job?" Jasper's melodic voice startles me. He shuffles onto the patio slowly. Rock and roll hasn't been nearly as kind to Jasper's body as it has to Fiona's. "Did that magazine offer you a job, Smithy?"

"You got the job, baby?" Fiona squeals. "Don't say another word. I'm going to run back upstairs and demand Monroe get out of bed to hear this. Monroe!"

"Mom, stop," Smith groans. "I didn't want all this fuss. Can we have a little privacy? I haven't even had a chance to tell Penny what's going on."

"Why do you need privacy to tell Penny that you got the job?" Jasper plucks a slice of papaya from my fruit salad with his bare hands, and I make a mental note to get another bowl. He's notoriously lax when it comes to handwashing. "We're all family. Give us the scoop, kid."

"Penny, do you mind if Smith shares his news with all of us?" Fiona asks.

"Not at all," I reply.

In fact, the idea of having Fiona here is comforting. If Smith has been offered some terrible deal, then she'll help me set him straight.

"Mom. Dad. You're killing me." Smith runs his hands over his face in exasperation. "I just want a minute alone with my wife."

"She doesn't want a minute alone." Jasper snatches a handful of mango and banana from my bowl. "God, this stuff is the best. You want some?" He points at my bowl.

"I'm good, Jasper."

"Does anyone care about what I want?" Smith's tone sharpens. "Or does everything have to be decided by committee like we're in a commune or something?"

"You mean consensus, Smithy." Jasper sits in what was formerly my chair. "A committee is a subsect of a community. A consensus means everyone gets to share their vote and opinion. Or at least that's how we did it when your mother and I lived on The Farm in Tennessee that summer. God, those were good days. Fiona, do you remember—"

"Fine." Smith throws his hands in the air in mock surrender. "You win. I was offered a position as a traveling photojournalist. Are you happy now?"

"What?" My stomach sinks.

"That's incredible news!" Jasper claps. "Bravo!"

"Oh, my love." Fiona wraps Smith in a hug. "I'm so proud of you. Tell us all about what this means. Actually, wait a minute. Let me get Monroe. She'll want to hear this."

Jasper hobbles into the kitchen to grab a bottle of champagne with Fiona behind him to fetch Mo. They're so proud and excited for Smith to have achieved something without their help, and for that I applaud them. They've offered their connections in the music industry to Smith a number of times, but as soon as Smith made it clear that he wanted to build his career on his own, they stepped back and respected his boundaries. No meddling in his affairs whatsoever, and now here they are, genuinely enjoying his success. Meanwhile, I've got a knot in my stomach.

"Traveling, huh?" I say softly. "What does that look like?"

"C'mon." He takes my hand and makes a beeline toward the front door.

"You're not wearing a shirt," I say. "They're kind of big on people wearing shirts outside here."

"We're not going outside." Smith pulls me into the building elevator. He pushes the ground floor button, but as soon as the elevator begins its descent, he presses the stop button. "We're going here."

"In the elevator?"

"Yes." He takes both my hands in his and squeezes them tightly. "We're having this conversation in the elevator where nobody can bother us. Is that all right with you?"

"Sure." I glance at the mirrored walls surrounding us. "Although, it kind of feels like there are eight of us in here."

"Well, it feels like there's a thousand of us in my parents' condo." He lets my hands go and leans against one of the mirrored walls. "I haven't told the magazine whether I'll take the job. I told them I had to talk to you first about the details."

"OK." I breathe deeply. "And what exactly are the details?"

"Look, the company is a start-up. It's literally two guys with a few computers and even fewer connections to the industry."

"Sounds sketchy."

"I thought the same thing, until I spoke with them and realized that these guys could build the next *Rolling Stone*. The one guy Marcus is so ridiculously smart when it comes to social media and search engines and all that geeky shit. He helped launch Instagram, and that thing is blowing up."

"But what does that have to do with music?"

"His buddy Donovan is a savant when it comes to finding fresh voices. The guy was singing Bon Iver's praises for years before he won Best New Artist. He saw Adele and Amy Winehouse perform in dive bars long before anyone in America knew who the hell they were."

"OK." I slowly exhale. "That's exciting, but where do you come into all of this?"

"They've been functioning mostly as a music news source for the past year. They run a few interviews, but a lot of their stuff is reporting what other publications have already come up with. Once they saw my portfolio and my connections in the industry, they realized that I could possibly be the missing piece to their puzzle." He pauses to catch his breath. "Pen, they want me to partner with them. They want me to build this thing with them, and then when I told them about you—"

"You told them about me?"

"That you're a writer." His eyes light up. "Well, they thought you'd be a great addition to the team too. We could work together. I take the pictures. You interview the musicians and write the articles."

I haven't seen Smith this happy in years. I don't even think he was this excited on our wedding day, and that day included Elvis walking me down the aisle and a Madonna impersonator marrying us. I want to be happy for him. It's what he wants and needs from me in this moment. He wants me to be excited for us, but I'm not. I don't feel it at all.

I don't want to write about concerts and bands. I don't want to interview musicians. I don't want to live out of a suitcase and travel from one coast to another. I want the plan that we came up with together. I want him to be able to work anywhere, like Dubai, and I want him to stay in that one place. I want to finish my novel and send it out to agents. I want to quit serving coffee to grumpy assholes who don't realize what they're actually ordering is a giant milkshake instead of real coffee.

"I know what you're thinking, Pen." He pulls me in close and drapes his arms around my shoulders. "And I promise you that your career isn't going to take a back seat to mine. You'll finish that book. We can both get what we want without having to compromise our own success."

This is the part where I'm supposed to seal the deal with a kiss. I'm supposed to tell him that I'll go anywhere with him and do anything to help support his dreams. It should be easy to say it. It should be easy to feel it. I mean, what woman doesn't want to travel the country with her husband? What wife doesn't want to support her husband?

He kisses the top of my head. "What are you thinking in that beautiful brain of yours?"

I should tell him the truth. I want to tell him the truth. It's never been hard to be honest with Smith. He's my person. He knows my flaws. He knows I can't parallel park and that, sometimes, if I scuff a car in a parking garage that's nicer than mine, I don't leave a note or try to find the owner because they're probably doing all right. He knows I usually cheat at board games just a little because I'm awful at them, and if he catches me, he'll pretend he doesn't notice. He knows I never remember to return library books and that I'm probably still wanted by Blockbuster for never returning *Titanic*.

Smith knows all the bad stuff about me, and he doesn't care. He loves me unconditionally. How can I disappoint someone who loves me like that?

"When do we leave?" I whisper.

"New Year's Eve."

"OK."

"OK, I can call Donovan and Marcus and tell them we're in?" Smith asks, practically jumping up and down.

"Under one condition."

"Anything. You name it."

"We stay here with your family until we have to leave. I know you wanted to go back home for Christmas, but I like it here. Do we have a compromise, Mackenzie?"

He lifts me up and kisses me hard and deep. "We do, Mrs. Mackenzie. We have a compromise."

The second he puts me down I know that *we* haven't compromised. I have.

Chapter 20

I had no idea it was possible for me to hate Smith Mackenzie more than I already did, but here I am, halfway through the main course of dinner, and all I can think about is him choking on a turkey bone. I'm not saying I'd let him die at the table. I'm not a monster. I'm just asking for him to pierce a vocal cord so that he'll finally stop talking about Dubai.

What's worse is the man seems to have virtually no memory of the fact that I was there with him. It was one of the happiest times of my whole life—certainly the highlight of our marriage—and he has no recollection, or if he does, he has zero desire to ask me about it. That would be the polite thing to do when you're a guest at your ex-wife's home. It might not be Emily Post worthy, but it would definitely make Dear Abby.

When talking about the exotic vacation you plan on taking with your future wife while at your ex-wife's Thanksgiving table, include the old ball and chain in the conversation so she doesn't spend the entirety of the dinner plotting your demise. Also, bring a dessert or casserole.

"Penny, you spent some time with Smith's family in Dubai, didn't you?" my father asks. "If I remember right, you enjoyed the food. Maybe your mother and I should consider traveling there first."

At least my dad remembers I went.

"Food was great," I say as unenthusiastically as possible.

I grab my phone from the table and pull up the group chat with Falon and Phoebe.

Penny: Now would be a great time to share your news.
Falon: Nope
Penny: Why?
Phoebe: still 2 hi ?

Judging by her grammar, I'd say Phoebe and Falon are more than just a little high. How long does a person stay high after smoking weed? Curse you, Nancy Reagan, for making me such a drug noob. I google it, which is about as useful as asking a Magic 8 Ball. There's math involved, but the general gist looks like one to three hours.

"Shit," I mutter under my breath.

"What's wrong?" Martin whisper-yells, attracting the attention of my mother and Nana Rosie.

"Keep your voice down," I hiss. "I just need to think."

"About what?"

Honestly, it's like sitting next to a five-year-old. It's worse, actually. A five-year-old can at least understand tone and body language. Martin is painfully oblivious to the fact that I'm dangerously close to stabbing him in the thigh with my fork.

"I need to change the subject." I shove a bite of turkey in my mouth. Maybe I'll be the lucky one who accidentally pierces her vocal cords. "I can't listen to them talk about Dubai anymore."

"I have an idea." Martin taps on his wine glass with his fork, which still has a slice of turkey hanging from the tines. "Ladies and gentlemen, we have an announcement."

Shit!

He's standing before I can stop him. Panic spreads through my body like wildfire. He moves to the head of the table, right next to my father. God only knows what this man is going to say. He's like a runaway train, and none of us are safe.

"Martin, are you feeling all right?" my father asks. "Your eyes look a little funny."

"He's fine, Carter," Nana Rosie says. "He's just had a little too much to drink."

"That's right." Martin winks at my grandmother. "I smoked a little too much wine."

"Martin." I smile nervously. "Come sit down. No need to embarrass yourself in front of your boss."

"Penelope, he's fine," my father says. "It wouldn't be a proper holiday at the Banks house if someone didn't have a little too much to drink. What's your news, Martin? It had better not be that you've been snatched up by a new firm. We've got big plans for you."

"Nope, that's not it." A ridiculous, dopey grin spreads across his face. "The news isn't even about me. It's about Penny."

Oh fuck.

Why does it have to be about Penny? What does that even mean? Is he going to tell everyone that he's my fake boyfriend? Is he—

"She has a new business venture, and it's a doozy."

"A business venture?" My father's eyes flicker between Martin and me. "Well, this is intriguing. Go on."

"Dad, we don't—"

"She's opening a book McDonald's," Martin interjects.

I'm having an out-of-body experience. My soul has left my body, and in some cruel twist of fate, it won't leave the room. Instead, I'm being forced to watch as Martin takes my pitch for an inclusive romance bookstore and turns it into a fast-food catastrophe. How is it possible that out of everything we talked about, the only thing that cemented in that blond head of his is McDonald's?

"You're opening a diner or something with books?" My mother makes a face. "Won't that be messy? If someone gets a little ketchup on a book, it's ruined."

"I'm not opening a diner, Mom."

"She's in a coven," Martin says. "There's three of them, and they all have special talents."

"A coven?" My mother's voice is shrill. "Isn't that a cult?"

"A coven is for witches, I think," Sarah says. "I don't think cults deal in witchcraft. I think they're more for religious zealots. So are you a witch or a zealot?"

"My daughter is just a witch or a religious fanatic." My mother covers her face with her hands. "How lovely."

"Mom, calm down," I groan.

"The coven is for smut," Martin says, as if that will somehow calm my mother down. "You know, the stuff she writes."

"Martin, I think you've possibly had a little more than too much to drink." My father dabs at his temples with his napkin. "Penelope, a little help here would be nice."

My father glares at me from across the table as if I'm the one who's somehow responsible for Martin's present state of mind. I mean, technically, I was responsible for that bong hit in the greenhouse, but Phoebe is the one who invited Mary Jane to dinner in the first place.

"I'm not drunk, Carter." Martin pats my dad on the top of his head. "Penny's idea is brilliant, but she's too scared to pitch it to you."

"Why would she need to pitch it to me? Penelope's never once felt the need to include me in her career endeavors." He crosses his arms over his chest.

"Martin, please," I beg. "This isn't the right time."

Never mind the fact that it's not even the right pitch.

"She needs money," Martin says. "Actually, she really needs a sound business partner, which is something you'd be great at. She just doesn't want to let you into the coven because—"

"Martin, stop." I stand and motion for him to come sit down. "Please. Dad, I'm sorry."

"Wait a minute." Phoebe stares wide-eyed at me across the table. "That's your big news? Your big news is that you need money? You wanted my big news to share the main course with your big news, and your big news is money?"

"Girls, let's calm down now," Nana Rosie says.

"What's with all this talk about big news?" my mother asks.

"Can we go back to talking about Dubai?" I pinch the bridge of my nose to stave off the headache that is most definitely on the way. "Or what about *The Bachelorette*? Remember when we were all happy watching other people behaving badly? That was fun."

"That's the reason you wanted to come here for Thanksgiving, isn't it?" Phoebe scoffs. "I mean, why else would you choose to spend time with us if it wasn't going to benefit you in some way? And to think, for half a second, I thought I could count on you to help out down here once we move."

"Move?" my mother asks. "What do you mean, *move*? Where are you two going?"

"I don't want to talk about it right now," Phoebe says.

"Australia," Falon says with a thousand-yard stare. "We're moving to Australia, where they don't even celebrate this crappy holiday."

Australia. She might as well have said the moon or Mars.

I thought Phoebe loved it here in Coronado. It crossed my mind that her big news might be moving related, but I just assumed that she and Falon bought a place of their own. What does she want in Australia? Her job is here. Falon's job is here. Both of their jobs are connected to our father's business.

I look down to the other end of the table for his reaction. Surely, she would've told my dad before announcing this to everyone. She wouldn't just blindside him like this in front of all of us. There's a fair amount of perspiration on my dad's face, and his skin tone is a little ashy, but his expression isn't one of shock.

"Is this some kind of joke, Phoebe?" My mother's voice shakes. "I thought you were going to tell us that you finally settled on a wedding date, or maybe that you guys had already eloped. Australia? Are you serious? When?"

"It's not a joke, Mom," Phoebe says, suddenly appearing much more sober. "We leave at the end of spring."

"How is your father supposed to find people to fill your positions in a few months? That's impossible."

"We already talked to Carter," Falon says softly. "A few months ago—"

"A few months?" My mother slaps the table with her napkin and glares at my father. "You've known for a few months that they were planning on leaving, and you didn't think to mention it to me? Is that why you've been talking so much about traveling? Were you trying to get me on board so that when my daughter told me she was moving across the globe, I would somehow be OK with it?"

My mother begins to sob. It's quiet at first. My father and Nana Rosie do their best to calm her down, but it quickly escalates to being dangerously close to a full-out ugly cry. Martin quietly slips back into the chair next to me. I don't know that he seems any more sober, but he does appear to be drastically more somber.

"All my children have left me." My mother sobs. "I've failed as a mother."

"Mom, you haven't failed," I say. "Phoebe, tell her she hasn't failed."

"I knew this was going to happen." Phoebe shoots a murderous look in my direction. "I told you that my news might be upsetting. That's why I had this planned down to the last detail, but then you showed up and so did all your drama. This is all your fault."

"My fault? I didn't say a word." I nod toward Martin. "And he wouldn't have, either, if you didn't insist on going all Cheech and Chong in the bathroom."

"What does that mean?" Sarah asks. "What's a Cheech and Chong?"

Of course she doesn't know who Cheech and Chong are. She's one of *Forbes*'s 30 Under 30, which means she's basically an infant, albeit a successful infant.

"It means they got high, Sarah," I snap. "Keep up."

"Hey, you don't need to be rude to her," Smith says defensively. "She's not the person you're upset with."

He's right. She's not the person I'm upset with. He is.

"You don't get to tell me how to act in my own house, buster." I toss my napkin on the table. "You are on my list."

"What the hell does that mean?" Smith throws his hands in the air. "I'm not the one making an ass out of myself in front of everyone like your idiot boyfriend."

"Is that me?" Martin asks.

"Who brought drugs into this house?" My father smacks the table with the palm of his hand like a judge with a gavel. "If there is one thing I will not tolerate, it's drug use under my roof. Whoever it is might as well go find a hotel room for the night."

The table falls silent. It's as if someone has sucked all the oxygen from the room, and we're all just waiting to pass out and escape this hellscape.

"It was me." Martin raises his hand. "I was nervous about how this weekend might go and—"

"It wasn't you." I shove Martin's hand back down. There's no need for him to make an even bigger ass out of himself in front of my father than he already has. "I'll take the blame."

"Oh, for heaven's sake." Nana Rosie stands up. "Carter, the kids all got it from me, and if you think that I'm going to go find a hotel room for a plant that is less of a threat than the oleanders out back, then you've got another thing coming. I've been growing it in the greenhouse since spring."

"Mother?" My father gasps. "What in god's name are you doing growing marijuana plants in our backyard?"

"I needed a hobby." She shrugs.

"But why not cross-stitch or crochet? Something more appropriate for a woman your age." He lowers his voice as if the entire table isn't watching this telenovela unfold in real time. "Do you smoke it too?"

"Good lord, Carter, it's a medicinal herb, not crack. But if you must know, no. And before you ask, I don't sell it either. I share it with friends, and occasionally the household staff."

"Household staff?" My father furrows his brow. "Do you mean Marie?"

You can practically hear the collective movement of everyone turning to face the kitchen, where Marie is standing with a tray of pie slices in hand.

"Are we ready for dessert?" she squeaks.

"Just a moment, Marie." Nana Rosie waves. She turns to my father and lowers her voice to a growl. "Carter, so help me, if you embarrass that woman, I will make it my personal mission to spend whatever time I have left on this earth making your life miserable, and then when that's done, I'll haunt you."

"Maybe we should take a brief recess before dessert," my mother says. "I need to collect myself. I'll ask Marie to clear the table before she serves the pie. We'll eat dessert at eight thirty. Everyone be on time."

It'll be a miracle if anyone shows back up at this table.

Chapter 21

Everyone clears out of the dining room like a classroom full of kids on the last day of school. I put Ozzie on his leash and head out front. I need fresh air. Honestly, after that dinner, I think I could also benefit from a lobotomy or at the very least an emergency call to my therapist. The lobotomy is probably all I can afford, especially now that my chances of getting my father on board with a loan are slim to none.

I'm about to turn down the street when I realize that I've got the wrong elderly Pomeranian on the other end of my leash. Mine is a leg lifter, while this one is decidedly a squatter. *Great.* I can add dog larceny to my list of screwups.

I turn back toward my house and see Smith and Ozzie half a block behind us.

"I swear I didn't mean to steal Harriet," I groan. "I also didn't mean to snap at your girlfriend, but I'm less sorry about that than I am about the dog."

"We need to talk."

There's a serious edge in his voice, and I don't like it. Suddenly, it feels like I'm sitting in the principal's office for ditching school. Smith doesn't have any authority in my life. I don't need to listen to anything that he has to say. It's his turn to listen to me.

"No. I need to talk, and you need to listen." I press my finger to his chest. "Why are you carrying around my engagement ring?"

It's like I've smacked him in the face with a pitcher of ice water. He stumbles over his emotions, until he finally settles on angry. "You went through my bag? I can't believe you went through my bag. Actually, I take that back. It absolutely makes sense that you would snoop through my personal belongings."

"Answer my question."

"Unbelievable." He shakes his head. "You're not going to even attempt an apology?"

"For what?" I say. "You asked me to go through your bag. You knew it was in there."

"I asked you to look for something to eat so our driver wouldn't pass out. Not so you could pickpocket me."

"I didn't pickpocket you," I snarl. "The ring is probably still in your stupid bag now in that stupid Tiffany box. And that's another thing. Why would you put it in a Tiffany box? I mean, is Sarah so hung up on labels that you're worried she'd turn down your proposal if it wasn't with a shiny new ring completely devoid of personality like she is?"

"Why are you hating on Sarah? She's been nothing but kind and gracious to you and your family."

"She looks exactly like me!" I stamp my foot and inadvertently scare Harriet. "Sorry, girl." I pick her up, but she wiggles out of my arms and bolts across the street. "Shit."

I take off after her before Smith can tell me not to. Nothing bad is going to happen to this dog on my watch. I can recover from just about everything that's transpired tonight, but if this dog ends up lost or getting hit by a car, I will never be OK. Never.

She tears through the Donaldsons' lawn, which, unfortunately for me, was recently fertilized. My heels sink into the manure-coated grass. I kick them off because there's no bouncing back from cow shit, but there's still a chance that I can catch Harriet. Clumps of manure and wet grass stick to my dress and thighs. I lift my dress up past my knees just as Harriet burrows into the Japanese boxwood hedge that separates the Donaldsons' yard from the Mackenzies'.

Her little legs are running full speed up the hilly yard. Meanwhile, my legs are running more like an old Ford Pinto. I reach the top just in time to see her furry tail dive to safety through the doggy door. I fall to my knees out of breath and roll onto my back. The sky is painfully dark and cloudy. I can't even find a tiny sliver of the moon. The sky looks so lonely without it.

I reach for my smoky quartz necklace, but it's not around my neck. Why isn't it around my neck? I start to panic, until I remember that I shoved it in the pocket of my cardigan when I refused to let Martin help me put it on. I dig my hands into my pockets, but I don't feel it. I sit up and start running my hands through the grass, but it's useless, even with the flashlight on my cell phone. My necklace could be anywhere, but considering my luck as of late, it's probably buried in cow shit.

"What are you doing?" Smith asks. He's standing at the edge of his lawn with his stupid travel bag on his shoulder. "I took Ozzie back to your parents' house, by the way. If you would've waited half a second, I would've told you that Harriet knows her way home."

The last thread of composure inside me snaps. I go from panicked to full-out distraught in a manner of seconds. Tears pour down my cheeks.

"I was trying to save her," I sob.

"Did she go inside the doggy door?" Smith kneels next to me. "Because unless there's an axe murderer in the house, I'm pretty sure she's safe now."

"I chased her through cow shit, and I lost my necklace." I start to wipe my tears away, but quickly realize that my hands are covered in bits of grass and manure. "And there's not even a moon out."

"The moon is always out."

"Well, I can't see it, and I don't have my necklace that your mom gave me after we got divorced. And I miss her, Smith. I miss her so much it hurts."

"Come here." He opens his arms to me. "I can't watch you cry like this."

"You can't hold me. I'm covered in cow poop," I wail. "And I'm still mad at you. I don't want you to give Fiona's ring to Sarah."

The moment I say it aloud, I realize how foolish I sound. I realize how unreasonable and selfish my request actually is. Fiona might've felt like a mother to me, but she actually was Smith's mother. He can give his mother's ring to whomever he wants.

"I'm not proposing to Sarah, Penny." He drapes his arm over me for half a second before pulling it back. "Come inside with me. Let me at least give you a towel to clean up with."

"Really?" I sniffle. "Can I go look in your mom's writing room?"

"Uh." He hesitates. "Why don't you just come into the kitchen first?"

He holds out his hand, and I let him help me up. Snot and manure be damned. I've wanted to visit this house for years. I'm not going to let the fact that I smell like a barn ruin it for me.

Smith unlocks the door, and I almost want to close my eyes. This feels like one of those big reveal moments. I know everything won't be exactly as I remembered it. Too much time has passed for that. But it should still smell like her. It should still feel like Fiona's house.

Except it doesn't. Not even a little.

"I thought you said you guys were going to start going through her stuff this weekend." My voice echoes in the big empty house. "Where is everything?"

"Mo got a jump on things last weekend. She had an estate company come out and move everything into storage."

My feet stick to the white marble floors as I follow Smith into the kitchen. It looks sterile. Gone are the colorful cabinets that Fiona hand painted, and so are the old, vintage appliances that she loved so much. Everything is stainless steel and gray and white. It's the exact opposite of Fiona in every way imaginable.

"The basics are here." Smith grabs a hand towel from a drawer next to the sink and runs it underneath the tap. "There's a bed in most of the rooms, and there's some furniture coming in next week for the living room. Mo wants to turn it into a vacation rental until we can figure out what we want to do with the place."

"So, there's no writing room?" I take the damp towel and wipe my face.

"There's not."

"I hate this. It doesn't seem fair." I shake my head. "I know I spent a long time without her in my life, but that doesn't take away from the fact that your mom was important to me."

"You were important to her too."

"I need to go find that necklace." I drop the dirty towel in the sink. "And my shoes. Then I've got to go eat pie with a bunch of people who hate me and wish I wasn't here, and a very stoned man who I've put in a really awkward position for the last twenty-four hours."

"Your family doesn't hate you, Pen."

"Trust me, they do."

Just as the words leave my lips, my foot slides across the tile and I fall on my ass. It's like the universe is trying to kill me slowly via humiliation. Like I'm this little field mouse and it's a rattlesnake bopping me on the head repeatedly until I just give up.

"I'm going to just sit for a second until the mud dries on my feet or until I die." I lean against the cabinet. "Whichever comes first."

Harriet's nails click on the tile. She's just as muddy as I am, but she has the benefit of it being socially appropriate to lick herself clean. She saunters over to me and curls up in my lap.

"Pen." Smith kneels down next to me, and in his hand is the small, blue Tiffany box. "The ring wasn't for Sarah. I like her. She's a fun girl to spend some time with, but I'm not ready to marry her. I don't know if I'll ever be ready to marry anyone again."

He opens the box, and there it is. My old ring. Fiona's ring. Our ring. It's somehow even more brilliant than I remember it being in the van. The light catches the moonstone perfectly, and for a moment, this place doesn't feel so cold. Not with a little piece of Fiona shining inside it.

"Why do you have it, then?" I ask.

"Because she wanted you to have it." He closes the box and sets it next to me. "It was in her will that if I hadn't remarried at the time of her death, the ring would go to you, as long as it had my blessing. And it does. It always would have. I couldn't give that ring to someone else. It's in that box because the ring was appraised and cleaned. There's a little paper tucked inside with how much it's worth, if you ever want to—"

"It's priceless," I say. "Thank you, Smith. This is probably the best gift anyone has ever given me."

"You might not want to share that bit with your boyfriend." Smith leans against the cabinet next to me. "I have a feeling that stoned or not, he wouldn't appreciate it."

"Martin's not my boyfriend." I rest my head on his shoulder. "I lied."

"Go on." He chuckles. "Let's get it all out in the open."

"I saw the ring in your bag, and I thought you were going to propose to a woman you've known for less time than I've known my air fryer, so I panicked and lied. Martin went along with it, as long as I agreed to get him out of playing golf with my father tomorrow."

"There's a lot to unpack there, but I'm going to bet that Carter is not going to want to play golf with Martin tomorrow."

"At least I held up my end of the bargain, then." I close my eyes and sigh. "I don't like who I am when I come here. It's like I become the worst version of myself, which only ends up pushing my family away instead of bringing us closer together. I know they love me, because they're good and decent people, and I love them. I just wish when we all got together it didn't feel like we were just tolerating one another. I want them to like me for me."

"How can they like someone they've never met?" He kisses the top of my head. It's not romantic so much as comforting. "Maybe you need to start by telling them your pen name."

"Maybe." I yawn. "I might need to work up to that."

"Maybe you can start by telling me."

"Fiona Nelson." I scratch the top of Harriet's head. "Nelson was Ozzie and Harriet's last name on *The Adventures of Ozzie and Harriet.* And Fiona, well, you know where that comes from."

"She would've appreciated the nod."

"I think so."

"You know, I've never understood why you named the dogs after that old TV show."

"My parents used to watch reruns of it all the time. Nana Rosie too." I smile at the memory. "*Ozzie and Harriet* was the first television portrayal of the American family. They were this perfect real-life family of four, with the kinds of problems that could be solved in under thirty minutes. They laughed together and at one another, but they always worked everything out. I think my parents wanted us to be like the Nelsons. I think, to some degree, I wanted that for you and me too."

I've never said anything like that about my marriage out loud. Not to Chelsey or Jackie. Not even to my therapist. What's even more surprising than making the admission is how relatively calm I feel about having said it. No instant wave of regret. No anxiety gripping my throat. Just me. Me and Smith in his parents' house, back where we started.

"I'm sorry we weren't like the Nelsons," he says softly.

"That's OK. The Nelsons weren't even like the TV version of their family." I sigh. "I watched a documentary in middle school where the family talked about how hard it was to keep up the perfect family image that everyone expected from them. So in a way, it's a good thing we didn't end up like them."

My phone buzzes in the pocket of my cardigan. I want to ignore it. I want to stay in this little muddy bubble for as long as humanly possible because I know I'll never get it back. Smith and I will never be alone in his parents' house again. Next week, this place will continue to morph into a vacation rental, and eventually, it will be sold to a new family. A small piece of my childhood will be lost again forever, and I'm just not ready to let it go.

"You going to get that?" Smith asks.

I'm about to tell him no when the front door swings open. Heels click against the marble floor, and instantly I know exactly who it is and exactly how not well this is going to go.

"Sarah." Smith starts to get up.

Her face is red, like she's been crying. God, I hate making people cry, unless they deserve it. She, unfortunately, doesn't deserve it. She gawks at me, which could possibly be because I'm covered in manure and not just that I'm sitting on the kitchen floor next to her boyfriend with an engagement ring.

"Your dad just collapsed." Sarah gasps for air. "He's on his way to the hospital."

"Oh my god. What happened?" I jump to my feet.

"We were waiting for you both to come back for dessert, and everyone was arguing again. You guys fight a lot. Like, way more than what's probably normal. Nobody could decide whether to eat or wait, and then he just sort of collapsed."

"Oh my god." My heart freezes in my chest.

"Wait, what do you mean, *He's on his way to the hospital?*" Smith asks. "I never heard an ambulance."

"He wouldn't let us call one." She covers her face with her hands. "Silvia drove him. Everyone except for Martin left. He and I stayed to find you two, and honestly, I kind of wish he was the one that found you both."

"I can call us a car," Smith says. "Penny, go get changed."

I'm out the door before he's finished giving me the direction. For the second time tonight, I race across the street. My feet thud against the pavement so hard it makes my teeth rattle. Just as I make it to my parents' driveway, my phone buzzes, and this time I answer it.

"Penny." Phoebe's voice is frantic. "Penny, oh my god, I've been trying to get a hold of you. Where the hell have you been?"

"What's wrong with Dad?"

"I don't know." She sobs into the phone. "We're at the ER and some nurses just took him back. He wasn't breathing right, and his skin was all gray and clammy. Where are you?"

"I'm at home. I just need to change and I'll be there. OK?"

"Penny, I need you now." She gasps. "I'm in the bathroom having a complete fucking breakdown. I can't be the one to hold everything together right now."

A car pulls in front of Smith's house.

"I'm on my way, Phoebe. Right now. I promise."

Chapter 22

It takes us just under seven minutes to get to the hospital. Smith and I pick up Martin, who was halfway down the street looking for us, and our driver broke nearly every traffic law imaginable to get us to the hospital fast. I'd like to think that he was in such a hurry because he could tell how concerned we all were, but I suspect that my lingering odor may have played a large part in his expediency. We make it into the waiting room just as the doctor assigned to my father arrives.

"Are you OK, ma'am?" The doctor waves her finger over me. "Have you been in an accident?"

"I'm fine," I say. "It's just a little manure. How's my dad? Is he going to be OK?"

"Carter's suffered a heart attack." Dr. Vance delivers the news so delicately that it almost takes the sting out of her message. Almost. "I know that sounds really scary, but the good news is that he's stable."

"Oh, thank the Lord," my mother breathes. "Can we see him?"

"In a few minutes," Dr. Vance says. "But then we'll need to take him back for a procedure."

"A procedure for what?" Phoebe grips my hand. "You just said he was stable."

"He is right now, but he's going to need a few stents put in to increase the blood flow to his heart and make sure this doesn't happen again. Your dad was very lucky he got here so quickly. Whoever thought to give him baby aspirin before putting him in the car was very smart. You likely saved his life."

"That was you." My mother kisses Falon's cheek. "I thought he was having a stroke, but Falon insisted we give him the aspirin."

"Well, good work," Dr. Vance says. "Not many kids get to say they saved their parent's life."

"Oh, I'm not his daughter." A mauve blush blooms across Falon's cheeks. "At least not yet."

"Then everyone is lucky to have you." Dr. Vance glances down at her watch. "I'm going to get prepped for surgery. I'll let Nurse Harper know that you'll be in to visit; however, I would like to keep it to no more than two visitors at a time. We don't want to overstimulate Carter. Why don't you all decide among yourselves who goes first?"

"Mom, why don't you go in first by yourself," I say. "Phoebe and Falon can go next, and I'll go with Nana Rosie."

"Actually, ma'am." Dr. Vance makes a face. "I hate to do this, but I can't let you go back into that room covered in manure. It just wouldn't be sanitary."

The thought of not being able to see my dad before heart surgery breaks me. I know she said he's stable and the procedure is small, but people die all the time going under. What if something happens to him? I'll never be able to forgive myself.

"Is there a gift shop where I can buy something to wear?" I ask. "Maybe I could shower in an empty room?"

"I'm sorry, but the gift shop isn't open, and unfortunately, this isn't a hotel, so I can't just let you shower here without being admitted." She offers me a sympathetic look. "I promise he'll be fine. Go home. Get yourself cleaned up, and you can see your dad after surgery."

I feel completely powerless. I can't exactly argue with the woman who's about to perform surgery on my father's heart, and the last thing I want to do is stress my family out. If I get upset, they'll be upset. So I do the right thing, which also happens to feel the most unnatural.

"OK." I turn to my mother. "Mom, you go ahead and see Dad. Give him a kiss for me."

"All right, dear." She nods. "I'll let him know you were here."

I watch her follow Dr. Vance down the hall. She looks so small and out of place. My mother's always been the type of woman who owns any space she walks into, but that's not the case right now. I've always known my parents were older, but it's not until this moment that I realize exactly how old they are. What if this is just the first hospital trip of many? The thought sends a shiver down my spine.

"Psst."

I look over my shoulder and see Martin and my sister waving at me from the opposite end of the hallway. Phoebe's holding open the door to a room and motioning for me to follow her.

"So, here's the plan," Smith whispers behind me. "Nana Rosie is going to keep the nurses' station busy. She's got a series of moles lined up for them to look at, and if that doesn't eat up enough time, she's willing to stage a fall. Falon has the front-desk lady occupied with insurance questions."

"What are you talking about?"

"Phoebe and Martin have a room staked out for you to shower in. I don't know what the clothes situation is, but I'm sure we'll figure something out. Worst case scenario, you wear a hospital gown." Smith gives me a gentle shove in the direction of the pirated hospital room. "I'm the lookout, but once your mom comes out, I've got to take over Nana Rosie's spot and run interference. Shower quickly. Got it?"

I want to hug him, but I can't. "Thank you."

"Thank your fake boyfriend." Smith nods in Martin's direction. "It was his idea."

I walk down the hall just fast enough to not draw attention to myself. The hospital is fairly quiet, and it looks like the staff is down to mostly a skeleton crew. Phoebe pulls me into the room as soon as I'm within arm's reach.

"I've already got the water running," Phoebe says. "The good news is that it's warm. The bad news is that I could only find hand soap for you to wash with and a hand towel for you to dry off with."

"What am I supposed to change into?" I pull off my cardigan. "Please don't say a hospital gown."

Phoebe points to the bed on the opposite side of the room, where Martin is standing in a pair of boxer briefs and an undershirt. The rest of his clothes are neatly folded at the foot of the bed. In any other situation, I'd be thrilled to see Martin half-naked, but my brain is quickly processing what half-naked Martin means in this context.

"Are you serious?"

"I'd give you my clothes, but I don't want to miss my chance to see Dad. It's either dress in drag or a hospital gown. Your choice." She covers her nose. "God, you smell like shit."

"Fine." I sigh. "And thank you."

"Thank Martin." Phoebe holds open the bathroom door. "The guy is literally giving you the shirt off his back."

I quickly close the door behind me, strip down to nothing, and step inside the shower. The showerhead barely reaches my forehead, and the water shoots out of it like a violent mist that stings my skin. My skin splotches an angry shade of red that's only exacerbated when I start scrubbing with antibacterial hand soap. I'm in and out in a matter of minutes.

"Hey, it's my turn to go see Dad," Phoebe shouts from the other side of the door. "Martin's on lookout and—"

"And what?" I fumble for the hand towel that's meant to dry my entire body. "Phoebe, what's going on?"

I can hear my sister talking to someone, but it's not Martin. The other voice belongs to a woman. Shit, it's probably a nurse. She's probably wondering why the hell there's a half-naked man in this room. Just wait until she realizes there's a fully naked woman in the bathroom. We'll be banned from the hospital for life.

"Here." Phoebe cracks the door and sticks her hand through. She's holding a floral dress identical to mine. "Change in plans."

"This is Sarah's dress," I say as much to myself as I do to Phoebe. "How did you get Sarah's dress?"

"Penny, I don't have time for this. Just put on the damn dress and come out."

She closes the door, and I do as I'm told. Sarah's the same size as me, so the dress goes on easy. When I open the door, her shoes are right there, waiting for me. The woman is basically like Mary Freaking Poppins. I expect her to be on the bed covered in a bedsheet or a hospital gown next to Martin, but she's not. Martin is in the chair by the window putting on his socks, and Sarah is next to the hospital room door. She has Smith's jacket draped over her and a look on her face that is definitely nothing like Mary Poppins.

"Sarah, thank you so much for doing this," I say. "Really, you didn't have to come here at all, and the fact that you did and you're letting me wear your clothes and—"

"Listen." Her voice is low and threatening in a chipmunk sort of way. "I don't know what I walked in on earlier, but let me make something perfectly clear. Smith is my boyfriend—not yours—and if you think I'm going to let some thirtysomething woman who still shops at Forever 21 steal him, you've got another thing coming."

"You have my word." I hold up my fingers in a peace sign. "Spice Girls honor."

"Huh?" She makes a face. "What does that even mean?"

I can't be mad at her for not knowing who the Spice Girls are. Not when I'm wearing her dress—a dress that happens to be from Target, not Forever 21—and her shoes.

"It means I don't want to steal your boyfriend." I glance over my shoulder at Martin. "I've already got a pretty decent one."

Even if he isn't real.

She moves aside and holds the door open for me. "For the record, I didn't undress in front of him."

"You're a solid chick, Sarah," I say. "I'll bring your clothes back to you ASAP."

Phoebe and Falon are still visiting with Dad when I make my way back into the lobby. Martin and Smith swap places as lookout, and Martin offers to find me a cup of coffee. I want to go with him. I want to thank him for coordinating all this, but he's in the elevator heading toward the cafeteria before I have a chance to say anything at all. Maybe I'm reading too much into things, but it almost felt like he didn't want to talk to me. Like getting coffee was as much of an excuse for him to have some space as it was to get me some caffeine. Not that I need any caffeine at this point. My body is buzzing with adrenaline.

I take a seat next to Nana Rosie in the lobby. She's sipping a cup of tea that smells a lot like bathwater and socks. "How are you holding up, Nana?"

"I'm all right, all things considered. Your father is a tough old bird. He's going to be OK." She squeezes my hand. "How are you holding up? You smell a hell of a lot better."

"Thanks to you guys," I say.

"Thanks to Martin."

"Right."

"You know, I'm no romance writer, but there's something terribly romantic about a man who's not afraid to bend the rules or look like a fool for the people he cares about."

"Yeah." A crooked smile takes shape on my face. "Though I'm not sure how much is Martin caring for me and how much is Martin being a genuinely great guy."

"Maybe it's both."

Maybe.

"Penny, Nana," Phoebe calls from across the lobby. "You're up." She nods toward the hallway where my father's room is. "They're taking him back in fifteen minutes."

"Come on, Nana." I hold my hand out for her to take, but she shakes her head no. "What's wrong?"

"You go on your own, dear," she says. "I'll see him when he gets out of surgery."

"But Nana, what if something happens?"

"It won't."

"But—"

"Penelope, I've had seventy-six years to tell your father that I love him, and he's had just as long to tell me." She pauses. "I've said everything I could ever need to say. The two of you have not."

I don't argue the point with her. She's right. There's enough unsaid between my father and me to fill the pages of an anthology. I can't possibly say all of it now, but at least I can make a start.

"I'll let him know you'll see him after surgery, Nana," I say. "Do you want me to tell him anything else?"

"No more doughnuts," she says, before turning her attention to an old copy of *People* magazine. "I'd add no more cigars, but I don't want to destroy his will to live."

"No more doughnuts it is."

My father doesn't look like a man who just had a heart attack. He looks like he's napping on the chaise in the den on Sunday morning after brunch. There should be copies of the Sunday *New York Times* and *Wall Street Journal* draped over his chest, rustling with the rise and fall of his breath. The crossword from the local paper should be on the end table next to him, perfectly completed in black ink.

I lean over his bedside and kiss the top of his balding head. A smirk spreads across my face as I think about how he'd say his hairline is receding, not balding. *Old men and action heroes bald, Penelope,* he'd always say. *My hair is simply adjusting to its current market conditions.* I watch his breathing while a nurse takes note of the numbers on his monitors.

"Can he hear me?" I ask her.

"Sure. He's not in a coma," she replies. "But he is heavily sedated."

"Oh." I hadn't expected for him to not be alert. "Do you know if he'll remember anything that I say to him?"

"I'm not sure." The nurse's voice is as soft as velvet. "In my experience, most people don't remember what their loved ones said, but they can tell that they were here. You can see it in their vitals." She points to the monitors next to him. "Since you came in, his heart rate is steadier than when his last visitors left."

This woman could be completely bullshitting me, but in this moment, I choose to believe that what she's saying is true.

I take his hand in mine and give it a squeeze. I remember when his hands used to seem as big as baseball gloves. He'd cradle me in them and lift me onto his shoulders when we went to the beach and my legs got tired from trudging through the sand. My mother would always insist that he put me down before he pulled a muscle, but Dad never listened.

One day, she'll want nothing to do with me, Silvia, he would say to her. *And then I'll have wished I carried her more.*

I don't remember the day I stopped letting him carry me. I'm not sure of the exact time in which I didn't want anything to do with him either. I just know that he was right.

Before the nurse leaves to check on another patient, she tells me that Dr. Vance will call him back for surgery soon, but I can stay with him until then. She closes the door behind her, and I suddenly become aware of all the machines connected to my father. I take some comfort in knowing that they're making sure my dad is OK. The beeps from all the different machines fill the room like the chirps of crickets on a balmy summer night. The soft shuffling of doctors and nurses outside the room going about their work as usual mimics the comforting din of the ocean tide. If I closed my eyes, I could probably fall asleep in this chair, holding his hand.

"I went through a lot of shit to get here tonight, Dad. Literally. Don't be surprised if the Donaldsons ask you to resod their front lawn."

I'm nervous. My dad isn't even awake and I'm still not sure what to say. Why is this so hard? Why can't it just be easy for once? All I could think about was how important it was for me to be here—to not leave the hospital—and now that I'm here, I feel like I'm wasting this opportunity to be real with my dad with zero risk of rejection. Something inside me is still worried I might disappoint him. My head knows it's not possible—it's not like he's in a position to keep score and rate everyone's performances—but my inner child isn't exactly on board yet.

I close my eyes and try to center myself. Smith's words from earlier poke at the back of my brain. *They can't be disappointed by someone they don't really know.* Maybe now isn't the moment to try to right every wrong or make up for lost time. Maybe now is the time to just say what I feel.

"I love you, Dad," I whisper. "And I know you love me."

When Dr. Vance's team arrives to take him into surgery, I give him one last kiss on the forehead and whisper Nana Rosie's new rule about doughnuts. I can't say for certain, but I think he might've smiled.

His surgery lasts an hour longer than expected, but as Nana Rosie predicted, he comes out of it fine.

Chapter 23

We decide to take shifts after my father pulls through surgery. It'll be hours before he can have visitors again, but my mother hates the idea of him waking up without anyone there. Martin agrees to take the first shift. He has work to do, informing the company of my father's health and making sure that everything continues to run as seamlessly as possible, so he says he doesn't mind staying at the hospital.

My mother and Nana Rosie are exhausted. We all are. Martin insists that we go home to get some sleep, and for the first time in family history, everyone agrees. I'm asleep within seconds of my head hitting my pillow.

∽

"I think I'll be able to get out of our lease." Falon breezes through the kitchen, where Phoebe and I are making lunch, with her wet hair twisted up in a towel. "We'll probably lose our deposit, but in the grand scheme of things, that's not such a big deal."

"Why are you getting out of your lease?" I cut a thick slice of left-over turkey and place it on top of a heap of mashed potatoes. They look at each other and then to me, as if trying to communicate telepathically about how honest they want to be. "What? Just say it."

"Mom and Dad are going to need help, Penny," Phoebe says.

"Dr. Vance said that Dad would be fine," I say. "He's on the road to recovery."

"Right." Phoebe nods. "But that road isn't a residential street. It's more like an interstate. There's no guarantee he won't have complications or other hiccups."

"Penny, I talked to Dr. Vance after I did a little research," Falon says. "Your dad is going to have to make some big lifestyle changes. Both of your parents will. Your dad needs to cut back at work. He needs to improve his diet. He might even need to do a little physical therapy. He banged his leg up pretty good when he fell."

"There are just too many variables for us to be so far away," Phoebe says. "They're going to need family."

"Plus, Nana Rosie isn't exactly getting younger," Falon adds. "We need to start planning for their next phase of life."

"What about me?" I ask.

"What about you?" Phoebe reaches across the counter and plucks the jar of mayonnaise out of my hands. "No mayo for Mom or Nana Rosie either. It's not good for their cholesterol. If Dad's diet is changing, then everybody's diet is changing."

"It's for me." I snatch it back. "And why are you guys acting like I won't be here to help? I can hop on a plane if they need me. We can hire a nurse to help around the house. We can get several. One for diet. One for exercise. Mom and Dad can more than afford for Marie to meal prep for them. I mean, you don't need to put your life on hold over this. We can make it work."

"I don't think Carter will like having a bunch of strangers coming in and out of his house," Falon says. "Plus, what's to stop him from firing them the second we're gone?"

"They need family right now, Pen," Phoebe says. "Australia will have to wait."

But I don't want them to have to wait. I don't want their dream to have to wait. Phoebe's been here for my parents whenever they've needed her, while I've been in San Francisco living my dream. I didn't realize it before coming here, but part of the reason I have the life that I do is because I haven't been burdened with the responsibilities that Phoebe has.

She and Falon don't just work for my dad. They don't just live in the same city. They actively participate in their lives. They have dinners together and go out together. They share a life, and quite frankly, I think the loss of that family connection would be far more devastating to both of my parents and Nana Rosie than any possible health crisis.

"Then I'll move here." I take a bite of my sandwich. "I'll help them get things squared away. I can write books anywhere. You guys take your adventure, and I'll hold down the fort."

"What about your bookstore?" Phoebe asks. "You can't run that from anywhere."

"I'll figure something out. Maybe my focus can be on marketing and social media, stuff that doesn't require me to be in San Francisco. I can fly out for special occasions."

I chew in silence as they mull over my proposition. Both seem a little skeptical, and I don't blame them. I haven't exactly proven myself as the most reliable person in the family.

Ozzie taps on my leg, begging for a slice of turkey. "I've kept him alive." I pick Ozzie up. "I mean, look at him, he's healthy and safe. I give him vitamins. I take him to the vet twice a year, and I walk him even when he doesn't want to go anywhere, because I know it's good for him. If I can keep a five-pound ball of fluff alive, surely I can keep three old people alive."

"Your pitch is that you haven't killed your dog?" Phoebe narrows her eyes. "That's what you've got to show?"

"Hey, it's more than what you two have." I set Ozzie down. "I see your Instagram. You two kill plants like it's a sport."

"Plants are hard to keep alive," Falon says defensively. "They've got too many variables. Some need full sun. Some need half sun. Some like to dry out completely. Some need to be misted daily. Some die if there are too many cloudy days in a row, and you know what I can't control? The weather."

"I'm also the only one who didn't get high last night. That has to count for something, right?"

"Don't be mad at me, Pen." My sister bites her bottom lip anxiously. "But what happens if we get settled over there and you change your mind? I mean, it's been two days and you haven't been able to make it through a single night without running out the door. I don't want to move across the world only to have to come back a few months later because you decide you can't deal with them."

A couple of days ago, her honesty would've hurt me. It would've made me defensive and reinforced the idea that my family doesn't have faith in me. Now I realize that their lack of faith is just as much my doing as it is theirs. They don't know me. My family knows a version of Penelope that no longer exists, and if I'm being honest, the Penelope that I morph into when I'm around them isn't someone I would trust either. But the real me—the Penny that I am when I'm back in San Francisco—she's the kind of person who is trustworthy. She's the kind of person who is willing to throw herself into the fire that is Thanksgiving with the Bankses because her friends are counting on her. And if they give me a chance, they'll see me for who I really am: a thirtysomething writer of smut who shows up for the people she loves. And still says no to drugs.

"If I run out," I say, "then I'll come back. I promise."

"Why can't you just promise to not run out?" Phoebe asks.

"Because that might be a lie, and I don't want there to be any more lies between us."

Phoebe and Falon exchange nervous glances.

"Let us think it over," Phoebe says.

"OK. But I'm going to cancel my flight in the meantime."

"Then you'll be stuck here with us. Are you sure you can handle that?"

I fight back the urge to say something snarky or crack a joke. I hug my sister instead, and I don't let go until we're both teary eyed. "I'm sure, as long as you're sure you can handle being stuck with me."

"I've never been stuck with you." She pulls away and her hazel eyes lock with mine. "And even though you can't pick your family, if I could, I'd choose you to be my sister, Penny. I'd choose you one thousand times over."

"Me too." I wipe back a tear. "I'd pick you one thousand and one."

"Show-off." She pulls me in for another hug.

⁓

It's late afternoon before Martin returns from the hospital. Phoebe and Falon take the next shift so Mom and Nana Rosie can be fully rested for tomorrow. Martin assures us that they won't be missing anything. He explains that my father has slept most of the day since the procedure. Dr. Vance assures us that everything went as close to textbook perfect as possible and not to worry. She says that some people just need sleep, and if there's anyone who needs a long rest after the past two days, it's my dad.

"Can we talk?" Martin asks after we finish a dinner of frozen pizza. Nana Rosie has instructed that all non-heart-healthy food be consumed before my father's return from the hospital, which is a task everyone under forty has taken very seriously. "Outside maybe?"

"Sure," I reply. "I'll grab Ozzie's leash."

It's cold out. Much colder than last night, but I don't mind it. There's a new moon, which makes everything feel a little better. Not necessarily warmer, but hopeful. I reach for my smoky quartz necklace, and I'm quickly reminded that it's probably buried beneath three inches of manure in the Donaldsons' yard. Fiona's ring is still in the Tiffany box next to my bed. I like knowing that I have it, but I haven't been able to bring myself to wear it just yet.

We make small talk, mostly about my dad. I get the sense that Martin is hovering around the real reason he invited me out for a walk, but I don't press him. Time is the least I can give him after all he's done for me and my family over the past few days.

We reach the end of my neighborhood, and I try to turn right down Orange as usual, but he grabs my hand and stops me. "I knew your dad was sick," he says. "Your dad started having chest pains a few days before Thanksgiving. I tried to get him to take it easy or go see a doctor, but he insisted that he was fine. I should've told you. I should've told all of you, but he swore me to secrecy. He didn't want anything to ruin this Thanksgiving."

I'm not sure what to say. Of course, part of me wishes he would've said something. I know it wouldn't have changed the outcome of my father needing surgery, but it's possible it could've prevented the heart attack. That's assuming my father would've allowed us to take him to a doctor. He's a stubborn man—an Aries if there ever was one—and so it's possible we would've still ended up at the hospital last night. The truth is that Martin was in a no-win situation, and as the unofficial queen of no-win situations, I can't really be upset with him.

Instead of being angry or making him feel worse than he clearly already does, I tell Martin what I want to hear whenever I find myself in a similar situation. "It sounds like you were screwed either way. And not in the good way."

"Definitely not in the good way."

"I'm not mad at you, if that's what you're worried about. But maybe keep that confession between just you and me?"

He nods in agreement. "I also need to apologize for my behavior last night. As you're aware, I wasn't exactly in my right frame of mind."

"I'm not even sure you were on this planet for most of the dinner."

"Regardless, I hate the fact that I stole your pitch."

"To be fair, that wasn't exactly my pitch." I chuckle. "You pitched the ultimate stoner's bookstore and burger joint."

"Penny, please be serious." The streetlight catches the bags under his eyes and the pain in his expression, and I realize that he's more than just apologetic about last night. It's been eating him up. "I need you to know that I will do whatever I can to help you get the money you need to open your bookstore. I'll loan you the money myself if I have to."

"Martin, it's OK. Truly. And I would never take your money."

"Why not?"

"Because I don't want it."

"But you need it."

"I'll get it some other way."

"It's not that easy, Penny." He sighs in frustration. "Business loans don't just grow on trees. The interest rates alone are enough to kill a business before it ever gets a chance to get off the ground."

"Martin." I grab him by the shoulders. His body is tense with the weight of the world. "This isn't your problem to solve."

"I know, but I don't want to be the reason your dream fails. I don't want you to remember me that way when you're back in San Francisco telling your friends about why you don't have the money you need."

"You won't be." I cup his face with my hands. "Martin, you're the guy who was willing to give me the shirt off his back so I could see my dad before his surgery. You're the guy who was willing to pretend to be my boyfriend so I didn't look like a fool in front of my ex-husband. You're not the kind of guy I'm going to bitch about to my friends. You're the kind of guy my friends are going to want to meet because guys like you, Martin"—I tilt my chin up so that my lips are only centimeters away from his—"they only come around once in a blue moon."

We kiss, and this time I don't pull away. Because this kiss isn't some act of old pent-up teenage rebellion. It's not me trying to disconnect from my problems or something new and shiny to preoccupy my time here. This kiss is real in all the best ways a kiss can be real. It's the first kiss of the beginning of something new.

"I'm not going back to San Francisco," I say when we've pulled ourselves off one another. "I'm staying here to hold down the fort once Phoebe and Falon move to Australia."

"What about your store?"

"I'll figure it out. If a single Kardashian can rule an empire from her phone, then so can I."

"This calls for a celebration." Martin laces his fingers through mine. "Preferably somewhere warm where your toes won't get frostbite in those Jesus sandals."

"These are not Jesus sandals." I point down at my Birks and socks. "Don't act like you haven't seen people wearing these all over the place."

"I'm not saying people don't. I'm just saying Jesus probably did too."

"Fine. Where is this warm celebratory place you have in mind?"

"That way." He points in the direction opposite the town. "It's a ten-minute walk. Maybe longer in shoes like that."

"There's nothing down that way," I say. "It's just more residential and a park."

"And a trailer park," he says.

"We're going to celebrate in a trailer park?"

"I own a trailer in the trailer park." He blows hot air on my icy hands. "I also own a decent propane heater."

"You're serious?"

"About the heater? Of course." He smiles and gives me a wink. "What do you say, Banks? If it makes a difference, I've got gas station doughnuts. I don't think they're as good as my pie would've been, but I've never been unhappy with one in my mouth."

"You should've led with that, Butler." I take his hand in mine. "Everyone knows that a woman of questionable morals can't resist a good gas station doughnut."

"You're a woman of questionable morals?"

"All the best women are."

⁓

Martin's neighborhood is charming and quaint. It has a Stars Hollow vibe to it with strands of white twinkle lights hung throughout. There's a smattering of mobiles that have probably been there since the park first opened in the eighties, along with some more modern tiny-house structures. His home is a cross between new and old. It's a refurbished Airstream trailer with a wooden deck built around it.

"Home sweet home." Martin flips a switch on the deck, illuminating two strands of Edison bulbs that span its length. "This is my little slice of Kentucky here in California."

"All this time you could've just gone home and escaped my family's shenanigans." I run my hand along the knotted pine railing. "This is beautiful, by the way."

"Thanks." He turns on a metal heat lamp between two wooden rocking chairs. "You and Ozzie have a seat. This will warm you up in no time."

"When you said you had a heater, I assumed you meant inside," I tease.

"You know what they say about assuming."

"Touché."

"And your family isn't so bad, Banks. They're just people." He unlocks the door to the Airstream. "I'm going to grab us the doughnuts. You want something to drink too? Coffee? Beer?"

"Coffee," I say. "Maybe with a little Baileys if you've got it."

"I do."

I rest my head on the back of the rocking chair, pushing it back and forth with my heels. The warmth from the heater radiates across my face, melting the frozen tips of my ears and nose. It's quiet out here. The park is guarded by a natural barrier of evergreens and bougainvillea bushes. It cuts out what little street noise there is and almost makes you forget that there's an entire ocean a mile away. It really is a little slice of Kentucky.

"Dessert is served." He carries a wooden cutting board with two cups of coffee and an arrangement of chocolate-frosted and powdered doughnuts in the center. "The powdered doughnuts have more of a biscotti texture at this point, ideal for dunking in coffee."

"Is that a nice way of saying you're serving me stale gas station doughnuts?" I take a white mug and hold it to my chest.

"Maybe." He smiles and eases into the chair next to me. "Or maybe it's my way to hoard the powdered doughnuts for myself because they're my favorite."

"Is this where you snuck off to yesterday morning?" I take a bite of chocolate-frosted doughnut. "Because I would've. In fact, I'm pissed at you for not telling me about this place sooner. Think of all the arguments I could've avoided."

"But where would be the fun in that?" He sips his coffee. "And no, I didn't come here yesterday morning. I had a phone call."

"From who?"

"Family." He tilts his head back and gazes up at the stars. "I have a son back in Kentucky."

"Oh."

"His name is Logan. He's twelve."

"Twelve. Wow."

"I was nineteen when his mother got pregnant. Twenty when she had him." He slowly exhales, his breath visible in the cool night air. "She was older. Twenty-five or so, and she was married. Before you ask, the answer is yes. Yes, I knew she was married. I was young and stupid and thought I was in love."

"That must've been hard," I say.

"I don't usually tell people that. I usually just lie and say we had a one-night stand or something. It spares me the awkward looks that usually come with admitting you slept with a married woman."

"Why are you telling me the truth?"

"Because I like you, Banks."

Maybe it's the clear night sky, the twinkling lights in the trees, or the liquor in my coffee, but right now, I can't help but think that Martin Butler is one of the best humans I've ever met. He's an old soul wrapped in a kind and gentle spirit. The fact that he looks like Thor is honestly the least interesting thing about him.

"I like you too, Butler," I say.

He takes my hand and holds it. We sway back in our rockers like an old married couple, with Ozzie sprawled out beneath the heater. The writer in me feels a sense of relief in knowing that moments like this exist in real life and not just on paper.

"Can I ask you something?"

"As long as it's not math," I reply. "Go for it."

"Why'd you stop coming around here? Was it the divorce? Was it your parents?"

"It was everything," I say.

But it was mostly me.

Chapter 24

Thanksgiving 2012:
The One with a Side of Divorce

It's the first time there's been only four of us for Thanksgiving, and never have I missed my sister as much as I do now. She's flying down from London for Christmas, instead of Thanksgiving, which means that today it's just me, my parents, and Nana Rosie.

My parents didn't even bother inviting over one of my dad's associates to set me up on a blind date with or one of his professor buddies to lure me back to school. They won't say it, but I think they're too embarrassed to have company over this year. Having a daughter with a divorce under her belt after a year of marriage isn't the sort of thing Carter and Silvia Banks like to brag about. I considered getting a shirt made up with the phrase *At least I'm not pregnant* on the back in bold lettering to remind my parents that things could be worse. I could be the divorced college dropout who is also barefoot and pregnant. But my parents aren't the best at looking at the bright side of things.

They are, however, incredibly gifted when it comes to being efficient. Within twenty-four hours of informing them that Smith had filed for divorce, I had a one-way ticket to San Diego. Upon landing, I had an attorney and a moving truck filled with my belongings from my LA apartment. Seventy-two hours later and I'm back in my childhood bedroom and have a plethora of interesting job opportunities to choose from, thanks to my mother. So far, my top picks include assistant to the vice president of the Daughters of the American Revolution, and secretary to the treasurer of the Women's Historical Society of Southern California. It's always been my dream to get coffee and take notes for busybody housewives who use charities as excuses to host tea parties.

"Penelope, you're sure you don't want both dogs?" My father peers at me over the brim of his reading glasses from across the table. He's got a stack of divorce papers next to his half-eaten slice of pie, and I've got a knot in my stomach that hasn't managed to untie itself since the appetizer course. This going page by page through Smith's divorce filing is about as painful as plucking out my eyelashes one by one. "Your mother and I are more than happy for you to keep both of the dogs here while we figure out living arrangements."

"Smith and I agreed that we'd each keep one of the dogs." I push my plate of uneaten pie to the side. "They're puppies, and it's too much work for either of us to take care of both of them. Plus, a lot of apartments in the city only allow one pet."

"Why would you need to look at apartments, Penelope?" my mother asks. "We have everything you could possibly need here."

"You know how to perform an exorcism, Mom?"

"You don't need an exorcism." She scowls.

I will if I stay here long enough. Already my mother has become obsessed with planning our calendars for next year. She thinks if I stay busy, then I won't have time to be upset about the fact that my marriage fell apart. Little does she know that I'm usually too exhausted during the day to be sad, because my insomnia makes sure that I don't miss a single midnight thinking about how I lost Smith.

"Fine. One dog each." Dad scratches his beard, examining one of the hundreds of documents my divorce has amassed. At this point, I'm fairly certain that the number one threat to the rainforest is divorce paperwork. "Now, your attorney noticed that you're also entitled to shares from that magazine you were writing for with Smith. What's it called again?"

"*Digital Slap.*"

"That's a terrible name for a publication." My mother shakes her head. "Sounds like some sort of online bullying group. You know that's on the rise right now. I saw it on *Live with Kelly*. Do you watch her show, Penelope?"

"I don't, Mom." I sip my now-cold coffee. "And Dad, I know about the shares."

"So you know you can cash them out? I'm not sure what the value is, but I could look into it. Seeing how fast these online start-ups crash and burn, I'd suggest cashing out now."

"I'll think about it."

"When?" my father presses.

"When what?"

"When will you think about it? You only have two more weeks to file a response with the judge, and there's still so much we have to cover. This is the problem with elopements. Two kids get so caught up in the idea of being in love that they let Siegfried and Roy walk them down the aisle before they've had a chance to think about a prenup."

"It was actually Elvis and Madonna," I mutter under my breath.

"Carter, give the girl a break." Nana Rosie rests her hand on top of mine. "We've already sat through an entire dissertation of her divorce in between courses, and I, for one, would like to put the kibosh on divorce talk for the rest of the evening. Thanksgiving is a time to appreciate family."

Hearing her say the word *family* stings. I know she means us here at the table, but I can't think *family* without thinking about the Mackenzies. I haven't spoken a word to them since the split, even though they're right across the street. Smith's house used to be my refuge when the walls in this house started to cave in. Now I can barely look at his house without feeling sick to my stomach.

The worst part is that I've never wanted to talk to Fiona more than I do right now. I want to cry on her sofa and tell her how hard I tried to be happy on the road with Smith. He tried too. I know he did. The fighting was both of our faults. I want to tell her that she was right, and that I should've listened to her. She told me that compromising my happiness for Smith's would only lead to resentment on my part and distrust on his end.

If you knew you didn't want this kind of life, why didn't you tell me, Pen? I can't walk away from the magazine now. I can't let Marcus and Donovan down because you've finally decided to be honest with me.

I relive that final argument with Smith nightly, and I'd give just about anything to talk about it with Fiona.

"Shall we talk money, then?" My father clears his throat. "I assume that you and Smith didn't have much of a chance to put money away while you were caravanning around the country like a pair of vigilantes."

"No." I take another sip of coffee. "Well, unless you can put a price tag on crystal figurines from gas stations."

"Excuse me?" My father groans.

"You said yourself that we were vigilantes." I shrug. "The only places we visited besides concert venues were gas stations, and crystal figurines were the easiest things to hide in my bra when we shoplifted."

"I'm switching you to decaf." My mother grabs the coffee cup from my hand.

"Do you have any money to live off of or not, Penelope?" my father asks. "It's a simple question."

"Of course she has money," Nana Rosie interrupts. "She's past twenty-five now. She has access to the trust I set up for her."

"I thought I had to finish college to have access to that," I say. "That's what Phoebe had to do."

"The trust was set up so that you could access it upon graduation from college or after you turned twenty-five," Nana Rosie says. "I thought your parents told you that."

"I guess it slipped our minds," my father says, none too convincingly. "Anyway, back to my original question. Penelope, what kind of savings do you have?"

I can't go back to my father's original question. At least, not without yelling and some choice words. The trust funds that Nana Rosie set up for my sister and me are sizable to say the least. I mean, they're chump change to the Hilton sisters, but they're still sizable. Phoebe was able to afford to go to Oxford with hers and not have to work for her first year in London.

If I'd had access to that kind of money last year, my life could look completely different right now. Smith and I would've had options. I wouldn't have needed to work two jobs. He might not have ever applied to *Digital Slap*, and if that never happened . . . maybe he'd be here now. No. We'd be back in Dubai with his parents, and everything would be OK.

"Penelope, are you still with me?" my father asks. "I need to get an understanding of your finances."

"You mean I could've had access to that money for an entire year?"

Neither of my parents make eye contact with me. Suddenly, they're both very interested in their pies.

"Penelope, what matters is you have access to it now," Nana Rosie says. "You can use that money to restart your life."

"Dad." My voice comes out like a growl. "Dad, why didn't you tell me that I had access to my trust last year?"

"I told you it was an oversight."

"Bullshit."

"Penelope Banks," my mother snaps. "I will not tolerate that kind of language. Your father and I made the decision to keep quiet on the trust because we worried about something like this happening."

"Something like what, Mom?"

The answer dawns on me the second the question leaves my lips. Divorce. She's talking about my divorce. My parents didn't want me to have access to my trust, because they thought Smith and I would end up divorced, and since we didn't have a prenup, a divorce would entitle him to half of it.

"Penelope . . ." My mother trails off. "We just—"

"Thought I'd get a divorce." My gaze flickers between my mother and father. "You two hoped my marriage would fail."

"We never hoped for that, Penelope," my father says softly. "But we had to protect you in case it did. Smith's family has made it very clear that they don't believe in helping their children succeed, and we couldn't bear the thought that your trust—the money your grandmother worked to ensure your future with—would end up funding his schemes."

"You don't know Smith at all, Dad. And the both of you don't know Jasper and Fiona either." I push out my chair. "Because if you did, you'd know that they'd give Smith the moon if he wanted it. Smith doesn't ask for anything from his parents. He wants to achieve his own success based on his own name and merits. And his future isn't a scheme. It's brilliant. You're both just too big of snobs to see it."

"We did what was best for you. If that makes us snobs, so be it." He crosses his arms over his chest in defiance. "That boy may not be OK with taking money from his parents, but if he's willing to abandon his wife after a year of marriage, I have no doubt he'd be fine with taking her money too."

"I need some air."

"I can't believe this." My father tosses his napkin on the table. "Your mother and I moved heaven and earth to get you home the moment you told us you were in trouble. Mind you, we hadn't heard from you in months because god forbid you remember to call us when everything in your life is going fine. And now, while we're in the middle of helping you sort through your mess, you have the audacity to insult us in our own home, on Thanksgiving no less. This is unacceptable, Penelope. I won't tolerate it. If you're going to stay under this roof for any length of time, you will treat your mother and me with respect, and trust that we have your best interests at heart."

"I'll keep that in mind, Dad." I grab my cardigan from the coat rack. "Don't worry. I'll be in by curfew."

I punctuate my outburst by slamming the front door behind me. The thwack is magnified by the marble floors on the inside and the ceramic tiles on the patio. It was a satisfying sound when I was a kid. The final word between my parents and me, and it was all mine. But now as I lean against the mahogany door and look up at the evening sky, I don't find any satisfaction in what just happened. The feeling is the exact opposite. Disgust.

I've been home only a few days, and already I've reverted back to being the worst version of myself. *If this is me now, what am I going to look like in a month?* The thought sends a shiver down my spine. I bundle myself up in my cardigan and walk down the driveway, careful not to let my gaze cross the street.

I will not look at Smith's house.

I will not add crying in the middle of the street to my embarrassing list of Thanksgiving accomplishments. I will make a left the minute my feet hit the sidewalk, and I will shield my eyes like a horse on a track if need be. My feet are already almost there. I can do this. If there is one screwup I will not make tonight, it's looking at Smith's house. I will—

"Penny?"

I look up, and there she is. Fiona's lounging in one of her pool chairs, surrounded by an assortment of votive candles. I wave like a fool, frozen in place, unsure of what to do or say.

"It's a new moon. You know what a new moon means, don't you?" Fiona unravels herself from the cocoon of knitted blankets piled on top of her. She grabs a tea light and a small slip of paper from the table next to her chair. "Come here."

I hesitate. As much as I want to talk to Fiona and listen to whatever nuggets of universe wisdom she has to share, I don't think I can stand on Smith's lawn and keep it together.

"I don't know," I manage to say.

"Meet me in the middle." She doesn't say it like a request or a command. It doesn't even come across as a question. "I want to give you something."

My feet start moving before my head has a chance to talk them out of it. It's five steps from my sidewalk to the middle of the street. I'm thankful it's not more. I don't think I could take another step without falling apart.

"New moons are lucky," Fiona says. "They symbolize new beginnings."

A lump forms in my throat. "No offense to the moon, but I don't think beginnings are all that lucky. They're pretty painful, if you ask me."

"It's not the beginning that's painful in my opinion. It's the ending that came before it. New moons represent that too. The end of one phase and the beginning of a new." She takes my hand, the one that used to have my engagement ring—her old engagement ring—on it, and places the slip of blank paper inside. "We don't always get to choose when one phase ends and another begins, but we can choose how we face it."

"I fucked it all up, Fiona." Hot tears cascade down my face. "I let him down, just like I've been letting everyone down my whole life."

"Disappointment is a part of life." She lifts my chin gently with the back of her hand. "Show me someone who's never disappointed their family or their lover, and I'll show you someone who's miserable inside."

"I was miserable." I gasp. "I was miserable at home. I was miserable at college, and I was miserable on the road with Smith. The only place I wasn't miserable was when I was with you guys in Dubai. I felt so alive and happy there. I never wanted to leave, and now I can never go back."

"You don't need to." She dries my tears with the sleeve of her sweater. "Happiness isn't a place you go back to. Happiness is a place you build and rebuild and then tear down and remodel a thousand times over inside you."

"I don't know how to start."

"You already have." Fiona presses the tea light into my palm. "Write down your dreams, hopes, and desires on a slip of paper, and burn them. My mother used to call it writing love letters to the universe. Set your intentions and trust yourself to follow through."

She pulls me into a hug, and I allow myself to sink into her arms like a child. Somehow, I know that this is my last Fiona hug for a long time, maybe forever, and I want to make a memory of it. When we finally let go, I notice that her eyes are glistening with tears. She's going to miss me too. We're going to miss each other, and I take a tiny bit of comfort in knowing that it won't just be me.

"One more thing. Smoky quartz for good travels and protection." She unclasps the necklace hanging from her neck and drapes it around mine. "Go write a love letter to the universe and yourself."

"I will," I say. "I promise."

And deep down I know that this is a promise I will not break.

Chapter 25

My mother and Nana Rosie take the morning shift with my father. They offer it to me, but the truth is, I'm not ready to be alone with my dad. I've built it up in my head that the next time we see each other will be the start of what I want our relationship to look like from here on out, and I'm not sure I've figured out exactly how to do that just yet. How do you reintroduce yourself to someone who's known you your whole life?

Thankfully, there are plenty of things that need attention at home, and lucky for me, some of those things include Martin, like stopping by my father's office. As my father's attorney, Falon needs some documents. While he hasn't officially made any decisions about his continued role in his company, we want to make it as easy as possible for him to delegate extra responsibilities to other partners in order to get the rest he needs.

"And if you happen to stop and get some ice cream"—Phoebe hands me her keys in the garage—"I wouldn't be mad about it."

"What happened to watching everyone's diet?" I ask. "You tried to deprive me of mayonnaise."

"I don't have to watch mine. I'm going to Australia, where I will likely be eaten by a spider the size of my thigh in my sleep." She lowers her voice and fixes her gaze on the back door. "Between you and me, I'm not sure I'm built for Australia. This was really more Falon's dream than mine."

"Between you and me," I say, "you should go wherever that woman wants to take you. She's pretty exceptional. Don't fuck it up."

"You want to take my bike?" Martin emerges from the other side of the garage, holding two helmets. "It's a little chilly this morning, but you can wear my jacket."

"Between you and me," Phoebe whispers, "he might be the only straight man I'm ever going to want to spend a holiday with." She pats my shoulder. "Don't fuck it up."

I put on the helmet and hang on as Martin drives us the scenic way through the city. I've written plenty of motorcycle montages in my books, but none of them come close to capturing what it actually feels like. Your heart feels like it's flying and falling at the same time. Like you can't catch your breath, but you're not scared. It's my second favorite thing I've ever done with a man.

It's been years since I've been in my father's office. The building has the exterior Victorian charm that's a staple of Coronado Island, but the inside is sleek and modern. At first, I think I'll wait in the lobby, but Martin tells me it might take him a while to go through all the files.

I'm not sure why, but I'm hesitant to go into my dad's office. It almost feels like an invasion of his privacy. Our home has always been my mother's domain. Sure, my dad has a den and an office there, but those spaces were carefully curated by my mother. My father's work office has always been sacred. When Phoebe and I were little girls, Mom would bring us to visit on Fridays. We'd take turns playing hide-and-seek under his big desk, or spinning in his massive leather chair until we were dizzy with laughter.

Inside, Martin sits at Dad's old cherrywood desk. It doesn't look nearly as big as it is in my memory. Immediately, I pick up the photo of me reading that Martin mentioned on one of our walks.

"Told you it was here," he says. "Come around on this side and see what else he's got."

There's a photo of Phoebe and Falon sitting at our patio table outside. They're holding glasses of margaritas and wearing ridiculous sunglasses with American flags on them. My mother likes to throw a big

Fourth of July cookout before the town parade. Even though I haven't been since high school, she always mailed me an invite.

I'll be there for it this year, I think to myself. *This year, I'll be there for all of it.*

"That picture of your mom and grandma might be my favorite." Martin points to a photo of the two of them sitting on a swing at a little B and B they used to visit every year in Napa. Mom is pregnant with me and Phoebe, her belly the size of a watermelon, and she's laughing because Nana Rosie's side of the swing is lifted higher than hers. "Your mom looks so happy there."

"She always said she hated being pregnant." I run my finger along the frame. "Guess I'll have to remind her of this."

Smith closes the filing cabinet next to my father's desk. "I've got what I need. You ready?"

I pick up the photo of me on his desk. "Can we stop one more place?"

He hands me my helmet. "We can go wherever you want."

"Then two more stops. Please."

⁓

It's late afternoon when Martin and I arrive at the hospital. Dad's visiting hours are restricted, but Martin was able to negotiate a few moments for me to be alone with my father. He looks smaller. As if the procedure to fix his heart somehow shrunk his presence.

"I'm just dropping something off, Dad," I whisper.

I don't expect him to respond. The desk nurse said they needed to adjust his pain medication, which would likely put him out for the rest of the night.

"This is the first book of mine that was published." I place a copy of *Once upon a Hot Summer Night* on his bedside table, and I perch myself on the side of his bed. "There's a bookstore close to your office that has several of my books, so if you want, I can get you more. I'm going to be honest with you, though." I pause to consider my words carefully. "There's

227

a lot of sex in this book, Dad. You can skip over most of it, if you'd like. I'll fill in the blanks for you if you have questions about the plot."

There's a tap at the door. Martin peeks his head inside. "The nurse says you have five minutes."

"OK."

"I'm going to wait outside in the parking lot. There's a woman in the lobby who won't stop discussing her bowels."

"I had no idea that you were interested in that sort of thing," I tease.

"I am a man of mystery." He winks. "I'll see you out there."

"You can stay if you want," I say. "I'm almost done, and it's cold outside."

He nods and takes the open seat on the other side of my dad's bed. Dad stirs a little in his sleep, and I take his hand and shush him the way he did to me when I couldn't sleep when I was a little girl.

"Dad, I want you to know that I'm going to stick around for a while," I say softly. "We're still figuring things out, but it looks like I'll be moving down here for a bit while Phoebe is in Australia. I want you to be able to recover, and I want to spend some time with you and Mom and Nana."

"Tell him that this won't affect your bookstore," Martin says. "Sorry. I didn't mean to interrupt. I just know your dad wouldn't like the idea of you putting it on hold."

"It's fine. The conversation is a little one sided now, anyway. I'm going to do what I can remotely. Social media and marketing. Maybe come up with a fundraising campaign to get things kicked off." I run my hand along the stubble on his cheek. "I'll be here, though, Dad. No matter what, you and Mom and Nana will have me around."

The nurse taps on the door, signaling our time is up. I take out two last items.

"I brought you some company." I place the photos from his office onto his bedside table. "In case you get lonely."

I kiss his head and promise to be back tomorrow and the tomorrow after that. No matter what.

࿆

After we drop off the legal documents with Falon, Martin and I decide to spend the night at his place. Phoebe suggested I take as many breaks from our parents' house as possible while she and Falon are there. The two of them talked things over with Mom, and they've agreed to give Australia a year. They also agreed to have a small wedding before moving in the spring so that my mother can finally throw a proper wedding. Phoebe claims it's the worst deal Falon has ever negotiated, but I think she is secretly looking forward to having a little more of the spotlight.

"So, have you told them yet?" Martin runs his hand along my naked back. We're wrapped in his sheets after a lazy and blissful love-making session. "The girls, I mean."

"About us?" I turn over and face him. "No. I usually don't share a play-by-play of my sex life with my friends. I wait until we're out having drinks, and then I just show them pictures."

"I hope you got my good side."

"Of course. I got a perfect shot of that tattoo on your ass."

"Oh really?" He chuckles. "And what does this ass tattoo of mine look like?"

"A big old heart with *I love Gilded Age spinsters* in the middle. Duh."

"I still don't know what that means." He smirks. "And I meant have you told your friends about you staying here."

"Not yet. I don't want to do that over text. They know he had a heart attack, but I'm going to save the rest for a video chat later."

"I know your dad is in bad shape, but I still think he'd like to help you out financially with the business."

"Maybe." I shrug. "But I also think that our relationship has a lot of healing that needs to happen. A loan or investment might complicate that."

"Possibly. What about this?" He motions between us. "Does this complicate things?"

"What could be complicated about us?" I nuzzle into the space beneath his chin and lay my head on his chest. "You're my ex–fake boyfriend who I enjoy having amazing sex with."

"It is kind of amazing." He kisses my head. "But I'm serious. If you need your space while you sort out what your life is going to look like here, tell me."

Ever since Smith and I divorced, I've been an expert in creating space. Space from my family. Space from men. Frankly, if my friendship with the coven hadn't started online, I'm not sure I'd have any friends at all. I was the queen of making space, and in a lot of ways, that space served me well. It taught me how to rely on myself. It taught me to figure out who I am and what I want in life. Space was absolutely necessary for me for a time, but I think now I'm ready to start filling that space with people who make me happy.

"I don't need space," I say. "But I do need a pencil and some paper. A candle too, if you have it."

"Are you sacrificing something?"

"Nope." I wrap the sheets around me in a cocoon. "I'm writing a love letter."

"To who?"

"To my longest-standing obsession." I point out the window of Martin's Airstream to the barely visible crescent. "To the new moon."

"I thought the new moon was yesterday?"

"She's OK if you show up a little late."

"Do you want company?" He hands me a small notebook and pen. "The heat lamp is all I have candle-wise."

"That'll work." I hold the door. "And I think I'll write this letter by myself, if that's OK?"

"I'd never dream of coming between the two of you. Take all the time you need."

So I do.

Chapter 26

"You know," I say to Ozzie after our third loop around the block before seven a.m. "Now that you're a swanky dog with a backyard, it would be really great if you started pissing in it, because it's getting really hard to always find an available Prius. Also, I think that Prius is starting to take it personally."

My phone chimes, reminding me that I have a video chat scheduled with the Smut Coven later this afternoon, because I am officially working toward being a responsible person who keeps reminders in her phone instead of inked on her hand. Ozzie has just rejected another truck when I notice a familiar black Pom on the opposite side of the street.

"Hey." Smith waves as he crosses the street toward me. "Are you screening my texts now?"

"Huh?"

"I just texted you."

I look at my phone, and sure enough, there's a text from "Martin" telling me to turn around. I really need to change Smith's name in my contacts.

"Sorry." I give him a hug. "I meant to reach out, but things have been a little hectic. Did everything end up OK with Sarah? She seemed a little unhappy finding us in your parents' kitchen the other night."

"She recovered." He shakes his head. "She's got a good heart."

"The best. She gave me the dress off her back."

"I'm flying out later today to meet her and Mo in Dubai."

"That's right," I say, pleasantly surprised at how unbothered I am hearing the word Dubai. "What time does your flight leave?"

"A few hours." He stares down at his feet where Harriet and Ozzie have taken to grooming each other. "I actually have a favor to ask you, Pen."

"Does she need to borrow one of my dresses now? Because we are the same size."

"Harry's getting a little old to be making long flights." He kneels down and scratches her graying snout. "I'd never kennel her, and I don't really have the kind of friends I trust to take care of her. Except for you."

My heart melts. "You want me to take Harriet?"

"Not forever. She's my longest-standing relationship with a woman. Just until after New Year's." He holds out her little pink leash to me. "What do you say, friend?"

"Yes."

I hug him until my arms hurt.

☙

I have the first shift this morning with my father. I brace myself for more of the same as yesterday, but to my surprise, my father is awake when I walk into his room. Not only is he awake, but he's sitting up in bed with a book. My book, to be exact.

"Good morning, Penelope." My father takes off his reading glasses and folds them in his lap. "Or should I call you Fiona Nelson?"

"When I was a kid, I went through that phase where I wanted everyone to call me Lamb Chop. Is that an option?" I move to his bedside and wrap him in a delicate hug.

"Penelope it is."

"I'm glad you're awake, Dad. You kind of scared the shit out of all of us."

"Myself included." He laughs. It's a weak laugh, but a laugh nonetheless. "Back to this book." He taps on the shiny cover. "I may be biased, and this is my first romance, but I've got to tell you, it's very well written."

"Thanks, Dad." I blush.

"The descriptions are very detailed. A little graphic for my taste in some parts. I had no idea there were so many ways to describe genitalia—"

"OK, Dad. Save the rest of your review for Goodreads."

"I will." He closes the book. "And while we're on the subject of you and books, I'd like to hear a little more about this bookstore you plan on opening."

"We don't have to talk about that."

"I want to." My father reaches for a yellow legal pad on his bedside table. "Now, I've looked over the reports that your friend Jackie sent over, and they're incredibly well done."

"How did you get the reports? And how did Jackie get your email?"

"I found her name in the acknowledgments of your book and I looked her up." He slides his glasses down his nose. "Why are you always so surprised that your mother and I know how to use the internet? Honestly, it's a little ageist."

If I thought I was having an out-of-body experience a few days ago at dinner, then this must be an otherworldly experience altogether. Carter Banks—my father—is talking about romance books and the Smut Coven. He's got a legal pad on his lap, and he's read Jackie's research and projections. How is this possible? How is this my life right now?

I'm not ready for all of this. I mean, I am. I've waited my whole life for my father and me to be on the same page about my career and my life. The fact that he's excited is an added bonus. But it feels like we're jumping too far ahead. In all this excitement, we're sweeping stuff under the rug. Stuff that will surely rear its ugly head the moment I have to tell Dad about the no-doughnuts rule.

"Dad, I'm sorry about Thanksgiving," I say. "And drinks before that. And the last ten years. And—"

"Penelope." He reaches for my hands. "I don't need you to apologize for anything."

"But I do, Dad. I wasn't fair to you and Mom. I haven't been for years, and I need to own it. I need to own it so I can do better moving forward."

"I think it's safe to say that neither of us were very fair to the other."

I nod.

"But as a parent, I am the one who failed here, Penelope. Not you." A single tear runs down his face. "All I have ever wanted for either of my daughters is a good life. I was just too stubborn to realize that my idea of a good life isn't the only good life out there. When I found out you were coming home for Thanksgiving, I was so scared that I'd do something wrong to make you want to leave again. I think that's why I worked so hard to make Smith feel included. I thought that if I could get him to like me, you'd do the same."

"I was worried you wouldn't like me." I wipe the tears from my eyes with the back of my hand. "I know you love me, but I didn't know if I was the kind of person you and Mom could like."

"It's impossible not to like you, Penelope, and I'm so sorry you ever doubted that."

We sit in silence for a moment. The white noise of the hospital fills the room. It doesn't feel awkward sitting in my dad's room with him. For the first time in a long time, nothing feels uncomfortable between us at all.

A nurse drops in with breakfast and to check his vitals. I make a few notes in my phone about his progress, which the nurse assures me is coming along nicely.

"Bankses are naturally resilient," he says to the nurse. "Just ask my daughter. She's the most resilient of us all. She's an author, you know. Penelope, show the nurse one of your books."

He's embarrassing me, and I've never been more happy to feel embarrassed. "Seriously, Dad?"

"Of course I'm being serious. Take my copy." He holds out the book for the nurse. "Penelope, I'm going to need you to pick up some additional copies for some of the other nurses and doctors on my team. I'll be sure to reimburse you."

"OK, Dad."

"Or maybe I can get some shipped to the room while I'm in here."

"Eat your food, Dad." I shake my head. "You'll be able to cover more ground as my publicist once you're back on your feet."

"Good point."

I freshen his water pitcher and organize the toiletries my mother sent with me, while he reads me some of the highlighted sections from Jackie's business plan.

"Now, Penelope," my father says in between bites of his heart-healthy breakfast, "I gather that you're going to need a little capital to help get this bookstore up and running."

"Well, yes, but I'll figure it out," I say. "I was looking into crowdsourcing."

"Isn't that what rock singers do when they throw themselves into a crowd during a performance?"

"Close but not quite."

"Well, never mind that." He shakes his head. "I have a small confession to make."

"Dad, I'm not taking your money. I don't want to complicate things between us, OK?"

"Penelope, I'm not offering you money." He hands me his cell phone. "Do you remember that last Thanksgiving you came to visit, when you and Smith were in the process of divorcing?"

"Yes, of course I remember. It was awful."

"Agreed. But there was one bright spot. You remember those shares you got from that magazine? The ones I told you to cash out and invest?"

I furrow my brow. "Vaguely?"

"I'll take that as a no. Anyway, it doesn't matter. Against my better judgment, I held on to them for you. I never thought they would amount to anything, but as it turns out, I was wrong." He taps his phone screen. "That's a screenshot of what those shares are worth now, should you choose to cash them out."

I don't understand everything on the document my dad is showing me, but what I do understand leaves me speechless.

"I hope you're not upset with me for never having them forwarded to your address in San Francisco." He lowers his voice. "I let my pride get the best of me at first. I figured if you didn't care about them, then why should I bother to bring them to your attention. Over the years, the little company started to do quite well, and there was a part of me that felt guilty for not telling you sooner."

"These are worth over $100,000, Dad," I finally manage to say as my initial shock wears off. "Am I reading it correctly?" He nods sheepishly. "That means I have over $100,000 to put toward the bookstore?"

"Well, there is the matter of taxes and such, but, yes. The bulk of that belongs to you should you decide to cash them." He clears his throat. "I take it you're not angry with me? You'd have every right to be."

Ten years ago, I would've been angry. Ten years ago, I would've seen my father's act of squirreling away money as a sign that he was preparing for me to fail. That he wouldn't have believed for a second that I could make it on my own in San Francisco as a writer, and if I was given access to those shares, I would mishandle them. That a life designed without his help could ever be anything but a complete failure. But I'm not angry with my father today. If anything, for the first time in a long time, I see a little bit of myself in him.

"You're stubborn, Dad."

"Your mother would say pigheaded," he chuckles. "But I like the way *stubborn* sounds much better."

"I guess we have that in common."

A warm smile spreads across his face. "You know, I think the most successful people in life are stubborn. Present company included."

Teenage me could never have imagined a moment like this. Adult me will never forget it. We spend the next several hours discussing business and creating a core memory for the both of us.

☙

Martin picks me up when it's time to swap out shifts. Nana Rosie is up after me, and she's armed with a stack of plant-based cookbooks.

"Your father is going to be a whole new man after I have Marie change his diet." She taps the cover of a book titled *Plants Are Friends and Food.*

I have a feeling Marie might finally retire if she has to cook anything out of a cookbook with cartoon vegetables.

I walk out to the parking lot and see Martin on his bike. My helmet rests behind him on top of his leather jacket.

"We really need to discuss those shoes, Banks." He nods at my Birks and socks. "I'd consider it a personal favor if you let me compost them."

"I suppose I owe you quite a few favors," I say. "I'll grant you three, but none of them can include getting rid of my shoes."

"Are you a genie in a bottle?" Martin hands me my helmet.

"That's what Christina says." I pull his jacket on. "So what are your wishes?"

He kisses me slowly, wrapping his arms around my waist. "First wish is that you'll spend the night tonight."

"Granted."

"Second wish is that you'll let me visit your bookstore in San Francisco."

"Done." I slide onto the back of his bike, cradling the helmet in my lap. "What's your last wish?"

"That you'll be my date to the company New Year's Eve party." He smiles.

"Real or fake?"

"Real."

"I'm in."

"Good. Then I can give you this." He reaches into his pocket. It's a necklace with a rainbow moonstone pendant. "I noticed you weren't wearing your old one anymore." My hand instinctively reaches for my neck. "The lady at the shop I got it from says it's supposed to symbolize new beginnings."

A wave of emotion I can only describe as utter contentment washes over me like a cool ocean breeze. He motions for me to move my hair out of the way, then drapes the delicate pendant around my neck and takes a step back to admire it.

"What do you think?"

"Beautiful." He lifts my chin and kisses me. "The necklace is nice too."

"Where are you taking me?" I pull my helmet on.

"Wherever you want to go."

"Home," I say.

For the first time in forever, I want to go home.

ACKNOWLEDGMENTS

It sounds cliché, but it takes a village to create a book.

To my brilliant agent, Joanna MacKenzie, thank you for being my champion. You are one of the best humans I know, and I feel incredibly lucky to have you represent my books.

To my excellent editorial duo from Amazon, Selena James and Kristi Yanta, thank you for seeing potential in my words and molding them into this story that I'm so incredibly proud to have written. Both Penny and I have come a long way in a short time, and we owe that to the both of you.

To my critique partner and forever friend Falon Ballard, you have no idea how many times you kept me going when I wanted to give up. You are the best thing I've ever found on the internet.

To my Pitch Wars mentor Katie Golding, you picked me at a time in my life when I really needed someone to choose me. Thank you for teaching me how to write.

To Lyssa Mia Smith and Jumata Emill, thank you for cheering me on. It's been a pleasure to read your words and to have you both provide a safe space for mine.

I would be remiss not to acknowledge how Brenda Drake's Pitch Wars mentorship program influenced, improved, and encouraged my writing. While Pitch Wars is no longer an active program, bookshelves around the world are better for it having existed, and I am forever grateful to have been a part of the program as a mentee and mentor.

To my extended family and friends who have encouraged and inspired my writing, thank you for supporting this wild dream of mine. Fair warning, if your name wasn't given to a character in this book, it is highly likely you'll find yourself in the next.

To my mom and sister, thank you for providing me with a lifetime of material. Little pieces of you both are weaved throughout the Banks family in all the best ways.

To my three children, my life would be so boring without you. I would be so boring without you. I hope you always want to come home for the holidays. Thank you for making me a better person.

To my husband, thank you for letting me be a whole planet instead of a moon. My dreams are real because you want them to come true just as much as I do.

And finally, I lost a member of my village during the creation of this book. Jim, I hope you get to see this book from wherever you're sitting, and I hope, for my sake, you actually read the ending.

ABOUT THE AUTHOR

Photo © 2022 Alexandra Yarborough

Brooke Abrams lives in the Sonoran Desert with her husband, three children, three dogs, and cat. She's quite literally never alone. Not even now. You can find her socials and writing-related news on her website at www.akabrooke.com.